Blackout

By
Tom Barber

*****

CW01212705

Blackout
Copyright: Archway Productions
First published: 10th September 2012
Second edition published: 23rd September 2014

The right of Tom Barber to be identified as author of this Work has been asserted by he in accordance with sections 77 and 78 of the Copyright, Designs and Patents Act 1988.

All rights reserved. No part of this publication may be reproduced, stored in retrieval system, copied in any form or by any means, electronic, mechanical, photocopying, recording or otherwise transmitted without written permission from the publisher. You must not circulate this book in any format.

This book is a work of fiction and, except in the case of historical fact, any resemblance to actual persons, living or dead, is purely coincidental.

The Sam Archer thriller series
by
Tom Barber

NINE LIVES

26 year old Sam Archer has just been selected to join a new counter-terrorist squad, the Armed Response Unit. And they have their first case. A team of suicide bombers are planning to attack London on New Year's Eve. The problem?
No one knows where any of them are.

THE GETAWAY

Archer is in New York City for a funeral. After the service, an old familiar face approaches him with a proposition. A team of bank robbers are tearing the city apart, robbing it for millions.
The FBI agent needs Archer to go undercover and try to stop them.

BLACKOUT

Three men have been killed in the UK and USA in one morning. The deaths take place thousands of miles apart, yet are connected by an event fifteen years ago. Before long, Archer and the ARU are drawn into the violent fray. And there's a problem. One of their own men is on the extermination list.

SILENT NIGHT

A dead body is found in Central Park, a man who was killed by a deadly virus. Someone out there has more of the substance and is planning to use it. Archer must find where this virus came from and secure it before any more is released.

But he is already too late.

ONE WAY

On his way home, Archer saves a team of US Marshals from a violent ambush in the middle of the Upper West Side. The group are forced to take cover in a tenement block in Harlem. But there are more killers on the way to finish the job.

And Archer feels there's something about the group of Marshals that isn't quite right.

RETURN FIRE

Four months after they first encountered one another, Sam Archer and Alice Vargas are both working in the NYPD Counter-Terrorism Bureau and also living together. But a week after Vargas leaves for a trip to Europe, Archer gets a knock on his front door. Apparently Vargas has completely disappeared. And it appears she's been abducted.

GREEN LIGHT

A nineteen year old woman is gunned down in a Queens car park, the latest victim in a brutal gang turf war that goes back almost a century. Suspended from duty, his badge and gun confiscated, Archer is nevertheless drawn into the fray as he seeks justice for the girl. People are going missing, all over New York.

And soon, so does he.

LAST BREATH

A Federal manhunt is underway across the United States. Three people have been shot by a sniper, and he's gone to ground somewhere in Washington D.C., his killing spree apparently still not over. As riots engulf the city and the manhunt intensifies, Sam Archer arrives in the city to visit his family.

Or so it would appear.

JUMP SEAT

A commercial airliner crashes into the Atlantic Ocean with hundreds of people on board. When another follows three days later, Archer and the rest of the team are assigned the case. At any moment, they know another plane could go down.

And to try and solve the case, Archer's going to have to go 35,000 feet up in the sky.

CLEARED HOT

A female CT Bureau detective and colleague of Archer's is shot in the head in an empty pool in Astoria. Archer learns she's been re-examining a strange case from seventeen years ago. On the morning of Tuesday September 11th, 2001, a FDNY firefighter showed up to work and committed suicide.

But no-one has ever figured out why.

TRICK TURN

At a pre-July 4th carnival in New York, an eleven year old girl is almost killed when a knife slams into a wall, missing her by a hair's breadth. No-one saw who threw the blade, but Archer and his NYPD team can guess why.

Her dead father was one of the most powerful mobsters in the city.
And someone seems hell bent on reuniting the girl with him.

NIGHT SUN

As Archer is sent to a federal prison to help transport an old foe to another facility, a situation erupts that leads to the escape of some other, extremely dangerous prisoners. One of them is an inmate with just six days left on his sentence.

But for a reason that quickly becomes clear, that's six days too many.

Also:
CLOSE CALLS

In a collection of three stories, familiar characters from the Sam Archer thriller series look Death right in the eye and don't blink first. Moments that forged the people they are today.
Moments they can never forget.
Their close calls.

HAND OFF

In this prequel novel, featuring two familiar characters from the Sam Archer thriller series, an investigation involving a dead famous athlete, another assaulted in a seedy strip club toilet and a vigilante going out at night delivering street justice draws the NYPD's attention.

Despite their junior status, Officers Matt Shepherd and Jake Hendricks are drawn into the case as quiet, unofficial investigators.

But also, as suspects.

To my mother, Alison.
A heroine in her own story.

ONE

It was a few minutes to midnight on a spring night in London.

Inside a medium-sized office on the top floor of a three-storey building in West London, a man in his late-thirties was just finishing annotating the last page of eleven sequential A4 sheets of paper, his brow furrowed in concentration as he worked. He was a politician, but about as far removed from the stereotypical type as you could get.

Unlike a number of people in that career who so often sported the pasty complexion and soft, flabby physique that came with too much time sitting behind a desk, the man examining the papers had skin tanned and weathered by years in warmer climates. He was built like a professional rugby player, powerful arms and shoulders with not an ounce of excess body-fat on his midriff. He had a dark-featured chiselled face, a warm smile when he chose to use it and possessed a charisma that perfectly suited his chosen path as a politician. Collectively, these attributes had earned him a legion of admirers and supporters not just in his constituency but across the country. He'd entered politics on a sheer whim a couple of years ago, and no-one was more surprised than he at the meteoric success he'd enjoyed so far.

However, as humble as the man was, it wasn't a fluke that he'd done so well. Officially, the tabloids said it was due to his *inspiring and morale-boosting speeches* and his *refreshingly straightforward and honest approach*. But as his campaign manager had told him, he ticked two very important boxes as a front-runner in the elections, two things that probably wouldn't make the bold print of the newspapers but nonetheless were qualities that none of his competition shared. Women wanted to sleep with him and men wanted to buy him a beer.

Handsome, eloquent and charismatic, he was very much a maverick in the Kennedy and Obama mould, someone the public could relate to and get behind, a surprise but sure-fire candidate for leader of the party in due course. *Show business for ugly people* was how politics was often described. The man working on the papers behind the desk in his office that evening was definitely an exception.

Changing one final word on the last sheet of the pile, the man dropped the pen on the page and stretched back in his seat, yawning, wearily rubbing his face. He'd been working on this speech for weeks, and tomorrow was the day he would finally deliver it. He knew its success would either make or break his campaign.

He was due to speak at 11 am to a worker's union across the city in Dalston, outlining his planned reforms and intentions for growth in the area if they chose to get behind him and help him get elected.

Their support was crucial. He knew he had the middle-class vote in the bag. If he got the Dalston backing, it would be a clincher. Get them on his side, win the seat and who knew what could happen next. Given his recent run of success, he was sure as the night was dark that he could get to 10 Downing Street one day. He'd always been an ambitious man, and as everyone around him had started to realise, his confidence was infectious. Day by day, public belief in the man was growing, matching the same inner sureness that he'd always had in himself.

He stretched the tight muscles of his neck from side to side, rubbing the day's worth of stubble that had accumulated on his chin and cheeks. Blinking fatigue from his eyes, he checked the clock on the wall across the room. He caught it just as the long hand ticked forward, nestled side-by-side with the small hand. 11:59 pm. *Time to head home.* He needed to be on his best form tomorrow and that meant a solid night's sleep, or as good a one as he could get considering the importance of tomorrow's commitments.

He rose from his desk, reshuffling the series of papers carefully into numerical order, then slid them into a slender brown folder resting on the desktop. Closing it, he placed the folder inside his briefcase and clicked it shut, spinning the two three-digit dials with his thumbs.

He was wearing dark suit trousers with a light-blue shirt, and the sleeves were rolled up to reveal thick forearms and a series of faded tattoos. Working here at night alone was usually the only time that he could get away with revealing them, the only other place away from the privacy of his own home. At all other times, he had to keep the sleeves rolled down which was a bitch in hot weather. Personally, he liked the ink-work, but he wasn't a fool and knew the common stigmas that were frequently associated with tattoos. His campaign manager had emphasised some potential supporters still on the fence could perceive them in a less than positive way. He thought his manager was being over-cautious, but at this point every vote mattered and the politician with the tattoos couldn't afford to become complacent. Once he was elected, he could roll his sleeves up, literally. But for now, in public and with elections still on-going, the ink would remain covered.

He pulled on the jacket and tightened his tie, then checked the rest of his office. He had everything he needed. Across the room, the tall windows were shut and locked, long red curtains drawn in front of them. He would be back here in six hours, but that gave him more than sufficient time for a rest and was all he really needed. He used to manage on half or a third of that in his former life, hunkered down in foxholes, bunkers or military camps in dark corners around the world. Six hours was plenty.

Walking around his desk, the man moved to the door and stepped outside, then shut and locked it behind him, the briefcase in his right hand. He stood at the top of stairs, the building around him still and quiet, the only sound the faint ticking of a large grandfather clock downstairs in the reception hall. His offices were above a law firm and an up-and-coming showbusiness agency, so the silence in the building was a welcome contrast to the constant hustle and bustle of the day. He figured there might still be some people in the law offices below, unfortunate souls who were pulling an all-nighter, working hard on cases and scouring legal documents that couldn't wait until morning. He knew how they'd be feeling. He'd slept here a few times himself on a couch in his office.

Double-checking he had everything, the man turned and moved down the carpeted stairs towards the ground floor. To the right of the front door was a reception desk and to his surprise, despite the lateness of the hour, his receptionist was still sitting there, her head down, hard at work on something, distracted. She was a sweet girl called Jamie, just turned twenty five. She'd knocked on the front door at the beginning of the year asking if there was any work going in the building. She explained that she'd graduated last summer from a well-respected university with a good degree, but unfortunately, with the current state of the economy, such qualifications no longer guaranteed a job in the City, or in any city in fact. The man had liked her instantly, admiring her resourcefulness and after approval from the law firm and the showbiz agency he'd offered her a spot running the front desk. She'd proven adept at her role, working from morning to night without complaint, juggling the needs of the law firm, the agency and the up-and-coming politician's office. Altogether, she did a fine job.

Just as the grandfather clock in the hall struck midnight, she sensed him coming down the stairs. She looked up and smiled. There was a pause as both of them waited for the twelve chimes on the clock to pass so they could hear each other speak.

'Good evening, sir,' she said, once the building was quiet again, the last chime echoing in the hall.

'What are you still doing here, Jamie?' the man asked, stepping onto the marble floor and approaching the desk. 'It's late. You should be at home.'

'I've got some exams coming up for my law course. Here's a good a place to study as any.'

'When are the exams again?'

'In a couple of weeks.'

'Well, good luck. I'll see you tomorrow. Don't stay too late.'

'Yes, sir. Good night.'

He nodded and moved to the door.

'Oh, sir?' she added.

He turned. Jamie reached for something on her desk and held it towards him.

It was a letter.

‘I almost forgot. This arrived for you about an hour ago. I didn’t want to come up and disturb you, but it’s addressed to you personally.’

He frowned and reached over, taking it and examining it in his hand, turning it over and checking both sides.

‘Mail? At this time of night?’

She nodded.

‘Did you see who delivered it?’ he asked.

She shook her head.

‘It just dropped through the letter box,' she said. 'As you say though, it seemed strange so I opened the door and checked outside. I couldn’t see anyone. Whoever posted it had gone.’

He looked at it in his hands, then shrugged.

‘OK. See you tomorrow,’ he said, and pulling open the front door, he left.

Outside, the man walked down a couple of steps and passing through a small black metal gate, he crossed a cobbled road and headed towards his car, a black Volvo, parked across the street. Although it was midnight, the street-lights lining the pavements clearly illuminated either side of the road, breaking up the shadows and providing light for anyone out and about. Although the pavements were quiet, the man could hear soft and slightly muffled activity coming from a pub up the street on the corner. The street itself was still, with no traffic. Most of its daytime residents were already at home, but a faint glimmer of light was still visible from slits and cracks in curtains that weren't entirely closed, most likely workers pulling a late one or people who lived here.

Putting his briefcase down on the cobbled ground, the man took the keys to the Volvo from his pocket and clicked his car open. He pulled open the door and climbed inside, slamming the door shut behind him. He placed the briefcase on the passenger seat and tossed the letter on top of it, then slid the key into the ignition and prepared to twist it.

But then he thought for a moment and changed his mind, taking his hand off the keys.

He glanced down at the letter.

He was intrigued.

Who the hell would drop off mail this late at night?

Reaching over, he picked it up. He ripped open the envelope, then pulled out a letter.

He unfolded it and started to read, curious.

He read it from beginning to end, slowly.

He only read it once.

Then he found two photographs inside the envelope. He looked at them both, staring at each one slowly, examining every millimetre, every pixel of detail.

And for the next hour, he remained where he was.

He didn't move.

He barely even blinked.

He just stared straight ahead, the letter and pair of photographs resting on his lap.

Not long after he read the letter, Jamie stepped out of the building across the street and locked up, but she didn't notice him sitting there in the car. She headed off down the pavement, turning the corner and disappeared out of sight, as the man sat motionless in the Volvo, staring unseeingly through the front windscreen.

After just over an hour had passed, he made a decision and twisted the keys, firing the ignition. He drove straight home, on autopilot. The next thing he knew he was parked outside his front door, in a quiet neighbourhood in the west of the city. He got out of the car and shutting the door behind him, walked up to the front door and entered his home.

He moved into the house quietly, listening, waiting. There was nothing. The residence was silent and dark. He placed his keys gently on a table by the door, and then headed straight upstairs. After a few moments, he came back down again slowly, in a daze, walked to the kitchen and took a seat at the table in the dark, all alone, a still black figure silhouetted by the moonlight from the open curtains behind him.

He sat motionless for some time. Then he rose and walked into his den next door. Pulling open the top drawer of his desk, he retrieved two separate items and tucked one into each pocket.

Then he walked back into the hallway, grabbed his coat and left the house.

He sat on a bench on the South Bank until morning. He watched the sun rise on the horizon, bathing the London skyline in an orange glow, the air fresh, the smell of salt from the Thames in the air, the city waking up from a deep slumber in front of him. It was one of the most beautiful things he'd ever seen. He felt unaccustomed tears well in his eyes as he looked at the view, the sun slowly bringing light to the city and the start of a new day.

He checked his watch. Then he reached into the inside pocket of his suit jacket and pulled out the letter and the two photographs. He took a lighter from another pocket and sparked a flame. He set the paper and photos on fire, watching them curl and burn away between his fingers, eventually dropping the smoking edges of what was left on the ground by his foot, twisted, black and destroyed.

He then reached into his pocket again and pulled out something else.

It was an old revolver, six bullets inside, the second item he'd retrieved from the desk in his den.

He put it in his mouth and pulled back the hammer with his forefinger.

He took one last look at the city in front of him.

And he pulled the trigger.

TWO

At the same moment that the old revolver fired, Officer Sam Archer of the Armed Response Unit also had his hands on a gun, twenty two miles across the city. He was snuggled in tight to the stock of a long sniper rifle, his breathing slow and smooth, his heart-rate as even as a slow-ticking clock. His left eye was shut and his right was looking down the scope, the fingers of his right hand curled around the brown pistol-grip of the weapon, his forefinger resting gently on the trigger.

Seven hundred yards away his target was still, unmoving. The morning air was cool and clean, with no crosswind to worry about.

He was aiming the crosshairs of the scope on the man's right eye.

The average length of a human head and torso is thirty six inches. The head alone is normally about ten. Archer had heard snipers talk about the *fatal T*, the region on a target's head where any impact from a bullet would be an instant kill. From the chin to the nose and either side on each eye, any round that went through that area would instantly sever the brain stem and spinal cord. A target would be dead before he hit the ground, and nine times out of ten before he even heard the shot that killed him. With a moving target, a torso shot was more reliable, as the target area was larger and any hit to a vital organ was effectively a kill-shot regardless.

But the man on the wrong end of the scope that morning was stationary.

And he was about to get shot.

The rifle in Archer's hands was a Heckler and Koch PSG1A1. The abbreviated name came from the German word *prazisionsschutzengewehr,* or *precision-shooter rifle* in English. Heckler and Koch had been commissioned to create the weapon by German law-enforcement after the Black September Munich disaster at the 1972 Olympics, when the Israeli Olympic team were ambushed by armed terrorists in the Olympic Village.

The West German police had been unable to engage the armed gunmen with their short-range weapons and eleven hostages had died, to the shock and horror of millions watching around the world on television. The heads of the German police force had ordered a long-range shooting weapon be designed specifically for their police teams, and Heckler and Koch had consequently come up with, still to this day, one of the most accurate sniper rifles in the world.

The weapon was dark and sleek, supported at the front for stability by a bipod. It had a side-folding, adjustable, high-impact matte black plastic stock with a vertically-adjustable cheek-piece to accommodate the varying body-types, heights and builds of different shooters. Older versions used to have a Hensoldt scope, but this latest model had an improved Schmidt and Bender 3-12x 50 Police Marksman II tactical scope, mounted on 34 mm rings. It was new and more up to date, with increased accuracy and further range than the Hensoldt, effective in all elements, rain or shine. The sight showed four lines coming together then narrowing into thin cross-hairs which were at that moment in Archer's hands, aimed on the iris of his target's right eyeball.

The rifle held a five, ten or twenty round ammunition box or could be loaded manually bullet-by-bullet, but Archer had gone with the five. It didn't disrupt the weight and feel of the rifle too much, and gave him sufficient reserve ammunition without having to manually load each bullet or weigh the rifle down unnecessarily. Inside the magazine were five polished NATO 7.62 x51 mm rounds, devastating rifle ammunition. Each bullet was a 175 grain, fairly heavy, but was the perfect blend of stopping power and accuracy. At 1000 yards, the fired bullet would contain more kinetic energy than a .357 Magnum round fired point blank. Dirty Harry would have approved.

Once the trigger was pulled, a bullet would leave the rifle at over 2500 feet per second, just about twice the speed of sound, and rotated at about 200,000 revolutions per minute. With longer shots a sniper had to worry about *spindrift*, where the constant turning of the bullet would carry it off course, but the target wasn't far enough from Archer on this occasion for that to be a concern. Each bullet was a hollow-point, boat-tail cartridge, designed to mushroom upon impact and create irreparable damage. Through a human head, the bullet would enter the cranium and expand, destroying brain tissue and rupturing the spinal cord, resulting in instant death. With terminal ballistics, a rifleman always knew what both the *crush* and *tear* factor of each round he put into his rifle would leave. Basically, what the round would destroy in the body and the damage it would leave behind. And in both regards, the NATO round was the pick of the bunch. If there was a better common rifle ammunition out there, no-one had discovered it yet or at least, had advertised it.

The PSG1A1 really only had one disadvantage. Once a shot was fired, the spent cartridge that had housed the fired bullet jumped out of the ejection port to the right, sometimes as far as ten metres away. In certain situations, retrieving the cartridge could be both a potential nightmare but a necessity for a sniper, especially if on a covert operation. However, for the police, that wasn't a concern, and aside from that very minor issue the PSG1A1 had a solid reputation as the most accurate semi-automatic rifle in the world. It was an outstanding weapon and the sniper rifle of choice for many police and law enforcement groups around the world, including the Spanish police, the Mexican army and the FBI's

Hostage Rescue Team. And the latest inclusion to that group was Archer's London-based counter-terrorist team, the Armed Response Unit.

The young blond police officer held the sight on the target's eye, his breathing barely noticeable. He was on the second of three final deep breaths. He inhaled slowly and exhaled for a third and final time, emptying all the air from his lungs. His heart-rate was slow and he felt calm, not a thought in his mind. He'd already taken the slack out of the trigger, halfway towards the two and half pounds of pressure it would need before the rifle fired.

And he gently squeezed all the way.

The weapon kicked back into his shoulder as it fired. The bullet took less than a second to reach the target and it hit him straight through the nose, a half-inch to the left of where Archer had aimed, right through the centre of the *T* of the *fatal T*.

An instant kill.

Down the shooting range, a hole appeared in the paper target, the sheet billowing back just a tad from the impact of the bullet, and Archer smiled. He glanced back over his shoulder at his best friend Chalky and two other officers, Porter and Fox, who were standing watching him, each with a set of binoculars in their hands. Chalky had his face covered by his palm whilst the other two laughed.

Checking that the weapon was empty, Archer applied the safety catch then rose, taking off his ear defenders and walking over to the trio of officers behind him. As he approached, Porter and Fox were still chuckling as Chalky shook his head, swearing under his breath. He'd taken a shot with the rifle just prior to Archer, but he'd only managed to clip the paper target's left ear. A painful injury for sure, but not a kill. And that meant this morning Archer was now eleven to nil up in their contest.

'I'll take cash or cheque,' Archer told Chalky, grinning at him and joining the group.

With his head still down, Chalky pulled a twenty pound note from his pocket and held it up. Archer took it with a wink and a smile.

The four men were an integral part of the ten-man task force of the Armed Response Unit, one of the two premier counter-terrorist squads in the city along with CO19. For the sake of operational ease the task-force was split into two sections, First and Second Team, and these four men comprised First Team, the quartet typically charged with the most important tasks in the field. Porter and Fox were both in their mid-thirties, experienced guys and as tough as they were professional, Porter solidly built and dark-featured whilst Fox had a more wiry build and sandy hair. Both men had been policemen for over a decade, and they were at that stage in their careers where they were in their physical and mental prime, experienced and seasoned officers.

Archer and Chalky were both still twenty seven, ten years younger than the other two but just as deserving of their spots. In the United States, an FBI agent could be as young as twenty six, and it was much the same in the UK for the counter-terrorist police force. They'd both been with the Unit for over two years and in that short time had proved themselves to be invaluable members of the squad, quick-thinking, fit and decisive. They were similarly built, both six feet and about a hundred and eighty five pounds, but Chalky had dark features whereas Archer had blond hair and blue eyes. The two friends were pretty evenly matched with the pistol and sub-machine gun that the Unit used in the field, but the recent arrival of the sniper rifle had seen Archer take not only a considerable amount of Chalky's money, but serious bragging rights in their contests.

Just before Christmas last year, the head of the Unit, Director Tim Cobb, had ordered every officer in the squad take a sniper course with the newly-arrived PSG1A1, at this range. A siege and hostage situation at a townhouse in Tottenham earlier in the year had left Cobb with the realisation that the task force was only really equipped for close-quarter confrontations. In the field, each officer was armed and proficient with an HK MP5 sub-machine gun and also a Glock 17 pistol, but Cobb had requested and been given official authorisation for the use of two PSG1A1 sniper rifles. In the army, snipers were the ultimate force-multiplier. One sniper could hold down an entire area for days at a time. In the U.S, their forces and statisticians had come up with the estimation that snipers in their army averaged 1.3 rounds per kill.

But in the police, sharpshooters gave them the distance advantage. Any emergency that called for a sharpshooter normally meant the enemy was at a single location, usually a bank or a hostage situation, and meant the shooter could engage the enemy unawares from a distance, not coming in through the front door. The arrival of the rifles had taken a real weight off Cobb's mind. He didn't want to get caught short as the German Police had.

Over a week-long period during the Christmas holiday four months ago, the entire team had become accustomed with the weapon under the tutelage of three snipers from the SAS, the British Special Forces squad. Each officer had fired hundreds of rounds with the weapons and all had quickly improved, learning the intricacies and technicalities of precision marksmanship. Archer in particular had proven to be particularly proficient, despite being the youngest man on the team. He was a natural, having taken to sharpshooting as he had to the pistol and sub-machine gun work in previous years, and by the end of the week he was the stand-out shooter in the Unit. The three SAS guys training him had been impressed. He'd even ended up outshooting one of them in a final challenge, much to the delight of his team-mates. However, the ARU's First Team were typically the go-to squad in operations, the first guys through the door, so Archer needed to be there on the ground and not far away from the action and up high with a rifle. As a consequence, the two best shooters of the six-man Second Team were assigned sharp-shooting detail if it came to it, but Archer was always there as immediate back-up if they needed him.

Fox and Porter stepped forward to take their turns with the weapon whilst Archer and Chalky walked through to the back of the range, headed towards a drinks stand to their right where there were a couple of tables and some empty chairs.

The range was about a twenty minute drive from their headquarters and was a second home to the Unit. North of the city up past Stratford, the range had separate areas for short-arms and long-arms fire. The entire team were officially required to retest on handguns and MP5 sub-machine guns every three months here, so the guys were extremely familiar with the place. Cobb encouraged constant practice to mitigate against any disasters in the field, so First Team had taken to meeting here three times a week, if they weren't on an operation, to work on their shooting. Soon after its arrival, one of the PSG1A1s had become a consistent fifth member of the group. The challenge of being precise with the rifle inevitably created competition within the team, and although Chalky had improved he was still to beat Archer in their head-to-head, a score-line his best friend seldom let him forget.

Returning his binoculars to a rack on the wall, Chalky poured himself a coffee with milk and two sugars whilst Archer went for tea, black, nothing added. The two men took a seat and watched as Fox snuggled in against the stock of the rifle across the range, Porter lying beside him like a spotter, binoculars to his eyes, ear defenders in place on his head. They were the only ones here on the long-distance range, but they could all hear muffled bangs and weapons' reports coming from the doors across the stone walkway to their right.

Archer watched as Fox clicked off the safety and settled in behind the weapon, giving it a dry click. He then carefully slotted the magazine into place and pulled back the slide, loading a round into the chamber. Seven hundred yards across the grass, the black paper target was mounted in front of a thick sand levee, the sun now shining down brightly. The morning April air was thin and clean, not a whisper of wind in the air, good weather considering the usual showers that time of year in the UK.

'So how's your girl?' Chalky asked, blowing on his coffee to get it to cool. 'The one in New York. What was her name- Katick?'

Archer looked at his tea.

'Katic. And she's not my girl.'

Chalky looked at him. 'What happened?'

'It didn't work out.' Pause. 'She met someone else.'

'Oh shit. I'm sorry buddy.'

Archer shrugged.

'Guess it wasn't meant to be,' he said. 'Probably for the best anyway. She's a Supervisory Special Agent in the FBI. People like that don't have time for personal lives.'

Silence followed. Chalky took a premature pull from his coffee and winced as he burnt his tongue. It was still too hot.

'You should go over there,' he said. 'Go and see her. Maybe she'll change her mind.'

Archer looked at him and shook his head.

'With what money?' he said. 'I'm even more broke than you, Chalk. And you know the way this job goes. I can't just pack up and leave for a week.'

There was suddenly a loud *bang* as Fox fired the weapon. They looked down the range from their seats and could just make out a white hole in the black right shoulder of the target. A hit, but not a kill. Anything three inches left would have been a different story. The sandy-haired officer looked up and cursed, clicking on the safety. He and Porter swapped places as the two other officers watched. Fox was six-five up against Porter, much closer in their head-to-head contest. But from the looks of things, it was about to become six-a-piece.

'So what's new with you?' Archer asked, drinking his tea and eager to change the subject.

Chalky grinned. 'I went on a date last night.'

'Oh really? Who's the girl?'

'Her name was Elaine.'

'Where'd you meet her?'

'Dating website. She's a lawyer.'

Archer looked over at him. ‘You’re kidding?’

‘That she's a lawyer?’

‘No, that you're on those websites.’

‘What’s wrong with that?’

‘Chalk, you’re twenty seven. Why the hell are you online dating? Go to a bar.’

Chalky drank from his coffee and shook his head.

‘You should have seen her, Arch,’ he said. ‘She was a real beauty. Divorced, late-thirties. She saw *police officer* on my profile and said that’s what attracted her. Said she’d always liked a man in uniform, and was looking for a new one after her ex-husband left her for a younger woman.’

‘Am I going to meet her?’

‘No. Don’t think I’ll see her again. Didn't even get a chance to show her my scar.’

Archer smiled. Chalky had taken a bullet in the back a year and a half ago, and after he’d healed, he'd found much to his pleasure that the bullet-scar had a very positive effect on women. He had all sorts of wild stories for how he’d got it, including surviving a mob hit and Archer’s personal favourite that he took a bullet for the Prime Minister. Chalky had never realised that the true story how he got the scar was actually far more impressive than anything else he could come up with.

‘Why won’t you see her again?’ Archer asked.

‘My card got declined at dinner. She had to pay. Don’t think she was happy about it.’

'You made her pay?'

'I hadn't checked my account in a while. But I'm skint. We don't get paid for another couple of weeks, and you keep taking all my money with that stupid rifle.'

Archer laughed. 'Are you serious?'

'That wasn't just it,' his friend continued. 'She kept banging on about my name. You had to put your real name on the website, and she said she'd only call me Danny, or Daniel.'

'Imagine that. That is your name.'

He shook his head. 'She said Chalky made it sound like I was a builder or plastered walls for a living. We'd only just met and she was already nagging me like we'd been married for ten years.'

Archer shook his head and laughed, his low mood evaporating, all thoughts of Katic and New York disappearing. His best friend's real name was Danny White, but everyone apart from his mother called him Chalky, an ironic nickname given his dark features. He used to hate it, but had now got used to it, and he never used his first name anymore. He and Archer had met when they both joined the police at eighteen and had been inseparable ever since. They were a perfect foil for each other. Chalky's exuberant personality meant he often needed someone to keep him in line, which is where his best friend came in, but in return he had a knack for lifting Archer's mood no matter how shitty he was feeling.

Across the range, there was another *bang* as Porter fired. This one went straight through the target's torso, around where the liver would be, and the paper gently billowed from the impact of the bullet. A kill. Porter looked up and smiled as Fox swore, then pulled the magazine from the weapon. As he inspected it and made sure the gun wasn't still loaded, Archer checked his watch.

'Oh shit. *We need to go, lads*,' he called. '*It's eight o'clock.*'

Across the range, Porter finished inspecting the weapon, then applied the safety catch. He folded down the tripod and carried the weapon and the magazine carefully to a black equipment case, stowing them inside. He clicked it shut and lifting it, he and Fox walked over to join the other two men to return their binoculars and ear defenders to the racks.

Archer and Chalky rose, draining their drinks, and after tossing the foam cups in the bin, the four men headed to the exit, Fox pulling a ten pound note from his pocket with his free hand and passing it to Porter with a shake of his head as they walked.

Given the difference in time-zone, 8:00 am in London was 3:00 am in New York City. Although it was known as the city that never slept, it often dozed, and as it was the middle of the night on an early Thursday morning most of the city's eight million residents, spread out across the five boroughs, were fast asleep. Above the still-open bars and bodegas and shimmering lights that glowed all night down below, the high-rise apartment buildings of Manhattan housed the wealthier of those eight million people.

And one new member to this club was a dark-haired man in his early forties, a man who still couldn't believe that it had happened to him.

He worked as a bodyguard-for-hire, not normally a job that came with an impressive pay. Truth be told, it was typically shitty, thankless work which involved a lot of hanging around and unpaid overtime. But he was a solid professional, well-trained and good at what he did, and a year's worth of employment with an Arab oil Sheikh and a sequence of ever-increasing salary bumps had meant the man could finally move out of his old, beaten-down, two-roomed apartment in Brooklyn and take up residence in a Manhattan high-rise. He now lived in a comparatively luxurious place, on the twenty second floor of an East 41st apartment building overlooking the East River, Queens and his old neighbourhood in Brooklyn across the water. The apartment had two bedrooms, an en-suite bathroom, a lounge, kitchen and washroom. The building had a gym and a large roof-space available to all the residents, and he found himself living in the same building as lawyers, accountants and businessmen, a world away from his old neighbourhood in Brooklyn.

Finally, after twenty years of toil and graft, the man felt like he'd made it.

Working for the Sheikh was a dream come true. The bodyguard still couldn't believe his good fortune at landing it. He'd been referred to the Arab through a businessman he'd worked for during a conference in New York in 2010, and when the offer of steady employment had been put on the table he'd jumped at the opportunity. At that point, he'd been out of work for almost two months, living on canned food, and was watching his meagre savings slowly dwindle away. And so far, the job had been everything he'd hoped for and more.

He'd been on numerous trips to the Middle East, basically paid vacations, flying First Class alongside the Sheikh every time. His boss liked to stay at expensive western hotels on the coastline, so the ample sun, sea and exotic women on view didn't hurt. And the cheques he received each month were ten times what he'd ever earned before, despite being mere drops of water in an ocean to a man as wealthy as his employer. The bodyguard had always been diligent in what he did, never afraid of a hard day's work, but now he couldn't help but feel that life was finally starting to pay him back.

The Sheikh was staying across town at the Trump International Hotel, by Columbus Circle, and his protector would be back over there at six a.m. sharp, ready and waiting to do what he was paid for and protect his boss when he went out and about. After all, he couldn’t afford to get sloppy or careless. A man as wealthy and powerful as his employer would always have enemies, and if the bodyguard let his guard down all this could be over. He worked five days on, two off, and he'd hit the sack around midnight, early for him, wanting to get a good night's sleep and start his upcoming five day shift rested and alert.

The man was flat-out in the wide double bed in the main bedroom, fast asleep, snoring gently, the open curtains of the high-rise apartment showing just a solitary tugboat moving slowly up the East River outside in the darkness far below. He had no wife or girlfriend or even a dog and was all alone, his hard and scarred body stretched out on the soft and accommodating Egyptian-cotton sheets. The silence was rhythmically broken by gentle snoring from the man in the bed, the only sound in the apartment. The place was dark and still.

The door to the apartment had no latch, only a lock on the handle.

It was silently picked with ease.

The door was pushed back smoothly and slowly, and a large figure in black moved silently into the apartment, shutting the door noiselessly behind him. The intruder was wearing dark gloves and medical wraps on his feet, and carried a stubby silenced pistol in his hands, a round in the chamber, the safety catch off, his finger on the trigger.

The door to the main bedroom was open and the intruder crept forward slowly, feet silent on the carpet. As the stranger approached the door, he heard the man's rhythmic breathing increase slightly in volume.

The newcomer slid into the room through the crack in the door, coming to a halt at the foot of the bed and stared down at the sleeping man. He was flat out on his back, like a guy who had just got in from a hard night's drinking, dead to the world.

The stranger in black raised the pistol double-handed, centred on the guy's face.

'Hey,' he said, quietly, almost a whisper.

The bodyguard in the bed stirred.

He opened his eyes and looked down the bed, lifting his head up, like a red and white bulls-eye target at the fair.

He frowned as his jumbled brain tried to make sense of what he was seeing.

There was someone standing there.

He blinked, confused, wondering if this was a dream.

It wasn't. The intruder shot him between the eyes. The weapon was silenced but there was a loud *thump* as the hollow-nosed bullet smacked into the sleeping man's forehead, instantly blowing the back of his head apart. There was a spray of blood, bone and brains and another white *thump* of feathers in the air as the bullet passed through the pillow and buried itself in the bed-frame behind.

The guy in the bed snapped back and was still, feathers floating down to rest on his forehead and the blood-stained pillow case, his eyes open and staring at the bathroom across the room as his head lolled to the left.

And the room was silent.

The figure in black took a confirming look at the dead man. He flicked on the safety catch to the silenced-pistol, opening his jacket and sliding it inside, then zipped up the coat. He turned and walked out of the apartment as silently as he'd arrived, pulling the door shut silently behind him, the wraps on his feet and the gloves on his hands shielding any prints and any evidence that he was ever here. Fifteen minutes later, the gloves, wraps and pistol were on their way to the bottom of the East River and the man was in a taxi on his way to John F Kennedy International Airport.

His direct, six hour flight to London would take off in the next couple of hours.

THREE

The journey from the shooting range to the ARU headquarters took just over twenty minutes. The black 4x4 Ford carrying the four officers passed pavements and street corners busy with bustling, purposeful commuters heading to the office, cups of coffee and briefcases everywhere you looked. Cutting and weaving an intricate path through the London streets, Porter did his best to avoid the heavy traffic wherever he could and get them over to their headquarters in good time.

Eventually, he turned left and pulled the car into the police station car park. He tucked the vehicle into an empty spot near the entrance, alongside two other black 4x4 Fords, the other official Unit police cars. He applied the handbrake and killed the engine, and together the four officers stepped out and shut the doors of the vehicle.

Dressed in blue jeans and a black sweater, Archer took a deep breath of fresh air and looked up at the ARU's headquarters in front of him. The building was a simple design, two floors, a long, rectangular Operations room above and a series of locker rooms, holding and interrogation cells and a gun-cage below. They were in the heart of the city, surrounded by glass buildings and with the echoes of traffic in the air all around them, but without knowing that this was a counter-terrorist police station one would think it was just another office building. Looking up at the roof and shielding his eyes from the sun, Archer caught a quick glimpse of the end of a black helicopter rotor.

Then again, the chopper was kind of a giveaway.

Along with the recent inclusion of the two PSG1A1 sniper rifles at the end of last year, Cobb had also been allocated a helicopter, funded by the Met's budget much to the envy of some of his colleagues. Fox and another officer called Mason had qualified for piloting the vessel, and although it had only been used a couple of times since its arrival in January, it had proved invaluable on both occasions. It was a Eurocopter EC135, a twin-engine helicopter popularly used across the UK by police and ambulance services. Weighing just over three thousand pounds, the helicopter could carry a pilot and seven passengers, and gave both air-support and essential visual aid for any crisis or emergency where they needed an aerial vantage point. Sturdy and compact, it was painted black with yellow lining and had *ARU* printed in bold white letters across the doors.

Down below, Fox opened the back of the Ford and pulled out the rifle in its case. Once he shut the door, Porter locked the car and the four men walked across the tarmac towards the entrance.

A young officer called Clark was sitting behind the front desk, a metal barrier preventing them from moving further into the building. He was a nice guy, just twenty six, and had replaced Archer as the youngest officer in the building. He'd recently passed the rigorous selection process, completing his training with flying colours, but given that there were no spots available Cobb had offered him the desk job until one freed up. The young policeman looked up as he saw them coming and nodded.

'Morning lads,' he said, as the four men walked in.

'Morning, Clarky,' Archer said. 'How's things?'

'Good, Arch. Yourself?'

'Can't complain.'

The four officers took it in turns to sign a pad on the front desk, checking the time on a clock on the wall above Clark's head.

'Staying out of trouble, Chalk?' Clark asked.

'Doing my best,' Chalky replied, squiggling his signature.

After Chalky dropped the pen back on the desk, Clark pushed a button under the counter and the metal barrier in front of them was released. The four men walked through into the police station, nodding thanks to the young officer. Fox headed along the lower corridor with the sniper-rifle to return it to the gun-cage whilst the other three men moved upstairs.

When they reached the second floor, the trio were surprised to see a large group of people standing around in the Operations area ahead of them. Normally the task force were all in the Briefing Room to the left, staying out of the intelligence team's way.

Such a gathering normally spelt trouble.

'Hang on,' Chalky said. 'This looks interesting.'

'What the hell?' Archer said.

Each man had a mobile phone he was required to carry with him at all times, but none of them had been notified of any crisis or emergency. However by the looks of things, something was going on. The trio moved down the corridor quickly and entered the Operations room. It was a square shaped area, lots of screens, computers and keyboards, and to the right the three newcomers saw that the entire six-man tech team had paused in their work at their stations. Behind them was a cluster of task-force officers who had filtered out of the Briefing Room to the left, and all of them were watching a large screen mounted on the wall across the room. The officers already standing there sensed the trio arrive, turning quickly and nodding greetings, but the whole level was silent.

Archer turned to one of the officers, the leader of Second Team, a big man in his late-thirties called Deakins.

'What's going on?' Archer asked.

Deakins didn't reply; he just pointed to the television screen. A female news reporter was standing on the South Bank by the Thames. They'd caught it just in time. She was about to deliver her report.

'Thank you, Fiona,' she said. *'I'm afraid it has been a shocking and deeply unsettling start to the day, as*

up-and-coming politician Charlie Adams committed suicide on a bench facing the Thames early this morning. Found with a revolver in his hand, he was killed by a single self-inflicted gunshot wound to the head. With elections fast approaching and Mr Adams with a strong following, people from his constituency have been left in complete shock by the apparent suicide. Mr Adams was well-known for being a former soldier, a man who served in the British Army for eighteen years and was a real inspiration and success story in his surprise move into politics. An investigation is already underway to try and understand why this tragedy has happened. We will keep you updated on this situation. He leaves a wife and six year old son. Back to you, Fiona.'

As the group watched the screen, Archer became aware of some movement to his right. Looking through the transparent glass of an office, he saw Director Cobb, head of the ARU, standing whilst watching the report on a television on the wall in his office. Unusually, Cobb looked slightly agitated, running his hand through his dark hair and with a worried look on his face. Normally cool and collected, his anxious expression was a surprise.

'Is Cobb alright?' he asked, to no-one in particular.

'Apparently he knew the guy,' Deakins said.

Archer looked up at the screen again, then shrugged. He didn't know anything about politics and had never heard of Charlie Adams before. Sad news for sure, but not a headline he would remember.

Turning, he walked over into the Briefing Room to the drinks stand inside and poured himself a cup of tea. Seeing the news report had finished, the other officers started to join him and slowly but surely, the place returned to normal, like a cassette that had been paused but with the play button pushed again.

But whilst everyone else across the floor shifted their attention from the television back to their workplace, Director Tim Cobb kept watching the screen mounted inside his office.

He was feeling a mixture of shock and total disbelief.

He'd arrived for work an hour ago, feeling good. It had been a marquee year for his Unit so far, two successful operations already in the bag. He was just turned forty one, but felt like thirty one, and had a beautiful wife and two sons he adored. His team, the Armed Response Unit, had become the premier counter-terrorist police force in the city, the particular favourite of the Prime Minister, and just last week the detail had demolished a drug-dealing ring that had been plaguing the city for months. From intelligence his tech team had gathered over months of wire-taps and bugs, his task force had performed four early-morning raids and seized over three quarters of a million pounds in cash and heroin, arresting seven men in the process with enough evidence to put them away for some considerable time.

However, watching the television screen, Cobb was starting to realise that the ship was never steady for long. A storm was always brewing. And that morning, lightning had struck the moment he'd turned on the television to catch the headlines.

Standing there in his office watching the news report, Cobb felt bereft. The news of the suicide was brutal and shocking. A wife left a widow, a six year old boy without a father. He hadn't spoken to Adams in over ten years, but he'd seen a great deal of him on the television recently and had watched his unexpected rise as a politician with great pleasure. He'd become the surprise candidate, his name on everyone's lips, and there was an ever-growing public belief that one day he would make Prime Minister. He was building an impressive following around the country and everyone liked him, something which was often hard to say about a politician.

He'd been a refreshing change and had effortlessly captured the public's support and belief in a way that his competitors could only dream of. As a handsome, charismatic war hero, Charlie Adams had definitely bucked the trend and had been a true breath of fresh air. He would have had Cobb's vote, no question. The man had been as strong as he was dependable, one of the finest men Cobb had ever worked with, and given the ARU's close working relationship with 10 Downing Street, Cobb had secretly been hoping that Adams would one day in the not too distant future become the new PM so he could have the opportunity to work with him again.

Watching the television, Cobb saw the screen change to a bullet-pointed summary of Adams' life. He sighed. Away from all the politics, Cobb had liked him as a person. Charlie had been a good man and an excellent soldier. He knew there would be a lot of former comrades and servicemen watching the report who would feel just as sad as he did at that moment, wishing Charlie had said something or asked for help instead of putting that gun in his mouth and leaving so many questions unanswered.

Turning, Cobb sat down behind his desk and watched the report shift back to the studio newsroom.

Something must have got to Charlie. Who knew what inner demons he was fighting. After all, he'd served all over the place with the army and been in some hellacious places in the darkest corners of the world. He'd been to Bosnia, Kosovo, Iraq and Afghanistan, right in the middle of all of the conflicts. God only knew the things he must have seen and the way they might have affected him. Cobb had only had a brief interaction with him just before the turn of the millennium, but he couldn't have done his job better, a true leader of men.

Definitely not the kind of man who would blow his own head off with a handgun.

Rising and feeling agitated, Cobb moved across the room to his coffee machine and poured himself a thick espresso, no milk, no sugar. He took it back to his desk and let the drink cool, looking back up at the television screen. The *Breaking News* banner across the bottom of the screen was running the headline on a loop, but the screen had changed, now showing a picture of Captain Adams in some faded combat fatigues, kneeling and smiling up to the camera, his SA 80 rifle cradled over his thigh, squinting in the sunlight. He was in a dusty courtyard, somewhere in Iraq probably, and his skin was tanned, his dark hair untidy, the beginnings of a beard on his face.

Nevertheless his broad smile and whole persona demonstrated that raw charisma he'd always had, the quality that drew people to him and made him such a good leader of men. Staring at the image on the screen, Cobb shook his head in disbelief.

Charlie Adams had killed himself.

Why?

Just over three thousand miles to the west, across the Atlantic, a forty year old man stepped out of a dark strip-club in a Washington DC outer suburb and walked wearily across the empty parking lot towards his car. His seven hour shift had just ended and he was wiped out.

He worked the door at the joint four nights a week, making sure the girls weren't harassed and that the guys who came in paid the eight dollar cover and didn't cause any trouble. It was a shitty job with a shitty wage, but it was all he could get. He needed the money because he needed to eat. He couldn't survive without it, but he hated coming to work here. The place was seedy and grimy and he couldn't remember the last time he'd seen someone run a mop over the floor. The lights on the sign outside didn't fully work, constantly buzzing and flickering, and it was depressing as hell inside.

The man hawked and spat on the ground as he walked, his footsteps echoing in the empty parking lot as he made his way towards his car, the only other sound the electronic buzz of the blue neon sign above the door of the club. It was called *Mermaids*, a run-down place out of the centre of the city towards the projects, far away from the political glamour of the Beltway and the college red-bricked cleanliness of Georgetown. It had been a quiet night, typical midweek stuff, only a few customers, losers still in shirt and tie from the office catching a quick sleazy view or maybe a private dance before they went home to their wives and told them they'd been forced to stay late at work. The sad thing was those guys were probably earning more in one day than he made in a month. He was supposed to be working the door till four, but business was so quiet they'd locked up just before three. It was his only job and he needed the money, so that hour's less pay had put him in a foul mood.

He walked over to his car, an unreliable piece of shit that didn't run like it should anymore, and pulled out his keys. He pushed the button but the car didn't beep.

It was already unlocked.

He cursed, pissed at himself that he'd left the car open all night. It was a miracle it was still here, given how close the strip-club was to the projects. If it had been stolen, he'd have been well and truly screwed.

Shaking his head at his stupidity, he climbed inside and shut the door.

He never even saw the man hidden in the back seat.

The stranger was small, dressed all in black, and had been lying in the shadows so he was close to invisible from the outside. In a flash, he lifted a piece of wire over the doorman's head and pulled it back hard around the man's throat, locking his arms tight.

The guy in the front seat's eyes widened and he started thrashing in panic, scrabbling at his neck as the wire garrotted him. Behind him the small man cinched it tighter, the wire slicing into the doorman's neck, cutting off his oxygen, the sharp wire splitting the skin.

The guy in the front fought vainly for about ten seconds, the blood vessels in his eyes bursting, his head turning the colour of boysenberry, his fingers grasping at the wire frantically as he was strangled. Behind him, the small man pulled it tighter still.

The doorman gave a final wheeze and then died.

The small man held the wire tight for a few moments longer, ensuring the guy was dead. Then he pulled it free, gathering it up into a ball and tucked it back into his pocket. Up front, released from the wire, the dead man slumped forward, his forehead coming to rest against the steering wheel, his arms limp, like he was drunk and had passed out while trying to start the engine.

The smaller man checked the guy's pulse with a gloved hand, making sure he was gone, then slipped out of the rear door of the car quietly, clicking the door shut behind him.

The parking lot was deserted, the city asleep around him.

No witnesses.

No-one around.

Popping his collar, the small man put his head down and moved off into the shadows. Four minutes later, the wire and gloves disposed of, the man was in a taxi heading straight for Dulles International Airport and his 5:05 am direct flight to London Heathrow.

FOUR

Almost an hour later, Cobb was still at his desk inside the ARU headquarters thinking about the Adams suicide. He was going over and over it in his mind in a loop, like the *Breaking News* banner on the news channel, trying to process what had happened.

Thinking hard, he suddenly reached forward across his desk and scooped up a black phone receiver from its cradle, pushing *1* on the keypad. The call connected to Nikki next door, the head of his analyst group, a dark-haired woman in her late twenties who did a great job running the entire tech team. He looked up and saw her grab her phone, not looking away from her computer, sitting with her back to him as she took the call.

'Nikki,' she said, seeing it was on the internal line.

'Nikki, it's me. Who's handling the Charlie Adams investigation?' Cobb asked.

'Hang on, sir, I'll check,' she said.

Through the glass of his office, he saw her place the receiver to one side and start tapping keys on her computer. He sipped his second espresso of the morning, the caffeine not helping his agitation. There was a pause.

'A Detective-Inspector Graham in CID,' she said.

'Can you find out if they've spoken to Charlie's wife yet?'

'Yes, sir.'

‘Thank you.’

Cobb put the phone back on the cradle and looked back up at the television screen. As he took another hit of espresso, he saw through the glass the sergeant of his task force, Porter, approaching his office door. He was dressed in some dark blue jeans and a grey sweater, the jumper emphasising his wide shoulders and strong frame.

Porter was an imposing figure of a man, but he was a gentle giant. He was one of those people who never swore, no matter how bad the situation or how frustrated he was feeling. He reminded Cobb of one of those big dogs at the park who remained aloof and kept their patience whenever smaller dogs nipped and bothered at them, never losing his temper or biting back, endlessly patient no matter what the provocation. Cobb had seen people underestimate Porter, mistaking his quiet patience for weakness, but every one of them had quickly discovered their mistake. He was strong and loyal, and like Charlie Adams, was someone Cobb had taken to immediately as a human being.

His predecessor, a tough-as-nails army veteran called Mac, had retired towards the end of last year and Porter had been a shoe-in as his replacement. Everyone had approved of his selection, and so far Port had proved to be an outstanding choice as a leader. The men on the task force all liked him, but more importantly they all trusted him, the most crucial thing when out there in the field. Since he'd taken over, Porter had led the team against a potential terrorist plot and also the drug-dealing ring that the Unit had smashed just over a week ago; the success of both operations had left no doubt in Cobb's mind that he'd chosen the right man to be Mac's replacement.

Although he saw Cobb watching him approach, Porter still stopped and knocked on the glass, respecting rank. Cobb nodded and Porter entered the office, closing the door behind him.

'Morning, Port.'

'Morning, sir.'

Stepping further into the office, Porter glanced up at the television screen, at the headline running on the lower portion of the television, black text on a yellow stream under the newsreader.

Breaking News: Political candidate Charlie Adams commits suicide on South Bank early this morning.

Porter looked over at Cobb and shook his head.

'Sad news.'

'Yes. It is.'

'Deaks mentioned he was a friend of yours?'

Cobb nodded. 'We worked together a few years ago.'

Both men watched the screen in silence as a photo of Adams in suit and tie came onto the screen. He was smiling and waving to a crowd on a podium, a lectern in front of him, either before or just after he'd given some kind of speech. Even out of combat fatigues and dressed in the suit the man still cut an impressive figure, the broad musculature of his shoulders and arms clear under the dark suit jacket, his eyes narrowed warmly as he smiled at the crowd.

'Did you know of him?' Cobb asked.

Porter nodded. 'Yes, sir. He gave a speech in my local area last month. Impressive guy. He had my vote, that was for sure.'

Pause.

'The report said he left a widow and a small boy. A real shame.'

'Yes. It is.'

Just then, the phone on Cobb's desk rang. He reached over and pushed a button for the loudspeaker on the phone.

'Yep?'

'Sir, I spoke to CID,' Nikki said, her voice filling the office. *'I have some bad news.'*

'What?'

'The wife and boy are both missing.'

'What?'

'No-one has seen or heard from them since the news of the suicide. Not family, nor friends. They've just vanished. The boy didn't show up for school, and the woman isn't picking up her phone.'

'What about the house?'

'DI Graham went round to talk to her, but no-one answered. When they eventually got inside, he and another detective found two unmade beds upstairs. The master and the kid's room. But the house was empty. No bags were packed though. Everything was

still there. Clothes, valuables, the whole lot. They haven't done a runner.'

'Maybe they had a fight,' Porter suggested, loud enough so Nikki could hear.

'*Seems unlikely,'* Nikki said. '*DI Graham said the neighbours told him they heard no noise last night, saw no-one arrive or leave the house. Adams was at the office until midnight anyway, so if they argued, it would have been over the phone.'*

She paused, as Cobb and Porter absorbed what she'd just said.

'Speaking of his office, I have more news for your sir.'

'Go on.'

'DI Graham spoke to the receptionist at Mr Adams' office. The girl said a letter came in the post for him late last night, around eleven o'clock, completely out of the blue. She said she gave it to him before he went home for the night, around midnight. She was the last person who saw him alive.'

Cobb looked at Porter, and both men frowned.

'Have they found the letter?' Cobb asked.

'No, sir. But they found the envelope in his car. Forensics took a swab from the seal and are already running it to try and match the DNA. They're also checking the envelope for prints or anything at all they can trace which might tell us where it came from. When they found his body, the report said there were black remnants of burnt paper by his feet. Two

different types. Standard sheet paper and photographic.'

Cobb nodded. 'Any details?'

'No sir. They were only singed edges, all curled up. The letter and photographs themselves were torched. Only parts of the edges are left, and those are black and charred.'

Cobb swore. 'What progress is DI Graham making re the two missing persons?'

'They are already going through her phonebook and contacting friends and family. He hasn't alerted the press yet, but he's going to let them know shortly and put out a plea for public help to call them immediately if there are any sightings. Adams' wife was starting to become recognisable to people, so he thinks that might help locate her.'

'OK. Stay on it. The moment it comes in, I want to know of any progress. If anything comes up that is relevant, let me know. And I mean anything.'

'Yes, sir.'

The call ended. Cobb shook his head and leaned back in his chair, looking at Porter.

'Shit, Port. What do you think?'

'I don't know,' Porter said. 'Maybe someone had dirt on him? Elections are coming up. Something from his past that he wouldn't want anyone to find out about? They put it in the letter and he felt it was worth killing himself over?'

'Bad enough to blow his brains out?' Cobb asked, frowning. He shook his head. 'No way. That's not the person I knew. He was a good man, through and through. He would never have done anything so bad he'd kill himself. And that doesn't explain his family going missing.'

Porter thought for a moment.

'I hate to say it, but kidnap?'

Cobb exhaled slowly, then nodded.

'Looks probable, doesn't it. Damn it. And the letter is definitely connected. Who delivers mail at eleven o'clock at night? Who knew he'd still be at his office? And why would he burn it?'

Porter nodded. 'Nikki said there were two kinds. Sheet and photographic. So probably text and photographs. Maybe a threat and a visual aid.'

There was a silence.

'Shit,' Cobb said again. 'Anyway, whatever happens, we'll stay close to it. It's not our investigation, but I damn well want to be kept in the loop about this. That press release about the missing persons will help.'

'You think someone will find them?'

Cobb looked at him.

'I hope so.'

Across the city in Mayfair, an American in a smart suit was making his way along Upper Grosvenor Street, carrying nothing save a briefcase, his expensive shoes clicking on the smooth concrete pavement as he walked.

Turning the corner to his left and checking the time on a Tag Heuer watch on his wrist, the man arrived in Grosvenor Square, the home of most of the foreign embassies located in London. The weather was good, the sun shining down, and the air was fresh, clean and mild. He paused for a moment, taking a deep breath and enjoying the view, then continued on his journey, heading along the western side of the Square and straight towards the United States Embassy.

The building stood out in the district, primarily because it was at least twice the size of every other embassy in the area. But it was also unique in that it was the only United States Embassy in the world not built on official US soil. A contentious dispute in the 1950s between the Grosvenors, an upper class English family and owners of the Square, and the United States Government had seen the Americans settle for a 999 year lease on the plot of land instead of outright ownership, a different deal from those usually signed in Embassy agreements. The Americans had requested that the section of the Square where the Embassy would be built become United States soil, but the Grosvenors refused. The Duke of Westminster at the time, a Grosvenor, had apparently attempted to resolve the on-going spat with a proposed deal. He told the Americans that if they returned all the lands 'stolen' by the United States after the War of Independence to the UK, then they could buy the site on the west side of Grosvenor Square and do whatever they wanted with it.

However, the Americans found a slight hitch in the proposition.

The lands the Duke wanted returned included most of Maine and New York State.

Unsurprisingly, the American Government refused the offer and consequently, were forced to rent the plot of land instead. So although not officially US soil, there were armed United States Marines standing guard at various positions outside the long building that morning, as there were every day. In any country around the world the US Embassy was a priority terrorist target, a chance to hurt the US without having to try and breach their borders, and the London office was at the top of that list given the Americans' and the UK's close relations and military coalition in conflicts around the world. It was especially well-defended, not only with manpower but with some of the most advanced and up to date security technology placed in and around the building. Such measures were for two reasons. The building was officially the United States Embassy in London.

But it was also the unofficial British substation for the Central Intelligence Agency.

Outside the building was a glass hut with an x-ray machine and body scanner. Seeing as an application for a US visa could only be approved after an appointment here, every day there was a long queue of hopeful people waiting to pass their bags and contents of their pockets through the machine and be patted down before they entered the building. Once inside, they were then shepherded to a long waiting hall to the left and told to wait for their final interview and hopefully, an approval. As a matter of course, they would be looking at a several hour wait at least before they got called, the entire process from joining the queue to leaving the building taking close to four hours, sometimes more, and it wasn't uncommon for someone to spend most of the working day in there, waiting to be processed.

Walking past the queue of people waiting to move through the security point, the American moved in through a side door to the hut as people stuck in the line looked on enviously. Two guards were working the x-ray machine and metal detector and they nodded at the man as he placed his briefcase on the conveyor, grabbing a grey bin and dropping a wallet and mobile phone into the tray. His dark suit was cut to fit, 42 regular with a 32 waist, so he had no belt, nor any spare change in his pockets.

'Morning sir,' one of the guards said.

'Good morning,' the man said.

He walked through the metal detector which didn't make a sound. Although he knew it wouldn't, the American still felt that moment of relief that everyone did when they passed through one of the machines and it didn't go off.

He retrieved his things from the tray, returning them to his pockets, then scooped up his briefcase and headed off towards the entrance to the Embassy.

He'd lived in London for over a decade and after a rocky start, he found that he liked it more and more with each passing year. He'd arrived here in 1999, fresh out of his training at Camp Peary just outside Williamsburg, Virginia, aka 'The Farm', where every CIA trainee goes to learn his craft and hopefully then graduate into a position with the Agency. He'd excelled at the paramilitary and tradecraft operations set up by the agency instructors, and being just twenty five at the time and a non-smoker, had been in excellent cardiovascular condition, cruising through all the fitness tests. He'd learned everything he could ever need in the field, from defensive driving and handling Zodiac boats to hand-to-hand combat and parachuting. He'd learnt interrogation techniques, manipulation and evasion tactics, how to deceive and turn the tables from having an enemy watching you to you watching him, and had finished the training fully expecting to become an NOC, a non-official cover, an operative who would work overseas with no official ties to the United States Government. Basically, a spy.

But then, at his final interview and to his dismay, the instructors had decided that they wanted him behind a desk. He'd scored very highly on the leadership and aptitude tests and they said his talents would be wasted undercover in some foreign country. Instead, they'd offered him a well-paid job in London in charge of a small team, and he'd had to adjust his thinking, determined to make the most of the opportunity given to him.

He'd been born and bred in Staunton, Virginia and found after he'd arrived in London in late-February 1999 that the weather in the UK was comparable and not such a shock to his system as it might otherwise have been. During his time here, he'd seen agents arrive on postings from Florida or California, and the frequently grey and gloomy weather had been a nasty surprise for them. He'd been one of the few students in his class in high school who'd enjoyed learning about British history, about their Kings and Queens, how their parliamentary system had evolved and the great battles they'd fought, such as Agincourt, Trafalgar and Waterloo. When the opportunity had arisen, he was excited to both begin his career in the CIA and come to live London and experience their culture first-hand. America was such a comparatively modern place that he'd grown to love living here, absorbing the history around him. He'd spent many a weekend going to the old churches and cathedrals scattered across the city, buildings older than any in his home country. Just last weekend he'd been eating lunch in a pub that was built in the 15th Century. A pub that was older than the formation of his nation. Even now, that sort of thing still blew his mind.

And aside from the history of the place, he'd found the lifestyle agreed with him too. Over the years several promotions had given him a substantial increase in salary over his peers and an apartment paid for by the Agency, both of which allowed him to live well in an expensive city. Physically most guys his age and position on the ladder had started to soften around the midsection, but he was thirty-nine years old and still looked fifteen years younger, having avoided cigarettes and excess caffeine his entire life, diligently maintaining the prodigious fitness he'd had back at The Farm all those years before.

In all, life was pretty good. He'd spent the last fifteen years trying to help others and his country, and felt as if he'd done a pretty decent job. He'd never harmed or killed anyone, and in his position as an Operations Officer was one of the best guys around doing what he did. He had a six man team under his command in this building and a further six agents scattered across Europe whom only a select few knew worked for both him and the CIA. The information his team had gathered over the past few years had proved invaluable to the United States Government, and they were a crucial part of the Agency's European intelligence gathering.

In a large and extremely powerful organisation, the man approaching the entrance to the Embassy had built a solid reputation for himself as a good leader and valuable employee. He'd worked his ass off to get where he was, with a silent determination that a lot of his peers often didn't understand. At this point, he knew if he played his cards right he could be looking at another solid promotion and a position of increased power, one he could perhaps use as a springboard to higher things or just as a smooth ride to retirement. If he didn't get promoted he was planning to hand in a transfer request and head back to Virginia in the next couple of years anyway, maybe take over running a team at the headquarters there. However, for now, he was happy with his job and his life in London. He felt as if he was doing a good thing here, something worthwhile, and for the moment he was content to keep right on doing it.

Walking up the path to the main entrance, the man pulled open the door and moved inside the building. The woman behind the front desk recognised him, giving him a nod and a smile as she talked into a phone. Members of the public applying for visas were directed to the large waiting room on the left, herded in and told to wait until it was their turn.

The CIA agent headed to the right instead.

Walking down the corridor, he passed through another metal detector and x-ray machine, and passing a final handprint and retina scan, a thick door in front of him buzzed and clicked open. He pushed it and walked into the heart of the CIA substation, heading towards his office. The hallway was cream-walled with blue carpet, two thirds patriotic, only missing the red. However, the CIA seal printed sequentially on the carpet compensated for that omission, the compass rose on the shield below the bald eagle as red as the *United States of America* writing on the golden scroll below. The man passed a number of familiar offices on the way, including a tech area where a number of analysts and intelligence officers were already working away at computers. He kept moving down the corridor, and eventually arrived at his own office, pushing open the door and moving inside.

Walking to his desk, he placed his briefcase to one side and picked up the remote to a television mounted on the wall across the room. He pushed the power button and flicked it on. He always liked to catch a brief summary of the headlines when he walked in, updating him on the most important and pressing situations taking place around the world.

Although the television had a range of channels, including CNN and the Fox Newsroom, the American liked to keep it on BBC World. The reports were unbiased and gave him a cliff-notes version of everything he needed to know at the start of the day. CNN and Fox were fantastic broadcasters, but even their own network heads would probably admit that most of their focus was geared towards events in the United States. Considering Jackson's job, he needed to know straight away of any crises in Europe, and BBC World could be relied upon to summarise the most important events. Many times in the past, his assistant had walked into the office handing over a first-hand detailed report from an agent who had been directly involved in something that was just coming up on the screen.

As he took a seat behind his desk, his assistant knocked on the door and entered. He'd left it open knowing she would. She was a few years older than he was, a woman called Lynn who was also from Virginia, not far from his hometown, Staunton. She'd been his assistant for almost three years, and they had a good working relationship, sharing a pleasant degree of mutual respect. She didn't take shit from anyone, no matter what their rank or position, an attitude that had definitely not helped her career.

However, she and her boss had developed a good rapport. He always made a point to treat her with respect and courtesy and he knew that she appreciated it and subsequently did the same for him.

'Good morning, sir,' she said.

'Morning, Lynn. How are you?'

'Very well, sir. Yourself?'

'Good, thanks.'

He watched the screen as a report came up, a black headline on a yellow banner, rolling onto the screen. *Breaking News: Political candidate Charlie Adams commits suicide on South Bank early this morning.* The CIA agent read the headline and a light-bulb faintly flickered at the back of his mind, like one turned on in a dusty cellar or basement in a house that had been abandoned for years, given a spark of electricity but struggling for full power.

Charlie Adams.

That name rang a bell.

It was familiar yet distant, tantalisingly out of reach.

Where had he heard it before?

'Charlie Adams,' he said to himself, out loud, watching the screen. He looked over at his assistant. 'You heard that name before, Lynn?'

'Only on the occasional news report, sir,' she said. 'Apparently he was a pretty big deal in British politics. People were comparing him to President Obama. Real up-and-comer.'

'How did he die?'

'Put a revolver in his mouth and ate a bullet.'

The man behind the desk frowned, thinking.

'OK. Anything for me this morning?'

'Nothing pressing, sir. But don't forget, you have a twelve o'clock with the Syrian ambassador. It's at a private conference room across town. I've arranged transport so you won't have to drive.'

'That's right. OK. Thanks, Lynn.'

She nodded to her boss and left, shutting the door behind her.

After she was gone and he was alone, the CIA agent continued to watch the screen, wracking his brains for any further recollection of that name. *Charlie Adams*, he thought, repeating the name to himself over and over in his head, trying to stir up some recollection. It felt significant somehow, like he should have remembered who the guy was.

Charlie Adams.

Where do I know you from, man?

Across London, another man was watching that same news report.

He was sitting in the dark, and he was alone.

Across the wide room to his right, a series of weapons were lined up neatly against the wall. There were six Kalashnikov AK-47 rifles with a stack of spare magazines, each one fully loaded, taped back-to-back in pairs for ease of reloading once the top one was empty. Alongside them were four MP5 SD3s, silenced sub-machine guns, and a stack of spare clips loaded with 9 millimetre Parabellum bullets. There was also a bazooka with spare ammunition in a black equipment case. And finally a Russian Dragunov sniper rifle, unloaded, which used the same ammunition as the Kalashnikovs.

The weapons had all been bought down at the Docklands illegally three days ago, cash in hand, sufficient threats made to the men who had sold them, warning them in explicit detail what would happen if they ever said a word about the transactions to another soul. Syringes and tourniquets would be used, and a power saw. The message was received loud and clear. No-one would ever know about the trade. The serial numbers on all the weapons had already been removed with acid, rendering them pretty much untraceable, and the man in the room had stripped apart, cleaned, oiled and reassembled each weapon, wearing gloves to avoid leaving any fingerprints.

The figure was sitting in front of a desk with a series of televisions on the desktop in front of him, one tuned to BBC World, the other to the CNN Breaking Newsroom.

The sound on both screens was off, but the footage was what mattered.

On the left, the BBC channel, the screen was still showing the *Breaking News* banner headline of the politician's suicide. To the right, CNN, a *Breaking News* report had just come in of a man found strangled in a parking lot in a Washington DC suburb.

On the table beside the screens, there was a list of names on a pad of A4 paper, eleven in all, one beneath the other, written neatly in a line down the left margin of the page.

Charlie Adams was near the top.

The man reached forward and took a pen in his large hand. He drew a line through the two words.

Adams was gone.

He moved his finger down the list slowly and drew a line through another name, the doorman strangled outside the strip-club in DC. The large man had received a phone call from JFK International Airport earlier confirming the death of the bodyguard in the New York City apartment, but he was still waiting for the television to report it before he put his pen through a name. Not that he didn't trust his man, but he'd learned long ago that a man wasn't dead until you saw his corpse. He was living proof of that. He wanted to see a body-bag on a gurney on the television before he drew a line through anything. His two men were already in the air, on their way across the Atlantic from the American East Coast, using the best counterfeit passports and identification money could buy. Passing through security and immigration would not be a problem. They would be here in the room beside him within the next eight hours.

In the darkness, the big man lifted the pen off the page and looked down at the list. With one of them killed in Iraq years ago by a truck-bomb, that was three confirmed down. Three for three. One hundred per cent success. The perfect start.

Which left eight to go.

He flicked his gaze to the next name on the list. Reaching into his pocket, he pulled out a mobile phone and pushed *Redial*, lifting it to his ear. The call was answered before the second ring.

'Sir?' a voice said, down the line.

'Are you in position?' the man asked quietly, in a foreign language. His voice was deep and low.

'Yes, sir. We're here.'

'The package will arrive soon,' the man said, checking a watch on his wrist, still talking in the foreign tongue. 'You know what to do. Kill whoever you have to if they get in the way. But make sure you shoot him in the head. No mistakes.'

'Yes, sir.'

Without another word, the man ended the call. At the same moment, the CNN screen popped up with a new headline, appearing on the banner under the male newsreader's face. It joined the other report of the man found strangled on the looping news-feed, the reports streaming along the bottom of the screen one after the other, vice-versa.

Breaking News: Man found shot dead in New York City apartment.

The screen flicked to a gathering of news-vans and an ambulance outside a Manhattan building, the time still early in the morning there, the sun just starting to come up in the distance. He saw the doors open and a black body bag wheeled out on the trolley, moving down the steps and headed towards the open doors at the rear of the ambulance. The big man's eyes narrowed with satisfaction.

He picked up the pen and drew a line through the dead man's name.

Four down.

Seven to go.

FIVE

Inside his office in the U.S Embassy, the CIA agent was still trying to place Charlie Adams when his assistant came in bearing coffee on a tray. He didn’t react as she placed the cup and saucer on the desk in front of him, the tapping of fingers on computer keyboards audible from the tech area next door. Normally affable, she noticed he seemed distracted and took her time placing a small jug of milk and sweeteners by the cup of coffee on the desk, waiting for him to turn and talk to her. He didn’t.

‘Can I get you anything else, sir?’ she asked instead, subtly trying to get his attention.

‘No, thank you,’ he said vaguely, looking at the screen, his mind elsewhere.

Turning, she glanced at the television he was glued to across the room, seeing the report of the politician's suicide.

‘A real shame,’ she said. ‘I saw him on the news last week. Seemed like a good man.’

Her boss looked over at her. ‘What was his background?’

‘He used to be a soldier in the British Army. All the papers here loved him. You can see why,’ she said, nodding at a photograph of him in a suit waving to a crowd that had come up on the screen. 'I wouldn't mind going home to that every night.'

The CIA agent switched his attention back to the screen, scanning the photo, as his assistant turned to leave.

And all of a sudden, the light-bulb flashed on.

He sat up straight.

'Hang on, Lynn,' he said, as she walked to the door.

He grabbed a pen and scribbled three names on a small pad, then tore off the uppermost sheet, walked around his desk quickly and passed it to her.

'Do me a favour and run these three names through the system. Check every database you can. Military, NSA, FBI, police, DMV, medical and prison records. Anything and everything you can access.'

'Yes, sir,' she said, taking the paper.

'Don't let anyone know you're doing this. Not a soul. Understand?'

'Yes, sir. Is something wrong?'

He didn't reply. He'd shifted his attention to the television instead.

His secretary paused for a moment, then realised she wasn't going to get an answer. She nodded, pulling the door closed, and headed off to her private workstation to start searching the names he'd given her.

Alone, the CIA agent saw the studio shot change to one of Adams in combat fatigues, smiling up at the camera in some dusty courtyard somewhere in Iraq or Afghanistan.

Is something wrong, Lynn had asked.

'I hope not,' the man whispered, staring at the photograph of the soldier.

The shape of Grosvenor Square and the space on the western side of the U.S Embassy meant the area facing the building was a popular area for public protest. Pretty much every day of the year a group of people from some organisation or another would be out there, claiming civil rights or protesting against political injustice, chanting and waving painted signs, generally wanting to kick up a fuss and let their voice echo around Mayfair. The armed US Marines stationed on the outside of the building were used to this, ready and alert for any trouble, but despite being repetitive and occasionally aggravating to those within the building, the protestors were normally pretty harmless.

Walking through the Square, a small man in a purple delivery uniform stepped past them as they chanted and walked straight towards the Embassy. He worked for FedEx, and had a box-shaped express package under his arm. It was addressed to the London CIA office.

He moved to the left and joined the queue of people waiting to go through the security hut, and when it was his turn he nodded to the security guards within, passing the package through the x-ray machine. The guard behind the machine looked at the monitor, but all he could see inside the box was a white blurry rectangle, aka stacks of paper. The usual.

It took the delivery man two attempts to get through the metal detector, forgetting a small set of keys in his pocket the first time. But once he'd walked through without a bleep from the machine and had been patted down and covered with the metal-detector wand, he put the keys back in his pocket, scooped up the package and walked up the path towards the entrance, pulling open the main door and approaching the woman behind the front desk.

'Delivery,' he said. 'CIA Office.'

She was busy talking to someone from the visa queue, but she looked towards him and nodded. He pushed the brown package on the counter towards her and slid an electronic pad on the top, stifling a yawn. She propelled herself over on her swivel chair, taking the plastic pen and quickly signed the screen, then returned her attention to the lady enquiring about her visa.

'Cheers,' the FedEx guy said, turning and walking back out through the doors.

He moved down the path and across the Square, heading back to his truck, and disappeared out of sight.

Back in the building, the woman finished dealing with the woman from the visa line, then turned and looked at the package. It wasn't addressed to anyone in particular, just *The Office*. She scooped up her phone and pushed 4 on the internal line, lifting it to her ear, connecting to the tech team next door.

'Delivery,' she said, putting the phone back down.

A minute later, a young male analyst appeared and taking the package, turned and headed back towards the offices, looking at the address as he walked. It wasn't addressed to anyone in particular so he had the right to open it. The guards on the second x-ray let him pass back in straight away, pushing a button so he didn't have to bother with the face and retina scan.

Once inside the sub-station, he took the package to his workstation and ripped the side of the parcel open.

But as soon as he did so, something unusual happened.

White powder from inside the package sprayed everywhere, all over his legs and arms and his workstation. Clouds of it puffed over the dark fabric of his trousers, as if he'd been baking a cake and had spilt the flour.

He jerked back, covered in the white powder, then looked at his hand and the clouds of it on his legs and on the carpet.

'What the hell?' he said.

Across the room, a female analyst sitting at her computer had seen what had happened. Whilst the guy with the package was still staring at the powder, confused, she realised straight away what was going on.

'Oh my God,' she said.

She jumped back out of her chair, covering her mouth and backing up, as the male analyst looked over at her.

Then it dawned on him what the powder was.

And his eyes widened in terror.

SIX

Inside the Briefing Room at the ARU's headquarters, Archer turned back from the drinks stand, watching as the rest of the team around the room kept themselves busy. For some reason he felt restless today, but knew he had to remain where he was.

Next door the intelligence team were working away as hard as ever, but part of being a response team often meant a lot of time was spent sitting around, waiting for a call, and in the meantime finding stuff to keep them occupied but which could be dropped immediately if a call came through. Usually some of the guys went downstairs and oiled and cleaned the weapons, plus the shooting range was pretty close by, so often members of the task force would go down there and fire off some rounds, ready to abandon at a moment's notice if they got a 'shout'. It was a fun way to stay sharp on the trigger and kill some time.

In the field however, the weapons were rarely used. It wasn't like the James Bond films, where 007 went around shooting everything in sight. That made for a good movie, but in reality the legal ramifications and paperwork involved whenever there was a shooting meant each officer had to be accountable for every single bullet he fired. The wrong trigger pull could cost any one of them their jobs. Behind every bullet was a mountain of potential paperwork and an inquisition.

Archer scooped up his cup of tea and walked over to the window. Glancing left, he saw someone had brought in some biscuits and some left-over cake that their wife or girlfriend had probably baked, but he passed. He never felt hungry in the morning and the tea was just about the only thing he could handle before lunch.

He put the foam cup down on the windowsill and looked out at London through the glass, the sun shining down, reflecting off the glass windows of the buildings around him. The clock on the wall to his left had just ticked to 10:10 am, and the city was wide awake now, going about its business, the cogs and pistons of the great machine working hard.

His mind started to wander and inevitably, as it had done so often in the past eight months, his thoughts turned to Mina Katic, the FBI agent an ocean away.

He missed her. A lot. He'd met her last summer when a turn of events had taken him on an unexpected week-long trip to New York City. Third-generation Serbian but born and bred in Chicago, she had dark brown eyes with long brown hair that had a hint of crimson in the sunlight. Feminine and beautiful, she was also just as tough as any man in the Bureau she worked with.

Although just turned thirty, she was already a widow. Her husband had died of cancer a couple of years previously, leaving her with a young daughter to look after. She and Archer had worked together on a case when he was out there and they'd become close. And ever since he got back he couldn't get her out of his mind.

But they lived different lives. She was now head of the FBI's Bank Robbery Task Force in New York and he was an integral part of the ARU counter-terrorist team here. Two people, the possibility of a life together separated by an ocean and two careers both had worked extremely hard to forge. Archer was half-American through his father, so he had a US passport and the option to live there whenever he pleased. No-one else knew it, but since he'd got back from New York last summer he'd toyed with the idea of moving there and applying to join the NYPD, just like his father before him, a fresh start in a place that had always fascinated him. Although his dad had been born and bred in New York, Archer had only gone on brief trips there as a child, growing up predominately in the UK, so hadn't experienced any real exposure to the city as an adult. But that trip last summer had planted a seed inside him and it had been growing ever since. He loved the UK, but he was also half American, and in a way half a New Yorker too.

And though he'd never admit it, ever since he'd got back last September he'd felt like a pair of thick shackles had been firmly attached to his feet.

He glanced over his shoulder at his team-mates. For now, London and the Armed Response Unit was where he needed to be. He had a good thing going here, a career he'd worked hard at, a good spot in a great police unit, solid colleagues and friends for life on the force around him.

Any woman in his personal life would have to wait.

And sadly, that included Agent Katic.

He took a pull from his tea and looked out of the window at the city again. He'd lied to Chalky earlier on the range when he'd said Katic had found someone else. That was bullshit. He'd only said it so Chalk wouldn't bring it up again. Her feelings for Archer hadn't changed; she'd called him at home just two days ago and told him she was thinking about him every day, hoping that somehow he could make the move and be with her in New York sometime soon.

But Archer was stuck. To be with her, he would have to leave the Armed Response Unit.

And right now that wasn't something he was prepared to do.

Returning his attention to the room, Archer shifted from the window and walked over to take a seat in an empty chair. Leaning back, he glanced to his right and saw Chalky buried in the sports pages of a newspaper, his eyes scanning the articles. Although his job often depended on even a minimal knowledge of current affairs, Chalk never read the front pages, only interested in the football and sports bulletins printed on the back. Archer looked over and read the front bold-print headlines of the paper facing him in Chalky's hands. He didn't see Charlie Adams' name anywhere. The newspaper must have gone out before the journalists had got news of the politician's suicide, but Archer knew for sure it would be all over them tomorrow.

'You know what's really annoying?' Chalky said, not looking up from the paper.

'What's that?'

'When you're reading a newspaper and someone else reads the back of it.'

Archer grinned at him. But before he could respond, he saw Nikki approaching the room with Cobb and Porter, moving fast through the Operations room.

They looked like they meant business.

'Look out,' Archer said. 'Here's trouble.'

The moment the trio entered, every man in the room stopped what he was doing and sat up, paying immediate attention.

Whenever these three entered the room at the same time, it meant something was brewing.

The room was silent and the relaxed atmosphere changed instantly from flat to charged.

'We've got a call, lads,' Porter said.

'A package was just delivered to the US Embassy containing some kind of white powder,' Nikki said. 'They think it could be anthrax.'

'HAZMAT are already down there, but they need back-up. This could be the start of something else'

Cobb said. ‘Everyone outside in two minutes. Get your kit and gas masks.’

As one, the ten-man team all rose and everyone moved to the doors without a word, dropping their papers, abandoning half-filled cups of coffee and tea all over the room.

Sitting around drinking coffee was nice, but this was what they were paid to do.

Inside his office across town, the CIA Operations Officer had been about to take a first sip from his cup of coffee when a wailing siren sounded around the building, jolting him, causing him to spill some of the piping hot liquid on his trousers and to jerk back on his chair. *Shit.* As he quickly patted his legs off with some tissues, wincing from the hot coffee on his legs, he heard a voice over the building intercom telling everyone to evacuate the building immediately.

Cursing, the man rose and pulling open the door to his office, walked outside. In the corridor, workers were rushing quickly past his office, heading towards the exits. It didn't look like a fire drill. These people were really hurrying out of the building.

He stepped out and caught a passing analyst.

‘What’s going on?’ he asked him.

'There's been an anthrax threat.'

His eyes widened. ‘Real?’

‘Yes, sir.’

He let the analyst go, and the kid rushed off. Closing the door to his office, the man went to make his way down the corridor with the others. But as he went to leave, he saw Lynn fighting her way towards him through the throng.

As people continued to flow past them, he noticed that she still had that list of names he'd given her in her hand.

She looked concerned.

'Sir?' she called, raising her voice to be heard over the alarm.

'Let's go, Lynn,' he said, turning. *'We need to leave the building. Walk with me.'*

They started moving down the corridor, side-by-side, the alarm above them still wailing.

'Sir, I have some news,' she shouted in his ear. *'I checked the names you gave me. I have to ask - are these men friends of yours?'*

He looked down at her. 'No. Why?'

'Well I'm very sorry sir, but one of them was found dead not an hour ago.'

The agent paused, right there in the corridor, people continuing to rush past, some of them bumping into him in their hurry to leave the building. Lynn stopped too, looking at his face for some answers, people streaming past them on either side.

'*What?*' he asked her. *'How?'*

'He was strangled in his car with a wire in a DC suburb parking lot. A Metro night patrolman found him.'

He looked down at her. 'The others?'

'Nothing yet, sir. I'll keep trying.'

Without a word, the man turned and moved through the door, headed for the exit. He suddenly felt very cold and extremely worried.

Two of the men down in the same morning.

An anthrax threat in the building.

This wasn't a coincidence.

He glanced out of the front of the building at the mass of people being cordoned off by police, HAZMAT vehicles already arrived, their team climbing into white bio-suits. As he moved through the front door, letting Lynn out ahead of him, he stopped and scanned the crowd nervously, searching for anyone who was looking back at him.

The cave echo of Charlie Adams' name in his mind was gone, replaced by four other words instead.

They've come for us.

Outside the ARU headquarters, in a black car parked outside the lot on the other side of the street, two men watched in silence as the doors to the police unit suddenly burst open.

The pair in the car were dressed in black military fatigues, boots on their feet, gloves on their hands. Stowed beside them were two AK-47 Kalashnikov rifles, balaclavas resting on the butt of each weapon. They'd duct-taped a second magazine to the underside of the one currently slapped into each weapon for ease of reloading, and each man also had three more stowed in pouches in their fatigues, close to Beretta 92F pistols that were tucked into holsters on their hips as backup firepower.

They watched in silence, side-by-side in the car, as the police officers ran to three black 4x4 Fords, all of them dressed in navy blue combat overalls, each man zipping up tactical vests and carrying MP5 sub-machine guns and black gas masks. The officers started pulling open the doors, climbing into the vehicles, and all three engines fired up.

They watched as the cars began to reverse out and then move forward to the parking lot exit. As the Fords started pulling out and speeding off, one of the two men in black pulled a mobile phone from his pocket and dialled a number.

The call connected to the man back at the command post.

'It worked, sir. They're leaving,' he said, an Eastern European accent.

Pause.

'Wait till they are gone. Then kill the man called Cobb. Like I told you, shoot him in the head. Give him the whole magazine.'

'Yes sir.'

The man in the car ended the call as the last of the three Fords turned out of the lot.

And the two men watched as the entire counter-terrorist task force left the police station unprotected.

SEVEN

Behind the wheel of the lead Ford, Porter put his foot down and the car sped off down the street, heading towards Grosvenor Square and the US Embassy, moving fast. When his predecessor, Mac, had been sergeant of the squad, Porter had been allocated driving duties due to his quality and speed. Now, with Mac gone and as sergeant of the task force, Porter could have offloaded driving responsibilities to someone else, but as he was the best guy behind the wheel in the squad, he insisted on continuing with the task.

Beside him, Fox was finishing adjusting a throat mic around his neck whilst Archer and Chalky did the same in the back seats, all of the officers now dressed in navy blue combat overalls, black tactical vests with mobile phones tucked in slots, plasti-cuffs, tools and spare ammunition zipped up over their torsos. Once secured, the black Velcro-bound strips on each man’s neck allowed the team to communicate on the ground, up to a radius of seven miles. Each man had a pressel switch on the front of his uniform and an earpiece tucked into his ear. If he wanted to communicate with the other men on the squad all he had to do was push the button and start talking.

As he finished adjusting his mic, Archer frowned. He'd caught a glimpse of something as they'd pulled out of the lot, something that had instantly struck him as odd.

Across the street, as they'd passed, he'd noticed two men sitting in a car. The North London area where the ARU headquarters was based was a business area, but these guys didn't looked like businessmen. They looked tough and out of place. The windows to the Ford were blacked out, so they didn't make eye contact with Archer, but he'd turned his head and glanced at them through the window as they pulled out of the lot and moved off down the street.

Beside him, Chalky finished with his mic and looked at the gas mask in his hands. It was an Avon C50 model, just about as comfortable a gas mask a police officer in this line of work could wear, an all-black ski mask and protective face seal combined with a solitary single filtration respirator that would stop any airborne toxin from entering an officer's lungs. In their training, every man on the team had become accustomed to wearing the mask on drills and exercises. The training had begun with all the officers huddled in a hut wearing the gasmasks. Then their instructor had unceremoniously tear-gassed the building. One by one, the recruits were ordered to remove the masks, to get an idea of what it felt like to suffer from exposure to the gas. Aside from being shot, it was up there as one of the worst experiences of Chalky's life. He'd staggered out of the hut, choking, his eyes and nose clogged up, struggling to breathe, rendered temporarily useless and totally incapacitated from its effects. He hadn't been forced to use the mask yet in the field, and looking down at it in the car was the first time he'd held it since that training over two years ago. It was stirring up some unpleasant memories.

'Question - what use is this thing going to be against anthrax?' he said.

'A lot of use,' Fox said, checking the safety of his MP5 sub-machine gun, as Porter turned the car to the right. 'It'll keep you alive.'

'Yeah, but HAZMAT have full body suits. I get a gas-mask.'

'Why don't you stay in the car then?' Fox replied.

'You alright, Arch?' Porter asked, noticing the blond man was unusually quiet, looking at him in the rear view mirror.

'Yeah,' the blond officer said, distracted, frowning. 'I think so.'

As Fox and Chalky continued their exchange, arguing about the benefits of the mask, Archer ignored them and made a quick decision. He pulled his mobile phone from a Velcro pocket on the left collarbone of his tactical vest.

He held down button *2*, and the call went straight through to Nikki back at the ARU's HQ.

Sitting at her desk, her tech team working around and behind her, Nikki was just pulling up a map of the US Embassy and the possible contamination zone, when the phone on her desk rang.

She scooped it up, not taking her eyes off the screen in front of her, still typing away.

'Yep?'

'Nikki, it's Arch.'

'What's up?'

'Do me a favour. Can you leave your desk for a moment?'

She looked at the schematics on the screen in front of her desk and at the busy tech team around her.

'Not really. Is it urgent?'

'Just do me a favour and go through to the Briefing Room.'

She shrugged, then rose and walked quickly through to the adjacent room. The place was deserted, littered with half-drunk cups of tea and coffee, newspapers abandoned on seats. She looked left and right around her at the empty room.

'OK. Now what?'

'Go to the window.'

She did.

'Look past the parking lot. Do you see two guys inside a car on the far side of the street? Black, license plate beginning FG6.'

Her eyes narrowed as she peered outside.

'Yeah. It's headed into the car park.'

As this exchange took place, the phone on Porter's uniform started ringing. It was hooked up to a hands-free inside the car, so he pushed Answer, returning his hand to the wheel.

'Porter,' he said.

'Sergeant, this is Dr Jim Keith from HAZMAT,' a man's voice said, filling the car. *'I'm here at the Embassy examining the package.'*

'How's it looking, doc?' Porter asked.

'I have some news. My team took a sample from the package and tested it here at the scene. The powder immediately showed up as just two ingredients mixed together. Hydrated magnesium silicate and sodium hydrogen carbonate.'

Pause.

'Is that bad?' Porter asked, the car speeding down the street.

'No, not at all,' Keith said. *'Quite the opposite in fact, Sergeant. It's talcum powder and baking soda. This isn't anthrax. It's a hoax.'*

In the ARU's Briefing Room, Nikki watched the black car suddenly speed forward through the parking lot and pull up outside the front of the building. The front doors opened and two men stepped out, dressed in black, balaclavas over their heads, black and brown AK-47 Kalashnikov rifles in their hands.

They slammed the doors shut and ran forward towards the entrance of the building below, each man pulling back the cocking handle on each, chambering a bullet.

'Oh my God,' she whispered, still on the phone to Archer. *'Arch, help!'*

EIGHT

At the front desk downstairs, Clark had his head down reading something so he didn't see the two men coming.

He looked up just as the front doors were barged open, and was momentarily frozen as the two intruders stormed inside the building. Before he could move, one of the two gunmen raised his Kalashnikov and immediately pulled the trigger, three bullets thumping into Clark's chest, the spent cartridges flying out of the side of the automatic rifle.

The force of the gunfire threw him back off his chair and the policeman collapsed back in a heap to the floor, blood and pieces of his torso spattered all over the reception area.

Upstairs, everyone stopped when they heard the gunfire.

Cobb was inside his office, still thinking about the Charlie Adams puzzle, but he froze when he heard the three gunshots. Unlike his tech team, who were sitting motionless at their desks and unsure how to react, he had no such doubts.

He leapt up from his seat, ran across his office and pulled open the door just as Nikki ran back into the Operations area from the Briefing Room, a look of sheer terror on her face.

'*Everybody get out!*' she screamed.

The tech team saw and heard her and panic instantly set in, flooding the room. None of the armed task force officers were there. These were all analysts, unused to combat or any confrontational situations.

They started to rise from their seats and scatter as they heard the slapping steps of boots racing up the stairwell, but Cobb took charge instantly, thinking clearly.

'*No! Everybody, in my office! Now!*' he bellowed, quickly pushing back the door to his office. *'Now!'*

The entire team responded to the order, running over into the glass-walled room, uncertain and frightened. Once the last person ran inside, Cobb dragged the door shut and quickly entered a six-digit code on a keypad on the wall, each button beeping as he pushed it. There was a *click* as the door locked.

Seconds later, two men in balaclavas ran into view dressed all in black, fearsome assault rifles in their gloved hands. They quickly scanned the level and saw the tech team huddled together inside the office through the glass.

One of the armed men ran forward and grabbed the handle to the office door, pulling on it as hard as he could repeatedly and violently, locking eyes filled with hatred with Cobb through the glass. But the door wouldn't budge. It was locked tight.

The man shouted something in a foreign language and stepped back to join the other man, both of them raising their AK-47s.

'Take cover!' Cobb said, pushing his team down behind his desk.

And the two men opened fire.

When the ARU headquarters had been built, Cobb's office had been made of standard, toughened safety glass. Not enough to stop a bullet but perfectly adequate for the walls of an office.

However, after an unexpected incident a year and a half ago when a terrorist had confronted someone from the building outside in the parking lot, Cobb had ordered the glass be refitted with bulletproof panes instead.

And at that moment, that decision saved every one of his tech team's lives, as well as his own.

The two AK-47s were on fully automatic. The bullets hammered into the glass, the savage echoing of close automatic gunfire and chipping glass filling the air, the bright muzzle flash from each rifle blinding and terrifying the tech team cowering inside. But the bulletproof glass did its job. Each bullet left a blurred white splodge and sharp jagged ripple around it on the reinforced windows as the glass withstood the onslaught. If it had been normal safety glass, everyone inside would have been torn apart by the gunfire in seconds. Cobb's intuition and sense of caution had saved every one of them from certain death.

Outside, each gunman's magazine clicked dry and one of them screamed a curse, running forward and hammering at the glass with the butt of his rifle repeatedly, trying everything in his power to smash it, screaming and shouting in a foreign language. Meanwhile, his partner suddenly paused, raising his head, then ran into the Briefing Room and looked out of the window. He shouted something back to his friend and the other man joined him, both of them peering down into the car park.

They both reloaded by reversing the clips in the AK, slapping the fresh mags into the weapons, and without hesitation the two of them opened fire out of the windows.

Unlike Cobb's office, the windows in the Briefing Room weren't bulletproof, and the rounds shredded the glass to pieces, the lethal hail of bullets and glass smashing down at the three ARU cars pulling up outside the building down below.

'Jesus Christ!' Fox shouted, as a spray of bullets hit the front of their car, riddling the bonnet, smashing the front headlights. Porter pulled on the handbrake and turned to the side as the gunfire smashed into the 4x4 Ford, the vehicle skidding to a halt.

The moment Nikki had whispered in terror down the phone and Dr Keith's voice had told the car that the incident at the Embassy was a hoax, Archer had put two-and-two together and realised this whole thing was a set-up. He'd shouted at Porter to get back to HQ as fast as possible, that this was a decoy. Porter hadn't needed to be told twice, pulling a U turn in the street and racing back to headquarters, the other two cars following closely as he gave the order over the radio. They'd roared back into the parking lot to the sounds of gunfire coming from inside their own station, seeing two harsh muzzle-flashes on the upper level, and then were met by a brutal barrage of automatic rifle fire as they sped forwards towards the entrance.

Down below, Archer was first out of the car. He pushed open his door, rolling out and moving to the side of the 4x4, and went to shoot back with his MP5. However, one of the two gunmen above saw him and directed his relentless fire at the blond officer, pinning Archer down, the bullets smashing into the car, blowing out the tyres. They were like sitting ducks down here, in the worst position possible, taking fire from an enemy from a far superior vantage point.

As he huddled behind the rear tyre, Chalky and Fox beside him, Archer realised that at least the car was stopping the bullets, which meant they weren't Teflon-coated *cop killers* as they were known on the street. If they had been, the officers would have been mere target practice, and the entire squad would have been mown down within thirty seconds.

The two gunmen had the height advantage, but the numbers advantage of the ARU squad allowed them to start to establish return fire. They were trained to make sure each bullet was accountable, but if they followed that ruling here they would be decimated. All rules had gone out the window. It was kill or be killed. The building was in the middle of a business area and the harsh sounds of the rifle fire hung in the air, echoing off the glass buildings around them, the two men above continuing their brutal onslaught.

Most of Second Team were forced to take cover, but from their position behind the lead car Chalky and Porter managed to start firing back. The cars were being shredded by the bullets from the AKs, all the windows now smashed, the sounds of bullets hitting metal and glass and the tinkle of spent shell-casings as they showered to the concrete adding to the constant harsh barrelling echo of the gunfire.

Chalky aimed over the back of the car with his MP5 and fired, hitting one of the two men in the shoulder. The guy shouted in pain and fell back, the Kalashnikov knocked out of his hands as he dropped out of sight. Beside him, the other man saw this and immediately retaliated, emptying his magazine in a merciless rage, shouting abuse behind the muzzle flash.

Once it clicked dry, he turned and disappeared back into the room.

'Move up!' Porter immediately bellowed.

Deakins was leading Second Team to the doors, but then the wounded man suddenly reappeared at the window, his AK-47 back in his hands, ready to resume firing. Fox fired and hit him again, smacking the guy back out of sight before he had a chance to aim and pull the trigger.

To the left, Archer was thinking about the whereabouts of the second gunman and took off across the car park, running to the left, headed around the building, his boots crunching on fragments of smashed glass and empty shell casings as he sprinted across the parking lot.

'Fire exit!' he shouted.

Porter, Fox and Chalky knew where he was going and the three of them were already following close behind. They sprinted around the building then slowed, all four of their weapons tight to the shoulder and in the aim.

Archer was the first man to reach the corner. He whipped around the brickwork, his MP5 aimed straight down the building and whoever might be standing there.

All he saw was a smoking Kalashnikov on the ground, jammed in the doorway of the emergency exit, the air stinking of cordite and oil from the hot weapon.

Archer ran over to it, then swore and looked around. The back of the ARU's headquarters didn't have the same space as the parking lot at the front, and surrounding buildings and streets were only fifteen yards away.

He looked over, seeing frightened pedestrians across the street, most of them looking back at him from behind makeshift cover.

There was no sign of the gunman dressed in black.

He was gone.

Meanwhile, Second Team had entered the building the other side, moving into the reception area. Leading the squad, Deakins saw bloodstains on the wall and spotted Clark's body slumped on the ground behind the desk.

Feeling his throat tighten, Deakins held his finger on the trigger, and led his team up the stairs.

On the second floor, the six-man squad moved cautiously down the corridor towards the Ops room, the men silent, each with his forefinger on the trigger of his MP5. Deakins glanced to the right and saw the terrified tech team huddled in Cobb's office, the glass on the windows damaged from gunfire but still intact, Cobb standing in front of his people. Deakins nodded to Cobb and keeping his MP5 in the aim, turned left into the Briefing Room.

The wounded gunman was writhing on the ground, two bullets in his shoulder, blood spattered on the floor behind him. He was lying amongst the debris of empty cartridges, smashed glass, spilt coffee, and scattered polystyrene cups and newspapers. His Kalashnikov was out of reach across the floor, the barrel smoking, but Deakins saw the man had a pistol in his hand, a Beretta 92.

'*Drop it!*' Deakins said, his MP5 in his shoulder, the hair-trigger on the man's masked face. '*Drop it!*'

Coughing, blood pooling under him, the man shouted something at him in a foreign language and spat a mixture of blood and saliva at Deakins through the mouth-hole of his balaclava.

Then he put the Beretta to his head and pulled the trigger.

NINE

An hour later, Archer finished making three strong cups of coffee and stepping past a group of Forensics detectives in white uniforms, carried them out of the Briefing Room. He walked into the Operations area and passed the cups to three members of the tech team, who were sitting together, their eyes wide, many of them nauseous from shock and spent adrenaline.

They all took the drinks without responding and he stood over them protectively, his MP5 slung over his shoulder. Turning, he looked at the scene around him.

It was one of utter devastation.

The Briefing Room was a sea of smashed glass, empty shell casings, spilt tea and coffee, and bloodstains. To his left, the glass on Cobb's office windows, despite being irreparably damaged, was still fully intact. It had done its job, saving the life of everyone who had been inside. A Forensics team had arrived, snapping photographs of the crime scene and zipped the corpse of the gunman who had shot himself up in a body-bag, dumping him on a gurney. They'd wheeled him outside to their van and the vehicle was already headed to their lab.

The team had also bagged and sealed the man's two weapons and magazines and were now taking every shell casing from the ground which they would run for prints and DNA to try to trace the weapons and the two men who had fired them. Outside, a pair of their detectives were examining the car the two men had arrived in. They'd run the plates through the DMV and Met log, and it'd come up listed as stolen less than two days ago. Across the parking lot several news-teams and a small crowd who had gathered behind some police tape that had been drawn across the entrance were being held back by Met policemen.

Detectives from CID and MI5 had arrived, having seen the news reports and offered their services, but Cobb had dismissed them all politely, saying this would be an internal investigation. The Prime Minister had contacted Cobb, checking if they were all OK, but for now no-one really had any answers. They all knew any possible clues lay with the dead body at the lab along with anything traceable on the weapons and casings.

There'd been another body-bag in the van alongside the dead gunman, containing the body of Clark. He was headed straight to the morgue, killed by the three gunshots to his sternum and upper chest. Thinking of the young officer, Archer shook his head angrily. He was only twenty six, and would have been defenceless when the two gunmen stormed the entrance downstairs.

In one way the Unit had been incredibly lucky.

But in another, they'd paid the heaviest of prices.

Turning, he saw Nikki sitting alone by her desk, a cup of coffee in her hands, a blanket around her shoulders. He walked over and took a seat beside her in an empty chair, making sure the MP5 around his shoulder was tucked out of the way.

They sat there side-by-side in silence, Nikki watching the forensics team sweeping up next door. Archer turned to her.

'You OK?'

'That was too close,' she said quietly, her eyes wide and looking ahead, watching the forensics team next door. They'd bagged and tagged the last shell casing and were now starting to clean the blood and brains from the second gunman off the floor, the acrid smell of bleach and disinfectant drifting into the Ops room. 'Who the hell were those guys?'

'I don't know. But we'll find out. Soon.'

Pause.

'I feel sick.'

'That's the adrenaline. It'll pass.'

She shook her head, her hands trembling from the shock. He looked down and saw ripples in the coffee from the tremors in her hands, like the shockwaves on the glass of Cobb's office.

'Little taste of what you guys go through in the field,' she said, forcing a smile.

He put his arm around her protectively and she leaned into him.

'That was too close,' she said again.

‘Jesus Christ, that was close,’ Fox said, side by side with Cobb, Chalky and Porter across the room. The three of them were examining the damaged glass on the exterior of Cobb’s office, well over a hundred white marks surrounded by jagged ripples.

Fox turned to Cobb. ‘Best decision you ever made, sir.'

'Not enough for Officer Clark though, was it?'

The three officers stayed silent.

'Are you OK, sir?' Porter asked.

‘I’m fine,' Cobb said. 'I just want some damn answers. Somebody's going to pay dearly for this. And I don't mean with money.’

As the three men nodded in agreement, Porter looked at Fox and Chalky and suddenly realised they were all still armed.

‘Sir, I’m sorry. I’ll get the men to stow their weapons.’

Cobb shook his head and turned to him. ‘No. I’m changing the protocol. Until we find out who those men were, I want every officer in the building armed at all times. That means Glock and MP5s, everywhere you go, spare mags in your pouches, all of you in full uniform with mic and earpiece. If one of the tech team goes downstairs to use the toilet, I want one of you with them in the next stall.’

The men nodded.

‘Yes sir.’

‘What did the Prime Minister say?’ Chalky asked.

'Like the rest of us, he wanted to know what the hell had happened and what this was about,' Cobb said. 'He said our entire team should consider relocating to MI5 temporarily until we find out what's going on and where those two came from.'

'Are we leaving?' Chalky asked.

Cobb shook his head, looking at the damaged glass in front of him.

'No. This is our home. We're not going anywhere.'

He turned to Porter, his face hard. Cobb's tech team may have been in shock, but he was in full control.

'I want Second Team guarding downstairs on rotation. Both entrances, armed and alert. No-one gets in without bulletproof ID, and no-one stows their weapons in the gun-cage until I say so. Clear?'

'Yes, sir,' Porter said. 'I'll tell Deakins.'

He walked off, turning the corner and headed down the corridor. Fox, Chalky and Cobb were left in a line, the three of them still looking at the damaged glass. From the outside, it looked as if someone had shot it repeatedly with a paintball gun filled with white balls, the spots surrounded by spider-webs of broken glass from the shockwave of each bullet from the Kalashnikovs.

Cobb reached over and touched one of them, feeling the sharp edges of the glass on his fingertip.

'What the hell was this all about?'' he muttered.

It took the lone surviving gunman about an hour to make it across town to the command post. He was no longer dressed in black. He and his partner had arrived outside the police station wearing civilian trousers and sweaters underneath their black combat fatigues for when the job was done. Once he was out of sight down a side alley and a sufficient distance from the police station, he'd pulled off his outfit and thrown it away with the balaclava he'd already removed.

He'd been forced to leave his Kalashnikov at the scene. No way could he run through London with that in his hands. But he'd pulled the Beretta from its holster and tucked it into his belt under his sweater, and had then made his way across the city back to the safe-house.

It was located on the 8th floor of a newly built office building. Rentals on each floor weren't due to start for another couple of weeks, so the ten storey building was completely empty and a perfect position for an anonymous command post. The man ducked in through the lobby and took the stairs rather than the lift, running up them two at a time. When he arrived on 8, he moved across the corridor and pushed open the door to a large room, a long, wide office, panting hard from the exertion.

The room was dark, almost pitch black, all the curtains drawn; in the darkness, he saw the large figure of his leader, sitting alone. In front of him there were two televisions, one tuned to CNN and the other to BBC World. The BBC screen was already showing footage from the ruined police station.

The big man by the screens turned and looked at the newcomer, his face and body dark, just the whites of his eyes visible in the darkness.

There was a pause.

'You're alone,' he said, in a foreign language.

'Yes, sir.'

'Where is Crow?' he asked quietly.

'They shot him, sir,' the man said. 'We failed. The man had bulletproof-glass as his office walls. We tried but we couldn't get to him.'

Silence. The leader of the group sat silently, staring at him. The surviving gunman tried to return his gaze, but failed as his leader looked straight into his eyes, his hulking figure silhouetted from the glare of the televisions behind him.

'Then why are you still standing there. You know what to do.'

The gunman looked at him, then swallowed and nodded.

'Yes, sir.'

With that he saluted, and turned and walked back out of the room.

The leader didn't see the salute.

He'd already turned his attention back to the televisions and the list.

Across the city at Grosvenor Square, the wailing sirens at the US Embassy had been silenced, and word had spread that the threat was just a false alarm. People were already moving back into the building, the HAZMAT team packing up their equipment and climbing back into their white vans, departing one after the other.

The crowds of Agency workers were relieved, none more so than the unfortunate male analyst who had opened the package. They all headed back inside, returning to their desks and the work that had been so suddenly interrupted. False alarms like this happened from time to time. Most were actually organised by someone from the Agency and used as an audit to test emergency protocols. On this occasion the building had emptied in a matter of minutes, so those in charge of the evacuation procedures were relieved, mostly because it had been a false alarm but also because of the speed at which the building had been cleared. They wouldn't suffer any reprimands for slow reaction times or disorganisation. The staff were well drilled.

Back in the Square, the protestors were still in place, undeterred, and their protests started to gather volume again.

But one person who wasn’t relaxing was the CIA Operations Officer who’d known Charlie Adams. Once the doors to the Embassy were reopened, he walked swiftly back to his office, moving as quickly as he could through the crowd of people. He needed to get on the system and pull a list. There were eleven names on it, and so far two of them had been confirmed dead in the past three hours, which was far too precise for his liking to be a coincidence.

Walking fast, he pushed open the door to his office and moved around the desk to his computer, then thought better of it and pulled his mobile phone from his pocket. He'd need someone familiar with all the government databases to do this, and couldn't waste time fumbling around trying to do it himself. For the first time in many years, he was going to disobey orders.

He pushed the number and waited for the call to connect.

'Operations Officer Ryan Jackson, London office. Access code 34321,' he said.

'One moment, please,' the woman on the other end said.

As he waited, Jackson found himself looking at the television in his office. In the commotion and sudden evacuation, he had left it on and there was new footage on the screen with a fresh *Breaking News* headline. However, it wasn't reporting on the hoax anthrax threat at the Embassy.

Instead, it was showing the ruined exterior of a two-floored building with a helicopter on the roof.

Some kind of police station.

He frowned and looked closer, waiting for the call on his ear to connect. It seemed a police squad across the city had been involved in some kind of gunfight. The news cameras were at the gates, cordoned off, but the shot had zoomed in and showed smashed windows, empty shell casings on the tarmac and three 4x4 Ford Explorers that had been torn apart by automatic gunfire. He read the headline.

Counter-terrorist police unit attacked by two gunmen.

The screen suddenly flicked to a man giving a short statement to the press by the gates. He was a dark-haired man, around Jackson’s age, in an expensive-looking dark suit and with a stern look on his face. His name came up on the screen below, just as it came up from the depths of Jackson's memory.

Director Tim Cobb.

Head of the Armed Response Unit.

The phone to Jackson’s ear connected. An operator asked how she could help him, but Jackson didn’t respond. He was staring at Cobb’s face on the screen, a man he hadn't seen in fifteen years.

He looked at the man and the devastation of the police station behind him. The operator asked him again how she could help him, but Jackson ended the call, lowering his phone and staring at the television.

So he wasn't imagining it, or being paranoid.

It was really happening. They were back.

And they were coming to kill them all.

At that moment, three thousand and thirty one miles and several time-zones across the Atlantic Ocean, a man in his late thirties stepped out of a large family home in a residential neighbourhood in upstate Connecticut. It was a dewy early morning, just coming up to 7 a.m. He shut the door behind him and headed down the path towards his car, stopping to push his son's toy tricycle out of the way with his foot.

His was a real success story. He'd left the military in 2004 after a turbulent career that had started in the Marine Corps. He'd then taken everyone off guard by launching his own business, supplying software equipment to companies in the area. People were waiting for it to fail. A southern boy, originally from Athens, Georgia, the man hadn't been an academically gifted kid, getting average grades in school, and he wasn't especially good with computers. He'd done some time in the military but had wanted a change, he said. It was just a matter of time, they all figured, before he ended up working dead-end security someplace or trying to re-enlist.

But the opposite had happened. Although he wasn't a genius by any means, the man had good instincts and was quick to identify opportunities in the marketplace. The quality of his product, hard work and the technical proficiency of his small team meant the company had grown at an impressive pace. It was now the premier supplier to offices and companies across the American East Coast. He was a self-made millionaire, had his own facility in Hartford and was on his way there that morning to finish up a big deal with a technological company based in Philadelphia. He had a wife, three kids and a house in one of the best neighbourhoods in the state, and he often had to pinch himself to fully appreciate his extraordinarily good fortune.

In the military, he'd been going nowhere. He had a poor discipline record and an even worse reputation. He'd been on his way to being kicked out of the Marines and realising he had nowhere to go, convinced them to let him enlist in the United States Army and give him another shot. Even then, it was a small miracle he'd survived without a serious incident in the years before he mustered out. He eventually came to the obvious conclusion that military life wasn't for him. Leaving the Army had been the best decision he'd ever made.

He headed towards his Mercedes, dark blue, less than six months old, fresh off the production line and parked on the street. He got a kick out of the envious looks other guys gave him when he parked at the golf club or at the Mall down the street. He unlocked the car, pulling open the door, and stepped inside, shutting it behind him.

Fastening his seatbelt, he put the key in the ignition and twisted it.

Given the advances in technology over the last decade, much like those the man had built his business on, the device rigged up underneath the Mercedes that morning would have been considered old-fashioned by those proficient with the finer points of car-bombing. Times had changed, such as when the six-shooter revolver suddenly found itself usurped by the 9mm pistol. The two bricks of C4 plastic explosive stuck underneath the Mercedes had been wired up to the car's ignition system in the middle of the night, a man lying there in the shadows under the car, spending almost half an hour wiring the charge. Most modern car-bombs were magnetic, triggered by the opening of a door or whenever pressure was applied to a pedal. Others used tilt fuses, one side full of liquid mercury, the other side the wires of an open circuit to the detonator. Whenever the car moved a certain degree, the mercury swished down into the wiring and closed the circuit, detonating the bomb.

But the man who'd wired up the Mercedes to the bomb had been out of the game for over a decade. He could be forgiven for being a little old-fashioned. But whatever the argument, one thing was for sure

His way still worked.

There was a split-second delay as the receiver half a foot beneath the man in the driver seat picked up the detonation signal from the ignition current.

Then the bomb under the car exploded.

The Mercedes erupted into a huge fireball, the vehicle lifted twenty feet into the air from the force of the plastic explosives underneath, the fireball burning the trees nearby, the shockwave smashing the windows of nearby houses, everything inside the car vaporised in an instant.

Down the street, the man who planted the C4 watched through the rear-view mirror of his own car. He'd been there for over four hours, watching and waiting for the man to step outside his front door, get inside the car and turn on the ignition.

As the flaming car landed with a thud, the shell continuing to burn, front doors of houses along the street started to open, curtains in windows flickering as neighbours peered out to see what the unexpected noise was. The man watching in the rear view mirror nodded with satisfaction, watching the Mercedes cook.

A confirmed kill.

The next moment, he fired the engine to his own car. He took off the handbrake, putting his foot down, and the car moved off quickly around the corner and out of sight, headed straight for Bradley International Airport and his 7:55 am flight to London Heathrow.

TEN

Back at the ARU's headquarters it'd just gone midday, and Deakins and Second Team were already downstairs guarding both exits, each man armed with his MP5 and the Glock in a thigh holster as backup. Hard as the clean-up team down there had tried, they hadn't managed to get rid of all the bloodstains by the reception desk, and the men stationed near the door found themselves glancing at them, Clark's blood still visible over the desk and wall, the air reeking of disinfectant and smelling like a hospital.

Upstairs, Cobb had just returned from delivering a statement to the press and was sitting inside his office talking with Archer, Chalky, Porter and Fox as the forensics team continued to work away in the Briefing Room and as the tech team recovered in the Operations area.

As the five men talked, the phone on Cobb's desk rang, cutting across the conversation. He reached over and picked it up.

'Cobb,' he said. He listened to the response. 'OK. I'm putting you on speakerphone. Four of my officers are in the room.'

He pushed a button, and then put the phone back on the cradle. Around the office, Porter, Fox, Archer and Chalky all listened closely.

'Director, this is Dr Kim Collins,' the other voice said, female. *'I'm here at the lab. We're with the body of the dead gunman. I have some news for you.'*

'Go on.'

'Age-wise, he's late thirties or early forties. We tried running his prints through our system, Special Branch and MI6, but nothing came up. He's not British and he doesn't appear to be someone we've encountered before. We tried Interpol, but that was a dead end. However, he has a series of tattoos on his body, on his arms, elbows and torso. They are distinctive. I've seen this type before. Definitely Eastern European.'

'Can you be more specific?'

'If I had to guess, I'd say Albanian.'

Cobb nodded as the four other men in the office listened in silence.

'OK. What else?'

'The man also has scarring on his torso and upper arm from several old bullet wounds. Coupled with the scar tissue on his right hand, I would say he's been in the military somewhere. The stitching on the bullet-wounds on his body is very rudimentary, the kind you'd see in the field, real needle-and-thread jobs, emergency repairs. Almost definitely obtained in combat.'

She paused.

'I also have something else for you. It's really quite bizarre.'

Cobb frowned. 'Go on.'

'When we ran this man's fingerprints and DNA, we came up with an immediate match for something else.'

'Which was?'

'The letter that was sent to Charlie Adams. This man sealed the envelope. The DNA from the saliva and fingerprints on the paper are a 100 % match.'

Cobb frowned, incredulous. *'What?'*

At that moment, a red-light came up on the phone from another call. Cobb reached over.

'Forgive me for one moment,' he said to Collins. He pushed the button. 'Cobb.'

'Sir, its Deakins.'

'Yes?'

'I'm on the reception. There's a man here who says he's from the US Embassy. He's asked to speak with you. Says it's extremely urgent. He's shown me ID. '

'What's his name?'

'Ryan Jackson. He's an Operations Officer with the CIA.'

The four officers noticed Cobb's body tighten.

Another pause.

'OK. Send him up,' he ordered.

'Yes, sir.'

Cobb didn't bother pushing the button back to Dr Collins at the lab. He just lifted the phone and put it down again to hang up. A silence followed.

'Everything OK, sir?' Archer asked.

Cobb sat back in his seat, his eyes distant.

‘No. I don’t think it is. Outside. I need to talk to this man alone.’

The four officers complied without a word and pulled open the door, moving out into the Ops room and out of the way.

After a few moments, Agent Jackson appeared, led along the level by Deakins. The other officers looked at him curiously. They saw a well-dressed man who was probably in his mid-thirties but who looked younger. He had brown hair and brown eyes and was dressed in a smart suit, light blue shirt with a dark blue tie. He looked fit and healthy, but at that moment also extremely worried.

He ignored everyone standing there, turning the corner and followed Deakins straight into Cobb's office, hesitating a brief moment as he came face-to-face with the damaged glass on the door.

Inside the glass-walled room after the two men had entered, Cobb nodded at Deakins, who turned and shut the door behind him.

Jackson stood there in the ruined office in front of Cobb. The two men looked at each other.

'Hello, Ryan,' Cobb said.

‘Hello, Tim,’ Jackson said, ‘It’s been a long time.’

Over three and a half thousand miles to the west, it was early in the morning in the town of McLean, Virginia. The sun had just begun its slow climb at the base of the horizon, shielded by clouds, the air muggy and damp. Officially an unincorporated community on the map, Mclean was a town with over 48,000 residents, many of them diplomats, members of Congress, or high-ranking government officials.

The reason for this concentration of population was that the CIA's headquarters were actually at Mclean, Virginia, not Langley as so many people thought. Other major companies such as Capital One and Hilton Hotels were also based out of the area, adding to both its prestige and wealth, the affluence of the area evident in the high-end shopping malls, golf courses and spa retreats scattered all over the community. Residentially, the census in 2010 revealed there were just over 17,000 separate households in Mclean, and despite being a predominately *government* town as people put it, at that time in the morning most of the residents were still asleep. The buses for the high schools in the area weren't due to roll around until just after 8 am, so it was still that blissful last hour in bed just before everyone had to get up and get going for the day.

But one young man was already up and had been for almost two hours, riding his bike through a series of suburbs and maple tree-lined streets. He worked the paper-round five days a week, the easiest money he'd ever make, thirty five bucks per shift. He was fourteen and hyperactive so he was usually up by this time in the day anyway, and much to the delight of his parents he figured he might as well make some money if he was already up and about.

He worked ten streets on his route, usually about twenty houses each side, so that added up to a lot of newspapers. Four hundred and four, to be exact. He'd worked out that he could carry eighty rolled up papers in the bag on his side, so he normally had to make a few stops back at the store to reload so he could finish his shift. When he'd started out, he'd carefully tucked each paper in each letterbox or walked up to drop it on the porch, but lately he'd started throwing them at the porches instead and had got pretty good. A friend of his who worked another route nearby for the same newspaper vendor had gone on vacation, so the kid on the bike had doubled up, offering to do his friend's route for an extra thirty five dollars. Seventy bucks earned by the time he ate breakfast and got on the school-bus. Pretty good.

He'd just turned down 41st Street, a stretch not on his normal route but one he was covering for his friend, and was a third of his way along, slinging the papers left and right, each one landing on each porch, some of them not even hitting the front doors.

As he moved down the street, he slung a paper to his left. It twirled through the air and landed. He glanced over to see he'd hit the mark as he pedalled past.

Suddenly, he pulled on the brakes, skidding to a halt, planting his feet either side of the bike.

The houses on the street all looked quiet, everyone inside still asleep or already out the door, but something had caught his eye. Being a wealthy area and with residents constantly out of town or on vacation, his boss at the paper gave him a new list every shift of houses to miss on his route, people who had cancelled their paper whilst they were away.

However, this front porch had a stack of newspapers on it. No-one seemed to have noticed.

It looked like there were over twenty there, hidden by the porch walls, heaped up by the front door.

The kid stepped off his bike, leaving it to one side, and walked down the path towards the house. It looked like most of the others on the street, a box-shaped, two floored brick house with a side garage to the left. The grass on the lawn was long, like it hadn't been cut in a while, and most of the curtains were drawn.

Moving up the path, the kid arrived at the porch and looked down at the stack uncertainly, pausing just in case whoever lived inside pulled open the curtains and started shouting at him.

But there was no movement from inside.

The curtains were still.

He knelt down and started rummaging through the pile. Eventually, he came up with a newspaper dated from March.

It was delivered three weeks ago to the day, Thursday.

What the hell?

He was used to the odd heap, maybe six or seven papers for someone who had forgotten to cancel for the week, but he'd never seen a pile this high.

Glancing back down the path, he saw the mailbox was jammed full of mail too, spilling out of the metal box.

Placing the paper back down on the pile carefully, the kid turned and walked back down the path. He'd report what he'd seen when he finished his route.

However, something about this place was making him uneasy.

Back in London, the second gunman who had attacked the ARU's headquarters had made it to the edge of the River Thames. He was on the South Bank, not a hundred yards from where the politician had killed himself earlier that morning, the smell of salt from the water hanging in the air. Pedestrians were walking past him from both directions as he stopped and looked out at the water. He could hear the distant calling of gulls and the sound of the small waves splashing as they hit the stone walls of the riverbank.

He stood there for a few moments then climbed over the railings, causing several passing pedestrians to slow, watching and wondering what the hell he was doing. The man shuffled back and positioned himself so he had his heels over the edge of the brick, his back to the water.

He looked up to the sky. Fifteen years of planning and he'd failed.

He knew what was expected.

He pulled his Beretta from the back of his waistband and flicked off the safety catch, then put the gun in his mouth, feeling the harsh cold metal of the barrel, tasting grit and gun oil.

And he pulled the trigger.

As people watching screamed, the back of the man's head blew apart and his body went limp as all brain function was instantly shredded by the bullet. He crumpled and fell back, his body tumbling towards the choppy water beneath him. As onlookers watched in disbelief and horror, the man's body hit the Thames with a loud splash. The current started taking the body downstream immediately as it also started to sink.

And within seconds it disappeared out of sight into the oily depths.

ELEVEN

‘How are you doing?’ Jackson asked, as Cobb passed him a cup of coffee, black, two sugars. He’d sat down in the empty chair across the desk, the damaged glass behind him and nodded thanks as he took the cup and saucer from Cobb, placing it on the edge of the desk to let it cool.

‘I’ll live,’ Cobb said, taking his own cup of coffee from the stand and taking a seat behind his desk. ‘How’d you find me?’

‘Saw your report on the television. My assistant pulled an address.’

‘I thought you’d be back in Virginia?’

Jackson shook his head. ‘Not yet. Been in London fifteen years and counting.’

There was a pause, formalities over. Both men knew what was coming next in the conversation, but neither wanted to address it, as if not speaking about it would make it less real.

‘I don’t think I want to know why you’re here,’ Cobb added.

Jackson looked at him.

‘You already do though, don’t you?’

Another pause. Cobb looked up at the ceiling, cursing under his breath.

'Jesus Christ.'

'Earlier this morning, a Metro squad car found a guy strangled in his car outside a strip-club,’ Jackson said. ‘Looks like he got taken by surprise. Someone garrotted him with a wire from behind. And on the way here, I got a call from my secretary that another body has been found in New York City. Apparently someone broke into the guy’s apartment sometime last night and put a slug between his eyes as he slept. He was working as a bodyguard for an Arab Sheikh, but he didn't show up for work. They sent someone round to check on him and found him in bed, missing the back of his head.'

Pause.

'Their names were Jason Carver and Derek Spears. A former United States Marine Captain and an Army Ranger Sergeant, respectively.’

He paused.

‘Ring any bells?’

Silence.

Cobb didn’t speak. Instead, he put down his cup of coffee slowly.

‘Holy shit,' he said. 'I hoped I was imagining the worst. But that confirms it.’

Jackson nodded, leaning forward and taking a sip of his coffee.

‘Add their murders to Captain Adams’ suicide and the marks on the glass behind me and a pattern is emerging, I'm sure you'll agree.'

He leaned forward, returning the cup to the desk but never taking his eyes off Cobb’s.

'We're in some seriously deep shit, my friend.’

‘How is this possible?' Cobb asked quietly. 'I thought they were all in prison?’

'They must have got out.'

'So why the hell didn't we hear about it?'

Jackson looked at him wryly. 'C'mon, man. Places like the jails they were in don't officially exist. They don’t exactly produce a roll call.'

Anxious, Cobb leaned back and flicked his eyes back up at the television, which was running through the morning headlines. Each one seemed to be related to those in the know, and spelled serious trouble for the two men sitting across from each other.

‘Do we have any information on them?’ Cobb asked.

Jackson shook his head. 'Nothing. I contacted my man in Belgrade on the way here. He's saying the Serbian government are denying any knowledge of a jailbreak. They’re claiming the men don't even exist. And their story checks out. These guys have no records left, no identification. None of them have used their real names in years, and no-one knows who or where they are.'

‘No files?’

‘Nothing.’

Cobb swore, then thought of something.

‘But wait a minute,’ he said. ‘How the hell do they know anything about us? No-one knew who we were. That was the whole point of the operation. You and I were here in London, for God's sake.’

Jackson shrugged.

'I don't know,' he said, turning and poking a finger at the television. 'But someone's been talking to them, Tim. Because they've tracked us all down.'

He paused.

'And that means you and I are next on that list.'

At the command post across town, the big man in the darkness was still watching the two television screens with interest. He saw a new *Breaking News* report of a second suicide on a bank by the Thames and nodded. Good. Like any man of honour, Grub did what was expected of him.

He'd known Grub since he was a boy. They'd grown up together, and he was sad that the man had been forced to kill himself. But he'd let himself and every other man in the team down. In a unit like theirs, such failure always came at a price.

But the big man in the darkness had another bond with his now dead colleague. They'd served time as cell mates together in the prison known as *Ferri*.

Or in English, 'The Pit'.

Fifteen years. Fifteen years he and his seven men had been held there, in the filth and the grime, surrounded by death and fear, a hundred miles from anywhere and with no hope of escape, left to rot. The prison at full capacity held three hundred inmates, all of them forgotten men. Every day was a battle just to stay alive. Prisoners around them were dying every day from dysentery or some other disease, their bodies often left in their cells for days before the guards bothered to remove them, the smell unforgettable, the constant stench of death unavoidable. It was freezing cold in winter and as hot as a furnace in summer. Every man in that prison was sent there to die, and with most of the inmates that was exactly what happened.

But in the midst of the total despair around them, the leader of the eight-man group had somehow kept his team going.

Stay alive, he'd said. *Hold on to whatever will stop you from giving up. Every morning you wake up is another night you survived.*

Another day closer to when we will escape.

And another day closer to when we get even.

Over the years they'd tried to come up with an escape plan. For a host of different reasons, none had been feasible. Other inmates had tried, but none of them were ever returned to their cells. They were taken into the exercise area in the middle of the dark cell block and shot in the head, the guards leaving the body there for a couple of days for the other inmates to see. They got the message. Any attempt at an escape would only end one way, your body left on that patch of ground to be picked at by the birds.

A man only ever had one chance to break out of *Ferri*.

The place was remote and well-guarded and the prisoners were deliberately kept malnourished and weakened to reduce the chance of any form of resistance. It had broken most of the other inmates. The majority of them died. And the ones who managed to stay alive usually went insane. It had almost broken the man sitting there in the dark command post. Most mornings they would wake up and find another inmate being dragged from his cell, a length of fabric tied around his neck in a makeshift rope, his body quickly disposed of. Another man who gave up. The option of suicide was always there, and they would all be lying if they said the thought hadn't crossed each of their minds.

But finally, just over three months ago, they'd escaped. From his cell the leader had co-ordinated a mass riot. It had taken time and patience, but he'd got the word out and it had quickly spread. His reasoning was that the prisoners had absolutely nothing in their favour except one thing; weight of numbers. If the other inmates did as they were told, together the mob could overrule the guards and have a chance at freedom. For too long every man in there had been looking out for himself, trying to escape alone or in a small group. There was strength in numbers.

If they all worked together, it was possible.

And it had worked. There were no showers in *Ferri,* so once a week, twenty prisoners at a time were walked out of their cells and taken to a dry wall where they were given one piece of soap between five of them and hosed down for just over a minute by a guard, two other guards standing there with sub-machine guns. It should have been eight prisoners at a time, but the guards had become lazy, eager to get it over with so they could head back to the comfort of their mess room. They were complacent, figuring the prisoners were too physically weak and demoralised to be a threat.

But the leader and one of his men, Spider, had taken the guards by surprise as they led them from their cells. Mustering all their strength, the two men killed them both with their bare hands as two of the others worked the mechanisms to open all the other cells. A mass riot had followed, the remaining guards beaten to death or hanged by the baying mob as the place was set on fire.

Leaving the other prisoners to wreak havoc in the prison, tearing it apart, the leader had gathered his men and headed straight to the guards hut, raiding their clothing stores and stocking up on food and water. The prison was a five day walk from anywhere, and it would be freezing cold at night. If they didn't prepare, they would die out there on the plains, and every day they'd survived inside that prison would have been for nothing.

And so, almost fifteen years after they'd arrived, the eight men had escaped.

They made their way across the biting cold of the valleys and plains towards Belgrade. The leader of the group had planned ahead. It was the main reason why he was still alive. Before they'd all been imprisoned he'd accumulated a significant amount of money, which he had stored in a secure bank account no-one knew about. After they got to the capital, the leader worked out a deal with a hotel owner on the outskirts of town, paying the man a handsome bonus on the condition that he tell no-one, not even his own family, that the eight men were staying there.

The leader and his men had spent the first month eating and slowly regaining their strength as best they could and living like human beings again. They'd recovered fast, the benefits of good nutrition, plentiful water and soft sheets to sleep on, and before long all of them were at a level of fitness which was sufficient for what would come next, all of them fuelled by a burning desire and appetite for revenge.

Once they'd eaten and slept enough, their bodies nourished and cleansed of the evils of *Ferri*, the leader had gathered his men and told them of his intentions. He still had a small fortune saved in that anonymous bank account, untouched in over fifteen years. It was enough to supply them with everything they could need to execute his plan. Food, clothing, weapons, fake documentation, plane tickets. He outlined what he was going to do personally, and had asked them if they were willing to follow him on the path he was taking, giving them the opportunity to leave and move on and enjoy a second chance at life.

But it was a redundant question. Every man in the room had instantly said *yes.* They'd entered that prison as comrades, but the fifteen years of hardship and ill treatment in *Ferri* had forged them into brothers.

The next step was acquiring information about the men who had ruined their lives, which had actually been relatively simple. Once they had fake passports and eight plane tickets, they'd flown to Washington D.C. and from there taken a bus out to a town called McLean in Virginia. Laying low and scouting out an information source, a few weeks after they'd arrived they hit the jackpot, a CIA employee with access to everything they needed.

Once they'd obtained what they were wanted, after some direct persuasion, they'd examined the data closely and realised the team would have to separate to get the job done. If they were systematic, taking down each target over a period of time, word would surely spread and the others on the list would be alerted, making the team's job of killing them much harder. At that moment, they still had the element of surprise, the most useful tactic in combat.

The men on the list had no idea they were coming.

No idea that they were all going to die.

Once weapons and plans of attack had been arranged, the eight man team was split into two groups, four staying in the United States, the other four travelling across the ocean to the United Kingdom.

And they'd begun to work through the list.

The leader had sent Bug to Washington to kill the doorman, the man called Carver. They had a number of options on where and how to do it, but the leader figured late at night outside the strip club was the best choice. No-one was around at that time, removing any potential witnesses, and no-one would discover his body until Bug was out of the country. Carver should have counted himself lucky. It was a blissfully swift death for him. In other circumstances, the commanding officer would have made it last for weeks.

He'd sent Spider to New York City to take out the bodyguard, Spears. That was just as straightforward. The guy had recently put his name down on a lease on a new apartment in Manhattan. He lived alone and had no partner. Spider would do the job late at night, taking the right precautions, then get out of the country after dumping the evidence in the River. And Bird had been sent up to Connecticut to kill the man who owned the software company. Out of some bizarre injustice, the exact same cruelty that had left the eight man team to rot in *Ferri* for fifteen years, it turned out that the man was now a major success, living a rich and prosperous life. Unlike the other two targets, he had a family and a business so he constantly had people around him. Bird wasn't a marksman, but he was good with explosives, and had rigged up a charge under the man's car during the night. Once the guy stepped in and put the key in the ignition and twisted, the C4 took care of the rest.

All evidence that the three killers were ever at the scene was either covered or destroyed. Bug and Spider would ditch their weapons, and Bird's would be destroyed when the car exploded. Right then, all three were already on their way across the ocean to London to reunite with the rest of the group. And once his job was done in D.C., the fourth member of the US quartet, Flea, would join them.

However, on this side of the Atlantic, the operation had had mixed success. Adams' suicide was a tick in the box. It had been one of his men's ideas to give the politician no other choice than to kill himself. They could easily have stormed his office or bombed his car, but Worm had wanted him to suffer. Not the physical kind of pain, but mental, the same kind of desperation the group had suffered every minute of every day in *Ferri*. Out of the eight-man team, Worm was the most inventive at this kind of thing. He liked his enemies to be in pain. If he was going to kill you, he wouldn't just do it there and then, he'd tell you a week in advance and let you think about it every night before he did it. The leader of the group knew bad things had happened to the tall, gangly soldier as a boy, his father and uncle abusive both physically and sexually, and he guessed the cruelty he possessed as a man had something to do with those scars he carried. For most of his men, killing a man was something they needed to do to ensure victory or stay alive, but for Worm, it was a pleasure.

The envelope delivered to Adams' office had contained a hand-typed letter and two Polaroid photographs taken by Worm, up close, taken in this very room. Worm, Grub and Crow had come for Adams' wife and the kid last night at their home, just before 11 p.m. They'd restrained and gagged the two, the boy pissing himself with fear, then brought them back here and tied them to two chairs. Worm had snapped a Polaroid of each, and scrawled in his best English a letter ordering Adams to kill himself, or his family would die. He told him why this had to happen.

The threats that followed were extremely specific and detailed. Surgery would be performed on the boy, and they would send Adams Polaroids during the long operation. Then the same would happen to his wife, an extensive, long procedure, documented with photographs that would all be sent to Adams in a neat pile, showing him all the pieces. And if he told a soul, especially the cops, or let anyone else see the letter and the photographs, work on the kid would begin regardless. He would never find them in time.

There was only one way this was going to end.

Worm had given the letter, the photographs and envelope to Crow and told him to handle the rest. Crow had sealed them all inside then delivered the letter to Adams' office late last night, knowing he was upstairs. The message inside the envelope was very simple.

If he wasn't dead by 8am, the boy would start losing limbs.

The commander of the group was somewhat taken aback when the man had gone ahead and killed himself. He was expecting him to put up some sort of fight or at least contact the police. But he was pleasantly surprised, and would congratulate Worm when he saw him next. Worm's predictions had proved correct. It gave the leader of the group great comfort to know that Adams died in agonising mental anguish, still not one hundred per cent sure his family would be safe. No bullet from an enemy would be more painful than one the man fired into his own head.

So Adams had killed himself but Crow and Grub had screwed up at the police station. They'd let the man called Cobb escape. An operational setback, but not a disaster. Both men had paid the ultimate price for their failure. The remainder of the team would get it done and kill the man, but it would take some extra planning now that Cobb knew there were men after him, much as it would with Jackson. Jackson's assistant had called ahead earlier to what she thought was the Syrian ambassador's office but was in fact speaking to Worm, and she'd asked if they could reschedule Jackson's noon appointment, seeing as something had come up today.

She'd unwittingly saved her boss's life.

So Cobb and Jackson were still alive for the time being through sheer luck. But they would die soon. He was as sure of that as he was that the sun would go down at the end of the day. At some point in the next forty-eight hours, Director Tim Cobb and CIA agent Ryan Jackson would both be killed. In a way, it would be even sweeter revenge as now they both surely knew it was coming.

In the dark room, the man flicked his gaze to the CNN newsroom, where Breaking Reports were just coming in of a man killed by a car-bomb in upstate Connecticut. A concerned-looking reporter was already on the street, the charred remnants of a car behind her, police tape pulled up and crowds of concerned residents gathered alongside the news vans and police cars.

He read on the screen that the deceased had been named as David Floyd, former US Marine Corps, and he left behind a wife and three children.

The commanding officer took the pen on the desk in front of him and drew a line through the man's name, nodding.

Six down.

Five to go.

The two McLean P.D officers who took the call to check out the house with the stack of newspapers were called Beckman and Vasquez. They'd been partners for almost two years and were a good team, Beckman a Sergeant, cool and calm of Polish-German heritage, Vasquez still just an Officer but with an energy and Latina fire for justice that would change soon enough.

McLean was a relatively quiet place, a good town to be a cop. Crime stats were low in the area. Pretty much everyone who lived here was either wealthy or on their way to be, or they worked for the CIA or Congress. Murders and homicides were minimal, usually less than ten a year, and the crimes that took place were normally financial, money-laundering or tax-evasion, not violent or physical. Beckman had been a cop for twelve years and had only ever drawn his piece three times, never having to fire it. Vasquez was coming up to her third year, but had only drawn hers once. There was no soaring murder rate or any turf wars between different gangs here, and the sense of community in the area meant the locals knew most of the officers by name.

The two cops worked five days a week, weekends off, and drove their beat in a squad car kept spotless by Beckman, covering an area of about eight square miles. They'd just taken a call from dispatch concerning a domestic enquiry. Apparently a kid who did one of the paper rounds had told his boss about a stack of papers on the front step of a property, and as the squad car pulled up outside, the two officers could see he hadn't been exaggerating.

Beckman applied the handbrake and killed the engine. Down the street, both cops saw the beginnings of activity from pretty much every house on the street. It was a family area, lots of people walking down paths and headed to cars, firing engines and driving off to work. The muffled noise of kids being rounded up before they were packed off to school, the yellow school-bus pulling up along the street, the activity that took place in most households across the country at that time in the morning.

But there was none of that kind of activity in the house to their left.

When they'd taken the call, Beckman had suggested that the homeowner probably worked for the CIA. He or she would have been called away somewhere unexpectedly. That was the nature of government work, after all. Vasquez had agreed that it was a possible likelihood, and when she'd checked the squad-car computer she'd found that the homeowner, a Peter Shaw, did in fact work at the CIA. But on the screen, it said he was an analyst, not the kind of guy who would be ordered off somewhere for three weeks. Maybe it was a cover. Maybe he was a field agent instead. But nevertheless, the two officers had to check.

Stepping out of the car, the cops shut the doors and walked up the path towards the house. Beckman stepped over the pile of newspapers and approached the front door.

He knocked three times, loud enough to be heard but not loud enough to wake the neighbours.

'Mr Shaw? McLean PD. Open up please, sir.'

Pause.

Nothing.

'Mr Shaw? Please come to the door.'

Nothing.

He turned and looked at Vasquez, who shifted her gaze to the door handle.

'Check it,' she said.

Beckman reached over and took hold of the door handle. He twisted it, expecting resistance and for the locking mechanisms to kick in.

But the handle twisted and the door opened.

It slid back, revealing a still and empty hallway.

The two officers looked at each other and simultaneously drew their service weapons, two Sig Sauer P229 pistols, from their holsters. One after the other, they moved inside the house, holding the weapons double-handed as they'd been trained, clearing the lower level.

It was silent, no morning activity, no man wearing headphones listening to music as he ate breakfast unable to hear the knock on the door. Vasquez turned right and headed to the living room, whilst Beckman went to the kitchen. Both rooms were empty, but there were clues that were making both officers increasingly concerned.

In the living room, Vasquez saw a heap of clothing on the floor, a woman's, not scattered as if it had been discarded in passion, but as if it had been torn off and dumped on the spot.

She walked over slowly and saw a nightgown and some underwear, both of which were ripped.

In the kitchen, Beckman saw what looked like the beginnings of a breakfast. There were two big bowls both half filled with what looked like some kind of bran cereal. Beside them, a carton of milk was open on the table. Beckman walked forward and sniffed it, then withdrew hastily, frowning. It was off. The rest of the kitchen was spotlessly clean and almost obsessively tidy, everything where it should be, mugs hanging from hooks, pots and pans all put away, the jars on the spice rack all lined up, their labels facing outwards. But there was one thing that caught Beckman's eye. Two things, actually. Their absence stood out seeing as everything else in the room was in place.

There was a wooden knife rack across the kitchen by the toaster.

And the two biggest knives were missing.

Keeping his pistol up, Beckman reached for his radio with his free hand, pushing the buttons either side of the handle clipped to his left shoulder.

'This is Sergeant Beckman. I need back-up at 41-44 41st Street. 10-54 in progress,' he said.

A 10-54. A call no officer ever wanted to make.

Possible dead body.

'Copy that.'

He turned and moved back into the hallway, joining up with Vasquez. The two cops glanced at each other, their faces mirroring their growing feeling of unease.

They looked up the stairs simultaneously. Vasquez took the lead, her pistol going everywhere her eyes did, the hair-trigger on the Sig making tiny little jumps in her hands as her heart pumped adrenaline around her body. She crept up the stairs, taking care to not make a sound, Beckman following immediately behind her.

There were two bedrooms, a small cupboard and a bathroom. The doors to three of them were open, and she could see from where she was that all three looked empty. Beckman moved up alongside her, and the two of them stood facing what must have been the master bedroom.

The door was shut.

They moved slowly forward, the two Sigs trained on the wood, and arrived outside the door.

Outside the room, Beckman turned to Vasquez.

Ready, he mouthed.

She nodded.

He reached for the handle and twisting it, pushed the door open.

Outside Cobb's office at the ARU headquarters, First Team were standing in a group, watching through the damaged glass as Cobb talked with Jackson. They'd been in there for about fifteen minutes, and even from here the four officers could see that the atmosphere between the two men was tense. Around them, the clean-up operation was still in full swing, the tech team sitting in their area and although still traumatised, were slowly recovering from their ordeal. But across the room, the four officers stood motionless, curious, concerned, desperate to be in the room with Cobb and Jackson and have some light shed on the situation.

On the far right, Archer stood watching Cobb, seeing the unusual anxiety on his boss's face. Even in deep shit, Cobb was always cool and calm. To spook him, something really must be wrong.

'I don't like the look of this,' Chalky said quietly, in the middle of the group.

None of the other men responded.

Watching the two men, Archer suddenly felt the phone on his tac vest vibrate and he pulled it out of its Velcro home. The screen was flashing and it was ringing quietly. He looked at the caller ID but it was a number he didn't recognise. He pushed the green button and put it to his ear.

'Hello?'

'It's me,' a familiar female voice said.

He saw the other three officers were looking at him, and he motioned *1 second* with his finger and walked off down the corridor.

'Hey,' he said. 'How did you get this number? This is my work phone.'

'C'mon, Archer, I work for the FBI,' Katic said. *'I saw on the news here that your police station got attacked? Are you OK?'*

'Yeah, I'm fine. They killed one of our guys though.'

'How many of them were there?' she asked.

'Two gunmen.'

'Who were they?'

'We don't know. We're trying to find out. There's a CIA agent here now talking with my boss.'

He glanced back.

'You heard of Ryan Jackson before? Apparently he's an Operations Officer.'

'Doesn't ring a bell. I can check him out?'

'I thought the Feds didn't have access to CIA files?'

'We don't.'

'So what are you going to use?'

'Google, stupid. Hang on.'

He smiled as he heard the tapping of keys down the line. There was a pause. He took a few steps back into the level and checked through the glass of Cobb's office. He and Jackson were still engrossed in conversation.

'Bulls-eye,' she said, as he returned to the top of the stairs.

'You found something?'

'Yeah. It's a news report from The Washington Times. Dated April 23 1999. CIA agent Ryan Jackson awarded Distinguished Intelligence Medal for Outstanding Performance and Service.'

'What does the report say?'

'Hang on.' Pause. *'He was twenty six at the time. There's a photo too. They had a presentation ceremony in DC where the Deputy Director of the CIA pinned it on his suit. All the top people from the Agency were there, as well as the Chief of Staff. Damn, Archer. This guy was a hero.'*

'What was it for?'

'It doesn't say. Just the official blurb- for performance of outstanding services, for

achievement of a distinctly exceptional nature in a duty or responsibility. He must have got it on a covert operation. They don't even hint in specifics at what he did to earn it.'

Archer nodded and turned, checking back.

Through the glass he saw Cobb scribbling something on a piece of paper, drain a cup of coffee and head towards his door, Jackson following close behind.

'Shit, I need to go,' he said. 'Looks like something's happening.'

'OK.' Pause. *'It was good to talk you.'*

'And you. It always is.'

He pictured her smile, the other end of the line.

'Speak soon,' she said.

He ended the call and slotted his phone back in its home on his vest, then walked quickly down the corridor, stepping past a Forensics detective in white coming the other way. He saw Cobb and Jackson were over by Nikki in the tech area, who was back at her desk although still pretty shaken up. Cobb spoke to her in a low voice, passing her the paper, and she nodded, then turned to her computer and started working away at something, seemingly keen to be distracted and get back into the usual routine.

Archer re-joined the other three officers, who sensed him return and glanced his way.

'Who was that?' Chalky asked.

'Wrong number,' Archer said.

Beside him, Porter gave a grunt of *I've had enough* and walked forward, approaching Cobb who had turned and was walking back towards his office.

'Everything OK, sir?' he asked.

Cobb turned and looked at Porter and the three other officers. Archer could see him weighing up his options, wondering if he should involve them in whatever was going on. Behind him, Jackson checked the time on his watch, then pulled out a mobile phone from his pocket and started texting something.

'We want to help,' Porter added, reading the situation.

Cobb looked at him, then nodded. *Very well.*

'My office,' he said.

He walked in, Jackson just behind him, and the four task force officers followed swiftly, moving inside and taking up positions around the room.

Cobb looked over at Chalky, who was closest to the exit.

'Shut the door, Chalk,' he said.

Chalky did so as Cobb looked at Jackson, who was leaning with his back to the wall on Cobb's right.

'May I tell my men what this is all about?' he asked.

Jackson nodded. 'Go for it. It's both our asses if you don't.'

So Cobb leaned back in his chair and he began to speak.

TWELVE

‘It was 1999,' Cobb said. 'I was twenty six, and was working on a six-month transfer detail at MI6. The war in Serbia was really taking off, and things in Kosovo were going from deep shit to worse. NATO had just got involved, As you may recall, there were two sides, the Serbs and the Albanians, the Christians versus the Muslims as the press liked to portray it, dubbing it a modern holy war. But to the rest of us, it was just a real damn mess. It was already a bad situation, but then NATO stepped in and started shelling Belgrade like it would fix all the problems.’

He paused.

‘I’m sure you know the history. They’ve been fighting over that land for centuries, as far back as 1389. A conference right here in London just over a hundred years ago officially stated that the Kosovo lands from then on would belong to Serbia and Serbia alone. But during the last century, the population in the area gradually became more and more Albanian. Serbia ended all self-government in Kosovo in 1989, and the police force became all Serbian. The Albanians in the region were pissed. They’d lost jobs, political rights and dignity. And soon enough, as the 90’s ticked by, they started to demand their independence, saying that the land wasn’t Serbia’s but theirs.’

‘But the Serbs disagreed,’ Fox said.

Cobb nodded.

‘And in 1998, the exact same as in 1389, the fight was breaking out all over the country again, across the plains and in the valleys, two sides going at each other just as they had six hundred years ago.'

He paused.

'Like all wars, some really bad stuff happened. Houses and villages were torched, women raped, villagers and civilians executed, entire towns razed and burned to the ground. Stuff that the BBC and CNN didn’t show in their reports.’

The room was silent as each man listened closely.

‘Anyway, I got called into my boss's office in March 1999, just before the NATO bombing of Belgrade had begun,’ Cobb continued. ‘To my surprise, there was a covert operation that he wanted me to handle. He claimed that he was passing it to me because he wanted to give me an opportunity to see what I could do, more responsibility, to see how I handled the pressure, etc. But even at the time I knew that was all bullshit. The fact is, no-one else wanted it. It should have been a military job, but for some reason that I never discovered, no-one would touch it, all making up long and elaborate excuses as to why it wasn’t possible. So it got passed down and I ended up being the schmuck who was too junior to say *no*. If I did, I would have been transferred straight out of there and stuck behind a desk. My career would effectively have been over before it had begun.'

There was another pause.

'What was the operation, sir?' Porter asked.

Cobb flicked his gaze at Jackson, who stood watching him silently, his arms folded. The American nodded and Cobb continued.

'Three soldiers from NATO ground forces had been kidnapped. One of ours, a British Army infantry Corporal, and two United States Marines. Intelligence reports said that they were being held somewhere in the Drenica Valley, a long gully in central Kosovo where a lot of the fighting took place. It was my job to find them and get them out. NATO had forces on the ground, but we had extensive access to undercover operatives, drones, bugs and wire-taps.'

He paused.

'I was working on this alone with a carefully selected team of six. No-one aside from the absolute minimum knew about it. My boss said that we couldn't risk any kind of leaks. If the press became aware of the situation, it could compromise the safety of the hostages. There would be ransom demands and possibly filmed executions.'

He nodded.

'Soon enough the team under my supervision found the three men by using a drone. It was just as they said. They were being held captive by a group of eight soldiers. I relayed this to my senior officer and he ordered me to organise the rescue operation, which was strange too.'

'Why?' Chalky asked.

'At MI6, they use covert and undercover operatives, secretive tactics, similar to the work the CIA does. We weren't a military hit-and-run squad and definitely not a rescue team. But nevertheless, he ordered me to handle it, and put me in touch with an American agent from the CIA to assist me. That happened to be Agent Jackson here.'

The four ARU officers looked over at the American, who nodded, his expression unreadable, his arms folded. Cobb continued.

'Given that two of the hostages were US Marines and that it was a NATO operation, Agent Jackson wanted American soldiers in the rescue team, as well as our own,' he said. 'Consequently, it ended up being a six-man squad, two teams of three. Captain Charlie Adams of the British Army in charge, Sergeant Derek Spears of the United States Rangers his second-in-command. And the official name for the unofficial rescue was *Operation Blackout*.'

He paused.

'The rescue operation would be performed by foot,' he continued. 'The captives were being held at a remote camp far away from both the Serb and KLA ground forces, out in the valleys towards Bosnia. We couldn't use aircraft near their citadel. RPGs and bazookas were one of the most commonly used weapons in the war and we didn't want to risk taking a hit. So the plan was to drop the team four miles to the east. They would infiltrate at night, move in, rescue the three hostages, then head back to the extraction point where it was safe to fly and for us to pick all nine of them up. We had to wait on the weather, and once it was in our favour, we were ready. Jackson and I were working together from a command post inside MI6, co-ordinating the operation. And on a Thursday night in late March in 1999, Operation Blackout was a *go*.'

He paused and nodded.

'They abseiled in and the helicopter left without drawing fire or any attention. These were good men, you know, really good. They were under strict orders not to shoot to kill unless absolutely necessary. The team worked their way inside the perimeter under Captain Adams' leadership. None of the enemy had a clue they were there, right under their noses. They moved right through the KLA camp, to the hut where the three hostages were being held. They got them out and headed back the way they came before anyone had any idea what had happened. Stealth over aggression, shadows over bullets. The helicopter picked them up at the RV point three hours after they dropped them off, and the entire team left unhurt with the three hostages, the mission a success.'

He paused. Leaning against some of the damaged glass, Archer glanced across the room at Jackson, who was standing motionless, listening.

He looked tense.

'Naturally, I figured my boss would be thrilled,' Cobb continued. 'It was a real coup. I was a young man, still twenty six, so naturally I was elated. The first big operation I'd run and it was a knockout. It couldn't have gone better. But then he called me into his office with Agent Jackson at four a.m. that morning, just after the operation had ended, before we'd even had a chance to leave and get some much needed rest. Obviously, with the nature of our work, we were both trained and familiar with discretion. Like everyone else, I'd signed the Official Secrets Act and Jackson the Espionage Act earlier in our careers. But we were each handed specially drawn-up agreements and ordered to sign them immediately. If we ever said a word to anyone about this operation, the ramifications would be incredibly severe. Even now, I'm breaking the terms of that document I signed by mentioning what happened. If the wrong person heard this, I could go to prison.'

'Why the silence, sir?' Archer said. 'I thought hostage rescues normally got leaked to the press? Good PR and all.'

Cobb looked at him. 'You're right. They are. Normally someone at Downing Street can't wait to tell the journalists. Such operations are real triumphs, something to lift the public, to reinforce their faith in our armed forces and government, showing our superiority over the enemy etc. But the document I signed was the most uncompromising I'd ever seen.

To my knowledge, everyone involved in Blackout signed one. So I moved on, and it's been fifteen years since I last thought about it.'

Silence.

'So why were they so keen to keep you quiet?' Chalky asked, by the door.

Cobb looked over at Jackson.

'Most of our operations were classified Top Secret,' Cobb said, his eyes boring a hole into the CIA agent, who looked at the ground. 'But something didn't seem right here. And I'm guessing they didn't tell me the full story. I should have known something was wrong when none of the military guys would touch it. This kind of thing is normally right up their alley.'

'But wait a minute,' Archer said, across the room. 'I thought NATO was working with the Albanians and the KLA. Why the hell would they take some of our own guys captive? We were on the same side.'

In his chair, his narrative complete, Cobb turned to Jackson.

'I don't know. Perhaps you would like to share? Why would they take three of our fellow countrymen hostage?'

The American paused and looked at him.

A long and somewhat awkward silence followed.

'*Speak*, Ryan,' Cobb said, his voice harder. 'No more secrets. It's too late for that. It's time we started sharing some history. Why would they take three of our guys?'

Jackson looked up at him ruefully.
'Because they were mass murderers,' he said.

*

Before Jackson could explain further, Nikki rushed over to Cobb's office and after knocking, quickly entered the room. She couldn't have entered at a worse time, but she had to talk to Cobb right away. None of the men paid attention to her. They all seemed to be looking at the American CIA newcomer.

'Sir, I found one of the names on the list you gave me.'

'Who?'

'Corporal Simon Fletcher, formerly British Army. He's under care at a hospice twenty five minutes from here.'

'Got the address?'

'Yes, sir.'

'So let's go.'

Cobb rose from his desk and moved outside into the Operations area, followed by the five other men, all of them turning left and headed for the lower level. Downstairs they found Deakins and another officer at the front desk, guarding the front entrance, MP5s in their hands. Archer saw that Clark's body had been removed, but he could still see faint blood stains on the floor and wall behind him.

'Is there a problem, sir?' Deakins asked.

'We need to head out for an hour or so,' Cobb said. 'First Team is coming with me. Hold the fort till I get back. You're in command.'

'Yes, sir.'

Cobb nodded and the six men walked to the doors. He peered outside, then turned and looked back at the five men behind him.

'We'll go in my vehicle and Jackson's,' he said.

Satisfied it was safe, he pushed open the door and moved swiftly to the cars. In the lot, the three ARU vehicles had been torn apart by the Kalashnikov gunfire so the men ignored them and headed for the civilian cars parked beside them. Cobb and Jackson pulled their keys and clicked open each car, the two vehicles giving two chirps as they were unlocked. Jackson climbed into the driver's seat of his BMW, Archer and Fox with him, whilst Porter and Chalky went with Cobb.

Both engines fired up, and Cobb took the lead, reversing and heading out of the lot swiftly. One of the two Met officers stationed at the perimeter lifted the yellow police tape, and the two cars moved underneath, past the gathering group of journalists, news-teams and members of the public, and headed off down the street, moving fast.

In the lead car, heading down the road, Cobb thought for a moment then pulled his mobile phone from his inside suit pocket and pushed *Redial*. The call connected to Nikki back upstairs in the Ops room inside ARU's headquarters.

'Sir?' she answered.

'Nikki, call my wife,' he said. 'Tell her to come straight in and bring the boys. Until this is over, I want them all under armed protection.'

'Yes, sir,' she said.

He ended the call, put his foot down and the car sped off down the street.

'Simon Fletcher,' Chalky said. 'Was he a member of the rescue team, sir?'

Cobb shook his head, his face hard.

'No. He was one of the hostages.'

Back at the command post, the big man sitting alone in the darkness saw the CNN screen flicker to reports of a double-homicide discovered in a family home in McLean, Virginia.

So they'd found the fat man and his wife. Finally. For a government town, they'd taken their time. He'd been expecting that discovery two weeks ago.

When he and his team had arrived in McLean after leaving Belgrade, they'd settled in a hotel and started to look around for what they were after. They'd eventually found it sitting in a local bar, three days later. The man's name was Peter Shaw, an overweight and disgruntled analyst who worked for the CIA. Spider had stopped into the joint for a beer, and had heard the overweight man complaining to a co-worker about how his talents were being misused, the two men sitting on stools down the bar nursing two cold Budweisers.

Once Bug and Flea had joined Spider and the fat man's friend had said his goodbyes and headed out, Spider had moved over and introduced himself, making up a bullshit story about his background and striking up a conversation. Over the next few hours, the three soldiers had proceeded to get Shaw increasingly drunk, encouraging him to talk and vent his anger about his perceived misuse by the Agency. Shaw had gone on and on about how his skills were being wasted by his superiors, how he was the best analyst you could find in the entire damn town and how he was sick of being overlooked for promotion again and again by people who couldn't do their job without him. The three men kept nodding in agreement, feigning interest and feeding him more booze, fuelling his dissatisfaction and in the process finding out what his security clearances were.

Once Spider told his commanding officer about Shaw the next morning, they agreed he was exactly what they were looking for. The next step was when to give the fat man the assignment. The team knew that they couldn't approach Shaw in his vehicle or anywhere near his office at the Agency headquarters. So they'd accosted him twenty four hours later, just before he went to work early in the morning. He'd opened the door, surprised to see his new friends from the bar standing on his porch. The men had stripped his wife naked in the living room and held a butcher's knife from the kitchen to her throat. She was as overweight as her husband, her pale fatty flesh marbled and stretched. Her nudity was an unpleasant sight.

The long blade to the fat woman's jugular, the leader had said very clearly and simply what they wanted. If Shaw complied, he promised that they both would live and they would leave them be. But if he failed or tried to tell anyone what was happening, the leader of the group would let his men start on his wife. Worm had taken over and told Shaw they wouldn't just cut her throat. They would start elsewhere, somewhere about a foot and a half south, and work their way up. There were all sorts of things they could use on her, he'd told the fat man. In all sorts of places. Cork-screws, peelers, chopping knives, a cleaver. After all, the kitchen was very well stocked.

Unused to such ferocity, Shaw had been almost speechless with terror, instantly compliant, nodding frantically and trying not to wet himself with fear as his former friends from the bar held the knife to his naked wife's throat. Despite being scared witless and a complete slob, he'd proved to be as good at his job as he claimed and had got the team what they wanted before lunch that morning. The team had remained vigilant, checking outside to see if this was a set-up or if Shaw had talked to the cops, but he hadn't.

When he returned, no-one followed him.

The CIA kept immaculate and up-to-date records on anyone who had ever been involved with the Agency's dealings over the years. Some tight, high-level security protocols had been in place with this file, but the information Shaw had rushed home with on the memory stick had been exactly what they were after, ten names and addresses of the men from that operation all those years ago. Only one man was missing from the list, but they already knew his name. Once the dominos were falling, one after the other, they would find him soon enough.

Back at the command post in London, watching the screen, the man saw police tape pulled up around the house in McLean, an ambulance team dressed in white working alongside a forensics team. He saw two large black body-bags wheeled out on two gurneys. Mr and Mrs Shaw respectively.

The commanding officer was a man of honour, but he was also ruthless. The safety and security of his men was his foremost priority and he knew sooner or later the Shaws would tell someone what had happened and could describe what each member of the group looked like. So once the fat man had returned with the information, the group had killed him and his wife. It had been relatively quick. They'd gagged the couple, taken them upstairs, then used two knives from the kitchen so as not to alert the neighbours. Knife-work was always messy. The pair of them had both bled like stuck pigs as Worm and Bug cut their throats, blood soaking into the white bed-sheets of their double bed. Each was around two hundred and fifty pounds, and blood had pulsed and pulsed out of their obese bodies onto the sheets and the carpet.

The bedroom looked like a horror film by the time the team had left.

Watching the fresh report, a lime-green light suddenly started flashing on the desk beside the television, lighting up the room like a large firefly. It was the screen of his mobile phone. The big man picked it up from the desk and answered it.

'Yes.'

'Sir, I have news,' a voice said. It was Worm.' *Jackson is with Cobb. They just left the police station. I don't know where they're going, but it must be important. They're not hanging around. I'm following.'*

'You didn't get a shot?'

'No, sir. I was parked down the street, and they drove too fast when they pulled out of the gates. They also have four cops with them. They're all armed.'

'Don't lose them. Report back when you know where the hell they are going. And don't screw up.'

He ended the call without waiting for a response.

He placed the phone back on the desk and looked down at the list of names in front of him. *Tim Cobb, ARU* it said there, in dark letters. *Ryan Jackson, CIA* just below it. Judging from Worm's report, these two now had an armed escort everywhere they went. The original plan for Jackson was to take him out during a meeting he had scheduled at noon. He thought it was going to be with the Syrian ambassador, but in reality he would have arrived at the meeting place, an empty conference room, and found himself walking onto plastic sheets, a silenced pistol put to the back of his head.

But it was now past midday and his assistant had called earlier to cancel the meeting, so the plan had been aborted. And now Jackson was with Cobb. Both would have made the connection by now and realised from the list of the dead what this was about. That explained the armed escort.

Alone in the dark command post, the big man cursed.

Killing Jackson and Cobb was going to be harder than he'd thought.

THIRTEEN

The journey to the hospice took just over forty five minutes. Cobb drove fast, but the midday city traffic was bad and they were delayed by queues and red lights. Nevertheless, they got there in pretty good time, just as the clock on the dashboard of the Mercedes ticked to 1pm. In Jackson's car not a word was spoken between the CIA agent, Archer and Fox on the journey. They were hoping to get some answers from Corporal Fletcher himself. Also, like loyal men, they didn't much feel like conversing with the man who'd withheld information from their boss.

As they turned into the parking lot behind the lead car, Archer looked out of the window from the front passenger seat and examined the hospice from the outside. It was a long, single storey building and looked newly built. Once the two cars parked side by side and the six men climbed out, Archer spotted a welcome sign with a map layout of the hospice a few feet away and walked over to take a closer look.

Judging from the map there was a three-acre garden the other side of the building, fenced off from the public where residents, if they were physically able, could enjoy some fresh air and some privacy. He scanned it quickly, looking for all entry and access points. He wasn't expecting trouble inside, but he heard his father's voice, a former sergeant in the NYPD, echo in his mind. *Make sure you know every way in and out of a place.*

It had been his dad's credo back in the 80's when he and his partner were after gang members and drug-addicts plaguing the city. If you were a landlord, you'd have to point a gun at some of those people to get them to move, but one knock on the door from a cop was enough to clear out an entire apartment like cockroaches when the lights were turned on. Archer had rolled his eyes as a kid when his dad told him about that stuff, bored, but as a man he'd remembered it and that advice had got him out of trouble more than once. Cobb stepped forward, joining Archer, and glanced at the map.

After a moment, he nodded and motioned for everyone to follow him inside.

Given the poor health and physical frailty of the residents of the building, the few people who happened to be near the entrance were extremely surprised to see six men, four of them armed police officers, walking towards the double-door entrance to the hospice. Not the usual sort of visitors.

All conversation in the reception area abruptly ceased as everyone watched the purposeful group enter. As Cobb approached the lady behind the front desk to explain why they were here, Fox and Porter remained by the entrance, checking the car park behind them to make sure they hadn't been tailed. Standing in the middle of the Reception area, Archer and Chalky looked around the interior of the building.

The place was clean with a lot of polished wood, shaped like a long bungalow and reminded Archer of a log cabin. It looked Scandinavian. Archer had spent time in a hospice before. His mother had spent her last few days in one a few years ago but much to his surprise, then as now, he'd found that the building didn't give him the yips in the way hospitals did. There was no smell of bleach or disinfectant, no crowding in the corridors, no drunken injured or people shouting, no impersonal staff. It was very calm and very quiet. Everyone who came here knew that their days on Earth were drawing to a close. But instead of being a desperately sad place, it felt peaceful. A pleasant environment which frequently took people who'd never visited a hospice before by surprise.

Archer realised the building was having a calming effect on him already. It'd been a tumultuous morning, but the quiet atmosphere was definitely soothing. He remembered Katie had mentioned that she'd spent a lot of time in one of these places when her husband was in the final stages of his cancer. He felt his throat tighten as he thought of her, but instantly banished any thought of her from his mind.

He couldn't afford to be distracted today.

If he was, it could get him killed.

Cobb showed his ID to the receptionist behind the desk, explaining who he was. She was a middle-aged woman, slightly frumpy, but with a pleasant face that right then looked pretty worried. Although Nikki had called ahead and told her Cobb and his team were coming, Archer realised she was a bit overwhelmed, and couldn't take her eyes off the four black MP5 sub-machine guns the officers were carrying. He guessed most people brought flowers.

After explaining why they were here and the pressing nature of their business, Cobb paused and looked down at the woman behind the desk,

'Is that OK?' he asked her.

'Yes,' she said, still staring at the weapons. 'Of course you can see Mr Fletcher. But could I ask you to leave those here please?'

She pointed uncertainly at the guns as if they would bite her.

‘I don’t want you to give our patients a heart attack. I have a secure room here where you can store them until you leave. I have the only key.’

None of the officers moved. The events of the morning had left them unwilling to relinquish their weapons.

Cobb thought for a moment.

‘Can my men keep their side-arms?’

She frowned at him, about to say *no*.

‘They’ll keep them holstered, out of sight,' he added, reading her expression. 'You have my word. I promise. But trust me, it's better for us all that they have them within reach.’

'OK,' she said after a brief hesitation, still reluctant but finally giving in. 'I suppose so.'

Cobb turned and nodded. The four officers checked the safety catch was on, then racked the cocking handle back and pulled each magazine from each weapon, ensuring the chambers were empty, much to the fascination of the few residents in the area watching them. The receptionist pulled a key from a drawer and opened up a room behind the reception, and one by one the men stowed their weapons neatly inside, taking the magazines and tucking them into spare pouches on their uniform. They wouldn't leave the weapons with any ammunition, just in case someone managed to get inside the room. Archer stepped back, relieved he still had his Glock 17 pistol in the holster on his thigh. It didn't matter where they were today, at their Unit, a hospice or even a church, they needed to be armed at all times. Some men had come to kill Cobb, and others were still out there somewhere.

And there was nothing that would stop them from trying again.

As satisfied as their compromise on the weapons would allow, the receptionist made sure the room was locked by trying to twist the handle. It wouldn't budge. She dropped the key in her pocket, turned and then looked across the desk at the six waiting men.

'Come with me,' she said.

Stepping into the lobby, she keyed in a six digit number on a keypad attached to an internal door, and pulled it open, passing through and holding it for the group. They followed and moved down the corridor into the building after her.

They passed rooms on either side occupied by patients; some of the doors were open and Archer could see people lying in the beds, some alone, others with families. He even saw one man with a dog curled up on the bed beside him, both of them asleep. Despite the circumstances, the sight of the two of them made him smile briefly. He remembered at the place his mum had stayed in that one patient had owned some racing stables, and she had one of her favourite horses brought to the hospice and led into the garden so she could be wheeled out of her room to pet and stroke him one last time. Archer had been in the room next door with his mother, and thought he was dreaming when the huge racehorse strolled past the window.

They passed a couple of elderly patients being helped to their rooms by a nurse, both walking slowly, using frames, the officers taking care to step past them carefully and respectfully. The two patients ignored the group, focusing on each footstep they were taking, but Archer saw the two nurses' look of surprise when they saw them.

Leading the way, the receptionist turned to the left, walking briskly down another corridor. She came to an abrupt stop outside a closed wooden door.

Number 32.

'This is it,' she said. She knocked softly.

'Come in,' a voice said, quietly.

She opened the door and the men followed her into the room.

As he walked in, Archer saw a blond-haired patient lying in the bed and managed to hide his surprise when he saw the man's frailty. Fletcher was pale and gaunt, his cheeks sunken. He was wearing pyjamas but they were hanging off him, his two pointy shoulders serving merely as a bony coat-hanger.

Archer looked around the room and saw a television on the BBC News channel, standing on a table in the corner. They'd caught it during a re-run of the bulletins, the screen showing the damage to the outside of the ARU's headquarters from the gunfight. The sound was muted, but the shot flicked to Cobb delivering his report to the waiting press.

From the bed, Fletcher coughed, clearing his throat, staring in confusion at the sudden influx of strangers who had entered his room. He looked totally bewildered.

'What's going on?' he asked.

*

'So we finally meet,' Fletcher said to Cobb and Jackson, after Cobb had explained to him who they were. 'I never had a chance to thank you two gentlemen for what you did for me.'

As he spoke, Fox and Chalky checked out of the windows which looked out over the rear of the building. They could see a large garden with a duck pond not far away from the building, surrounded by benches. The outskirts of the garden was lined with trees and shrubbery, providing a natural screen of privacy for the residents and their visitors. There were a few people out there walking around, several elderly patients, a young, tall, dark-haired man moving slowly beside an older grey-haired man, probably his father, looking around and enjoying the sunshine. The receptionist had just departed, both to leave the policemen alone with Fletcher and also to get back to her desk.

Chalky and Fox drew the curtains shut and across the room, Porter locked the door behind him. Archer flicked on the light on the wall and stood beside Porter, looking at the former soldier in the bed. The guy looked exhausted, ten or fifteen years older than he actually was. He had a sheen of cold sweat on his waxy face, his eyes sunken, but he looked back at them all in turn, curious.

'It's nice to have guests. My family haven't been in a while. I'd offer you all a seat, but there are only two,' Fletcher said, forcing a weak smile.

Chalky and Fox folded their arms, staying by the curtains. Cobb took up the offer and sat on one of the empty chairs. No-one took the other. Archer and Porter remained standing beside Jackson, the door locked behind them, and together the six of them encircled the sickly man in the wide bed.

'What kind of cancer is it?' Archer asked, breaking a few moments of silence.

Fletcher looked over at him.

‘Stomach. I’ll be dead in three months. Puts all my shit into perspective.'

Pause.

'But Nature knows what she's doing. I don’t deserve to live anyway.’

There was another pause. They all knew what the next question would be. It was just a case of who would ask it.

‘What happened?’ Porter asked quietly. ‘In Kosovo?’

Fletcher looked across the room at Cobb and Jackson.

‘So that’s why you’re here.’

They both nodded.

'It’s OK?' he asked them.

'Speak,' Cobb said. ‘No more secrets today.’

The sick man took a deep breath, wincing from the effort as air filled his lungs.

And he began to talk.

FOURTEEN

‘There were three of us,’ Fletcher said. ‘Me, Carver and Floyd. We all met at Camp Bondsteel. It was the main NATO military base over there, and it was a hell of a place to be. I'd been in the Army for over ten years at that point. Went to the Gulf. Bosnia. Been in some good camps, and some pretty bad ones. But Bondsteel was the best military base I’d ever been to in my life. It had everything. A cinema, school-rooms, two cappuccino bars, football fields, recreation rooms. You name it, they had it. They had the best hospital in Kosovo too. They even had a Taco Bell and Burger King.'

He paused, taking a breath. Archer noticed the effort from talking was already causing more beads of cold sweat to form on the man's brow. Simple talking and having a conversation for this man was like going flat out on a treadmill on the highest incline.

'Most of that stuff was there to keep the troops entertained, you know? Back then, it wasn’t like it is now in Afghanistan, or Iraq. The action was few and far between, and it was pretty damn boring. NATO bombers were just about to start hitting Belgrade, but the Serbs and the Albanians were only interested in engaging each other. We were like an umpire on a tennis court, watching it go back and forth, trying to keep score.’

He winced again as he took another deep breath, the effort causing one of the drops of sweat on his brow to slide down the side of his head. He licked his lips with a dry tongue, then turned his head to the side, looking at a small table. There was a cup of water with a straw there. Fox read what he wanted and moving forward, he picked it up, holding it closer as Fletcher took a drink.

'Thanks,' he said, leaning back in the bed, continuing. 'Anyway, the camp was the main base for the US Army in Kosovo. I was one of the only Brits on site, but that wasn't intentional. I shouldn't even have been there in the first place. I'd taken two bullets, one in the leg and one in the chest from a sniper. We were out on a peace-keeping patrol when I got hit, and the nearest hospital was at Bondsteel. I was told I had to stay there until I was fit to travel and return to my battalion.'

He coughed. It seemed like his body just wanted him to shut up and lie back.

'Once they'd patched me up and I'd recovered enough to be released from the hospital, I had a lot of time to kill. I was hanging around, waiting for some transport to be released to pick me up, but it was all committed elsewhere so I had to wait. Everyone there was US Army or Marine Corps and as I wasn't officially there, there was no chance of me being called out on patrol or anything, nothing to break up the days, plus I was still recovering. Although there was stuff to do on site, I got bored as hell quickly, spending all my time alone. I watched all the movies they had, and got sick of Burger King. So, to keep busy, I used to do down to the shooting range.'

He paused.

'The standard weapon for my squad was the SA80,' Fletcher continued. 'Typical English weapon. Solid, straight-shooter, gets the job done. Zero glamour. Not the kind of gun you'd ever see in the movies. But the Americans, they did it different. They had M-16s and Berettas. I got friendly with the quartermaster down at the range and he let me work out with one of the M-16s.'

He paused, and licked his lips, his tongue already dry again.

'It was a lot of fun. I'd never handled a weapon like that before. I spent all day there on the range, drilling the targets, getting used to the feel of the rifle. Given the amount of spare time I had, I got pretty good with it. Seeing as I never had to answer any roll call, I spent most of my days down there. Other soldiers would come and go, but there was one other guy who was always there, almost every time I was. His name was Floyd. David Floyd, a Private, US Marine Corps. Southern boy, out of Georgia. Spoke like one of those cowboys in the movies I used to watch as a kid. He was off the frontline too. He'd broken his ankle and was having to wait to heal up before he could return to duty.'

He paused.

'Now I came from a strong battalion in the British Army. We had some good shooters, believe you me. But Floyd was surgical. He was one of the best I'd ever seen. The quartermaster told me he was down there for hours every day. Soon enough, we got talking. People get to know each other on base, but I was a newcomer, an outsider. I didn't know anything about him. Turned out he was a real loner. Didn't have any friends there aside from one other guy.'

'Carver,' Jackson said quietly.

Fletcher nodded.

'Yes. After we got friendly, he introduced me to Carver, who was his Captain. Should have told me something then. Officers and NCOs are not usually mates. It crossed my mind - why wasn't Carver hanging out with other officers? Anyway, I'd heard about him from the quartermaster. *Stay away from that asshole,* he said. *For your own good.* Carver had a bad reputation, and I mean really bad. There were all sorts of rumours about him, but the guy on the range wasn't exaggerating. People hated him, mostly men under his command. Floyd was the only one who seemed to have any time for him, but his men wouldn't have pissed on him if he was on fire. He constantly punished them for trivial stuff, abused his privileges, stuff like that. There was even a rumour that he'd gang-raped some girl with two other guys back in Bosnia. From the sounds of it, it was a miracle that he'd never been fragged out in the field.'

'Fragged?' Chalky asked.

‘Killed by one of his own men,’ Jackson said.

‘But we clicked straight away when we met,’ Fletcher continued. ‘He seemed OK to me. Never gave me any grief. Anyway, we became a trio, me, him and Floyd. The three of us would meet up and go shooting together at the firing range. I wasn’t due to be picked up and taken out of there for a few weeks, so I had a hell of a lot of spare time on my hands and I spent most of it with the other two.’

He paused.

‘Soon enough, we started spending more time together outside of the range. Carver had access and privileges that Floyd and I didn’t, being a Captain. He used to go to the stores and get bottles of Jack. We'd get loaded up in his room.’

He paused and swallowed.

The room was so quiet, every man heard it.

‘So one night, we were in Carver’s room. We had some metal going on the speakers, and killed two bottles of whiskey between us. As it normally did, the conversation turned to shooting. Floyd had never even fired his weapon in combat before. He was your typical jarhead. He’d been there for almost a year and hadn’t even taken a shot at the enemy. And Carver had only ever shot at two enemy combatants in his entire career, killing neither, which pissed him off something special. It was eating away at him, just like this cancer in my gut.'

Pause.

'So Carver suddenly said that he wanted to go hunting.'

Fletcher coughed, then shook his head and looked at Cobb.

'Worst decision of my life,' he said. 'One of those moments where you'd give anything to go back and make a different choice, you know? I was drunk out of my mind. I said yes and so did Floyd, figuring we'd just fire off a few rounds out on the plains and drive back. So Carver got into a Humvee and fed the guard on the gate some bullshit excuse about a late-night rendezvous and we went out there, M-16s a piece, stacks of spare clips in the back of the wagon.'

He paused again. Archer saw the man's eyes weren't focused on anyone in the room anymore. His mind was back in that vehicle and reliving the drive that night. From the look on the sick man's face, Archer guessed it had happened thousands of times since.

'Floyd was wasted, full of bravado and out for blood, and so was Carver,' he said. 'He almost ran us off the road three times he was so tanked. Sitting there in the back of the truck, I started to realise that all those warnings about Carver were right. He was crazy, out of control.'

He stopped, taking a breath. His rising emotions weren't helping his sick body.

In the room, no-one made a sound.

'In that area, the Kosovo army, the KLA, were taking on the Serbs in the valleys. One of their units had evacuated all their women and children out to a township fifteen miles from our camp, to keep them well back from the firing line. Carver knew all about it from the latest reports. So he took us on the dirt track and headed straight there.'

He paused again, closing his eyes.

'Soon enough, we arrived, and stepped out of the truck,' he said, swallowing, his voice starting to tremble slightly. 'There were only three men in that town guarding the women and the kids. Two of them came up and asked what we were doing there. They weren't being aggressive; they were just doing their jobs.'

He swallowed hard again.

'Floyd started arguing with them, but then Carver just lifted his rifle and shot them in the head. *Bang bang*. Two shots. Killed them both.'

Pause.

'And from there, the floodgates opened,' he said. 'The two of them just went berserk. They were going hut to hut, through mag after mag. They hosed down kids as they ran up the street, reloading fast whenever their clips clicked dry. They shot pregnant women. And laughed as they did it. I stayed where I was by the Humvee, my rifle in the truck. I couldn't believe what they were doing. I thought it was a bad dream. But I couldn't stop them. They would have turned around and shot me too.'

He blinked, tears in his eyes.

'A lot of the women and kids tried to run to the hills for cover, but they were all mown down. The pair of them must have killed close to thirty, forty people, probably more. All of them women and children apart from three guards.'

The room was silent.

'Afterwards, when everyone around us was either dead or dying and their bloodlust was satisfied, both of them began to realise what they'd just done. They started to panic. Carver said we should head straight back to camp and pretend it never happened. Deny all responsibility. He said he could get us out of it, and would come up with some back-up plan that could cover us. So we jumped in the Humvee, turned around and left as quickly as we came. Leaving behind a camp littered with dead bodies and soaked in blood.'

He swallowed.

'But we never made it back. The last surviving guard or someone else must have called in the attack over a radio from somewhere. Our Humvee got hit by a bazooka as we were driving back to Bondsteel and the next thing I knew we were captured.'

'By who?' Archer asked. 'The KLA?'

Fletcher shook his head.

'Yes and no. Technically they were KLA at the time. They were a renegade Special Forces Unit. I found out later that the KLA expelled them after the war for stuff they did.'

'Why were they expelled?'

Fletcher blinked.

'War crimes. Back at Bondsteel, we'd all heard tales about them. They were called the Black Panthers. Entire Serbian villages were being found deserted in the area, clothes and possessions still inside the houses. Everyone gone, vanished, no blood, no bodies, no traces, never seen or heard from again. That was their handiwork. No-one knew why or what had happened to the people. Word had spread. They were close to being expelled by the time they kidnapped us, but later the KLA commanders said they were too savage for their organisation, that their interests weren't the same as the liberation's anymore.'

He paused.

'The Black Panthers. Albanian Special Forces. Some of the toughest bastards on the planet. And it turned out the people in the camp we murdered were their wives and children.'

FIFTEEN

A long silence followed as everyone in the room absorbed what Fletcher had just said. In the bed, the man's eyes were vacant, like looking at two windows with nothing beyond, his mind taken back all those years to that terrible night.

Eventually, Cobb broke the silence. This was all news to him too. Across the room Jackson was leaning against the desktop by the television, his arms folded, his head down. Clearly he already knew all about this.

He also knew what was coming next.

‘So what happened?’ Cobb asked. As he spoke, he glanced over at the American, but the CIA agent kept looking at the floor, avoiding eye contact.

'They took us back to their camp, tied us up, then beat the shit out of us,' Fletcher said. 'The whole group, punching, stamping, pistol-whipping. I thought I was going to die. They almost killed us there and then. Broke my nose and both my orbital bones. Smashed up Carver's arm. But then their Captain appeared. Most intimidating guy I'd ever seen. He was huge, camo paint covering his face, big AK in his hands. Even through the darkness and the paint, I could see the rage in his eyes. He looked at me and I almost pissed myself with fear. He ordered his men to do something in Albanian, and the next thing I knew we were thrown into one of the huts and locked up.'

He paused.

'So what happened?' Archer asked.

'They left us for a day. They even fed us, and gave us water. But then one of them walked in and said we were going to play a game. He was a big guy, almost as big as their leader. I think he was his right-hand man. He had big spider tattoos on his elbows. He spoke in English. He said the game was called *eeenie-meenie-miny-mo*. The guy did it with his finger, and it came to a rest on me.'

He swallowed.

'Straight afterwards his men dragged me outside and four of them held me down on the soil, no-one else around for miles, I was looking up at the stars.' He blinked. 'Then they got a set of bolt cutters and took off my small toe. One snip, and it was gone.'

With a great effort, he pushed back the bed covers and lifted his feet out of the bed, laying them on the sheets.

The men looked at his feet.

Seven of his toes were missing.

'The guy with the spider tattoos told me no-one knew we were there,' Fletcher continued. 'No-one was coming for us. And they were going to kill us over the course of the next three months. A piece at a time. First the toes. Then the fingers. Then the feet, and the hands. Then the arms. Then the genitals. Then the eyes and tongue. Then the head.'

The room was silent. Fletcher's chin trembled.

'They dragged me out there each night and took seven of my toes, one by one, over the course of a week. They didn't touch Carver and Floyd. They let them watch, telling them that once I was dead, they would be next.'

Pause.

'Then, on the eighth night, we were rescued. Six men came in the dark and got us out. The other two could move, but I had to be carried.'

He shook his head weakly.

'Neither of them paid any sort of price for what they did, unlike me. I never recovered properly. My body started to heal, but my mind and conscience didn't. My whole life ruined because of Carver and Floyd.'

By the windows, Chalky shook his head, his arms folded. His face was hard.

'Bullshit,' he said. 'You were there. You could have stopped them. But you stood there and let them kill those women and children.'

There was a long silence. Fletcher didn't respond.

'So what happened next?' Archer asked.

'We were taken out of there by chopper. Not to Bondsteel, but somewhere else. They gave me morphine for the pain as we took off and the next thing I remember was waking up in a hospital in Birmingham, back in the UK. There was a man sitting there beside my bed dressed in a suit. I didn't recognise him. He told me I had to sign a form, even before I was fully awake. He said that if I left the army immediately without a fuss, there would be no follow up to what happened that night.'

He paused.

'But he said if I ever spoke about it to anyone, anyone at all, the punishment that would come my way would be incredibly severe. And from then, until this moment, I've done exactly what he said. I've never said a word about any of it to anyone, ever. Gladly, I might add. I just wanted to move on as best I could and make the most of a second chance. Minus seven of my toes.'

He coughed.

'Guess it doesn't matter now. Nature is getting rid of me for them. Dead men don't talk.'

He paused.

'But it's always confused me,' he said. 'Why would they go to so much effort to save the three of us after what we did? We weren't important. Just three grunts, a Corporal, Private and Captain. Why weren't we punished and hung out to dry? The whole world deserved to know what happened to those people. At the very least Carver and Floyd should have been court-martialled.'

'So should've you,' Chalky said.

Cobb turned and looked at Jackson.

'I think this is where you fill in the blanks,' he said.

Silence. His arms still folded, Jackson looked up at him.

'Why weren't we punished?' Fletcher asked him from the bed.

Pause.

'Because Carver's father was in the CIA,' Jackson said, eventually.

'So what?' Chalky said, by the window. 'They still murdered all those women and children. Who cared if his father worked for the government?'

Jackson said nothing.

'How high up was his father, Ryan?' Cobb asked Jackson, his voice even, putting two and two together.

Pause.

'How high?' he repeated.

'Deputy Director,' Jackson said, eventually.

'Holy shit,' Fox said, as every man in the room looked at Jackson.

'I don't believe this,' Cobb said, almost at the same time. 'No wonder everyone was sworn to secrecy. Carver's father was one of the heads of the damn CIA?'

Jackson nodded. 'That's right.'

There was a long, somewhat uncomfortable pause as each man processed what they'd just been told, none more so than Fletcher, lying in the bed.

'You know three of the men who rescued you have died today,' Cobb said, looking down at Fletcher.

The sickly man looked up at him in surprise.

'What? How?'

‘One shot himself. Another was garrotted, and the third was executed in his sleep.’ He pointed at the television. 'You saw the reports of the attack on the police station?'

'Yes, sir.'

'That was my Unit. They were trying to kill me.'

Fletcher stared at him. He was sweating even more, the pillow behind his head already sodden.

‘They’re coming for revenge,’ he said. He looked at Cobb and Jackson. ‘They're after everyone who was involved that night. Which means you’re both on the list.’

'And so are you,' Archer said, quietly, by the door.

Fletcher licked his lips, looking back at Archer, fear in his eyes.

‘Look, I’ll talk to the Met,' Cobb told him. 'We’ll get some extra security here, guarding you, till this is over.'

Fletcher shook his head.

‘Don’t bother, sir. I’ll be dead before long anyway. And if they come for me, no-one will be able to stop them. God doesn’t want me to live anymore. Maybe it’s just my time.’

He paused.

'You know, every night that I lay there in the hut in agony, I used to pray over and over again. I promised God that I'd be a better man if I made it out of there, that I would do good, that I would spend the rest of my life trying to help people instead of hurting them.' He shook his head. 'But I didn't keep my promise.

I've done nothing worthwhile since. So maybe it's about time they came back and finished the job.'

'Can you tell us anything about these men?' Archer asked him. 'The Black Panthers?'

Fletcher nodded. 'Like I said, they are Albanian Special Forces. Once I healed up, I wanted to know who the men were who did that to me. I read everything I could find about them. But I can tell you they were the toughest group of soldiers I've ever seen. Their own army didn't want them, they were so ruthless.'

'How can we beat them?' Chalky asked across the room, from the window.

'You can't.'

Fletcher paused and coughed again. It seemed as if his stamina was almost gone. Across the room, the silent television flicked to show a *Breaking News* report of a car-bombing in upstate Connecticut, US.

No-one saw the screen change.

'How do we find them?' Archer asked.

'You won't. They'll find you.'

'OK, so what do we do?' Chalky asked the room, irritated. 'Just sit back and wait?'

Fletcher turned to him. As the man spoke, Archer found himself looking at the man's severed feet again.

'You want my honest advice?' Fletcher said to Chalky, his voice raspy, his throat dry.

Chalky nodded. 'Go on.'

'Hide.'

Just outside the parking lot of the hospice, a teenager in a matching white *Adidas* tracksuit leaned against the wall, smoking a cigarette and looking into the car park. He'd been walking past, heading down to the bookies to place some bets on the Premiership football this weekend, when something had caught his eye. He'd stopped and lit a cigarette, and was now taking a closer look at what had grabbed his attention.

His name was Leon. Just turned nineteen years old, he'd been in and out of juvenile detention centres and then prison since he could remember. He'd just finished his most recent stint twenty two days ago for breaking and entering. He and two friends had gone after an expensive apartment in Fulham that they knew belonged to a Premiership footballer. The guy was on over a hundred grand a week, so they knew there would be plenty of cash-value stuff to steal inside.

Leon had been cautious and planned ahead, waiting outside in the car with the other two and watching the player head out with his girlfriend on a Saturday night. However, every alarm went off the moment they picked the lock and stepped inside the front door. There were cameras all over the building and on the street outside and although they got out, two days later Leon and his two pals were hauled into Hammersmith and Fulham in handcuffs and booked. It was the latest in a growing list of convictions, the first of which was a simple fine for possession of marijuana, and was a list he knew without a doubt would get longer.

He'd started when he was thirteen. Like most kids in his area, he used to go down to the park and sniff glue or smoke puff, drink bottles of cider and try to get lucky with the local girls. But then he'd begun smoking more and more, and by the time he was sixteen he'd developed a fondness for cocaine that had taken all of his money. By that point he'd already stopped going to school. He couldn't remember the last time he'd been. And two months after his sixteenth birthday, his mother kicked him out of the house after finally having enough of him stealing from her. He didn't only take cash, he stole stuff in the house that was worth anything and traded it in, and the final straw was when he stole a favourite necklace from her dresser and pawned it for fifty quid.

Out on the street, broke and alone, he'd started staying at hostels, with friends or at homeless shelters. He'd also started pick-pocketing to keep himself going. He didn't have any qualifications and no way was he going to do manual labour or construction jobs for a living. Although he'd been nervous about pick-pocketing at first, worried he'd get caught, he'd been surprised at how easy it actually was. Given the congestion and close proximity of passengers on the trains on the Underground, a simple two finger dip into a handbag or pocket when everyone was jostling to get on or off the carriage reaped great dividends. He often worked with a partner, the two of them standing either side of a target on the train to box them in during the rush hour, pretending to be fellow passengers jammed together in the packed train carriage, but robbing them blind instead.

A lot of immigrants from Eastern Europe had started working the Underground too, and given the increase in thefts, the Met had started putting undercover cops down there in an attempt to catch them. Most of the Poles and Romanians couldn't spot a copper if he came up in uniform and tapped them on the shoulder, but Leon and the group he ran with could smell them a mile off.

Moving out of the Underground to avoid the police, they used Paddington as another haunt. The station was large and always busy, and its position as a main transport hub meant it was usually full of tourists with their heads buried in maps, disorientated and distracted. It was easy. Pick out a tourist and get one of you to grab their attention. Ten seconds later, when the distraction left and the tourist turned back, they find their bag they'd put on the floor beside them is gone.

And whoever had stolen it had now vanished into a crowd of constantly moving, anonymous people.

But it hadn't all been successful. Leon had been nicked a couple of times pick-pocketing, having to pay fines and do a short stint of community service, but as he got older and more confident he'd forgone the secrecy of pick-pocketing unsuspecting victims and moved up a level to armed robbery instead.

He was careful about his targets. A lot of thieves thought that young women were the easiest demographic to go after, given their physical disadvantage and that they were easily intimidated. But in fact they were one of the worst to confront. All those women groups, magazines and adverts on television had made sure a lot of girls were more prepared than they used to be. The fear of attack meant many of them now carried wailing button-alarms or even pepper spray, even though it was illegal, in their handbags. A friend of his had been maced by a girl a few years ago after he tried to mug her, and he still talked about how it was the worst couple of hours of his life. Women were often more alert than men, expecting trouble. It served a thief best to leave them well alone.

Leon took a draw on his cigarette, leaning against the wall, watching the hospice car park, and smiled. No, the best targets for mugging were posh kids or tourists. The toffs were soft as dog shit, unused to violence and easily intimidated, and one look at the knife in Leon's hand would get them scrabbling at their pockets like they couldn't wait to hand over their stuff. The tourists were equally soft. They were out of their comfort zone and easily scared, especially with the threat of violence and a big knife in their face.

Things had gone well for a while, but then the riots in 2011 had happened and Leon got nicked by an undercover cop. He wasn't doing anything different from the other rioters. It was just bad luck.

He'd been out of the door of an Argos store across town with over two grand of stolen goods in his hands, a mask over his face, but then he got levelled by some copper who picked him out of the crowd and took him off his feet with a punch. The guy restrained him, and two weeks later Leon was in the dock and given a sentence of thirteen months. He'd just turned eighteen, so juvenile centres weren't an option any more.

For the first time in his life, Leon was going to prison.

Leaning against the wall, he drew on his cigarette and narrowed his eyes, blowing out the smoke. A lot of lads from his area wanted to serve time. They felt it gave them street-cred and reputations on the estate as hard men. But Leon knew the moment he walked into that place that he was in deep shit. This wasn't a two or three weeker at some soft-as-shit juvenile facility, with lots of team-building exercises and counselling with biscuits and cups of tea. As he was led to his cell in the middle of the queue of new inmates, the prisoners already there shouting and baying at the new meat from their cells, he knew he was looking at over a year in that place.

And he knew he needed to make friends quick.

Luckily, he had. A lot of the rioters started getting sent down there, and they quickly grouped up, watching each other's backs as best they could. But Leon didn't join them. Instead, he started spending all his time with his new cell-mate, a huge black guy named Luther. Luther was on a two year stint for armed robbery, a career criminal who'd been on the wrong side of the law his entire life. He was from Croydon and made his living robbing drug dealers. He was a guy Leon had actually heard about on the street. Although never actually coming across him, his name definitely preceded him.

Leon never let it show, but Luther saved him in there. Luckily for Leon, the bigger man had taken to him straight away, acting like a mentor, and Leon had spent almost every moment outside the cell with him, both to learn from the man and also so he was protected. Shankings and gang-rape occurred almost daily, the guards turning a blind eye most of the time, but Luther was a guy who no-one messed with. He was six-five and thickly muscular, he and his gang monopolising the weights area in the yard every time they were out of the cells, working out for hours at a time and loading up on steroids smuggled in from the outside through the kitchen workers. Luther had started out doing hit-work for a gang in Brixton, and although Leon never knew for sure how many people the bigger man had killed in his lifetime, he knew it was more than you could count on your fingers and toes. He'd educated Leon about the benefits of crime, how to cheat the justice system and how to make the most profits for when he was back out on the street and ensure he never got sent back. *As long as you don't kill anyone, you're good,* Leon had said.

Or if you do, make sure no-one ever finds the body.

Given his size and being well aware of how much he intimidated people, Luther said that he'd moved from murder into robbing dealers and gang members, and although Leon's physique changed dramatically over the months from hitting the weights with the older man, he knew that using his size like Luther wasn't a path he could go down when he got out. *Play to your strengths,* Luther had said. Leon had told him about his past, dipping on the Underground and stealing wallets and purses, robbing posh kids and tourists on the street for maybe a hundred quid a pop. But after spending time with Luther, the younger man realised he'd been selling himself short. There was a hell of a lot more out there if he had the balls to go after it.

He was in the wrong game.

Leon had educated him about burglary, how he could make more profit from one empty house than he could from robbing ten tourists. He'd told him the ways around an alarm system and how to get anyone to open a safe. *With the men, it's easy,* he'd said. *Don't bother with idle threats or violence. Just strip them naked, get a sharp knife from the kitchen and put it to their balls. Works every time*. With women, he explained that the threat of rape was often sufficient. *But women are tougher than men,* Luther told him. *You have to know how to push their buttons. If they have a family, pull the kids out of bed and put a blade on them. Ninety nine times out of a hundred, they'll open sesame.*

Leon had grown close to the older man and had been sad the day he left him behind. But he'd walked out of that place a changed man, physically and mentally, his body no longer a boy's and his brain full of new knowledge. He'd heard a saying once and now he understood what it meant.

A man had to go to prison in order to learn how to become a criminal.

Since he'd left prison, he'd followed Luther's advice explicitly. Aside from his recent three-weeker, he'd been out eighteen months and had knocked down six mansions in Surrey and a townhouse in Chelsea, the profits huge, way into six figures, close to a mil. It was only his mate's sheer carelessness at the footballer's flat which meant they'd got caught, the idiot not checking the alarm system properly. Leon had learned another lesson that night. Never depend on other people.

So from now on, he worked alone.

Taking a last draw on the cigarette, he flicked away the butt, letting it smoulder on the pavement. He'd been wandering past the building, some kind of hospital or old-people's home, and had seen two cars in the parking lot that had instantly caught his eye.

One was a silver Mercedes. It looked less than a year old, fresh off the line. He didn't know enough about licence plates to judge what year the car had been registered, but that didn’t matter. It looked new and it looked expensive. He figured he could get five figures for it easily at a chop shop he knew in Hackney. The other car was just as nice, a black BMW. He'd had to make a choice, but he'd already gone with the Mercedes. He preferred silver cars anyway.

Pushing back off the wall with his foot, he pulled a tennis ball from his pocket and started to walk into the parking lot. He saw some old man was sitting on a bench across the tarmac by the wall, but what looked like a nurse was helping him up to take him back inside the building, leaving Leon all alone in the car park.

He smiled, bouncing the tennis ball on the ground as he walked.

In the joint, Luther had taught him how to steal cars. He’d explained that the movies got a lot of shit wrong, but they also got some stuff right, and a lot of the high-tech shit they showed like pin guns and diagnostic blank keys normally worked. It would just cost you thousands of pounds to get the equipment. But Luther had taught him a trick, one so incredibly simple that Leon couldn’t believe more people didn't know about it.

The lock to most cars had the grooves for the key. Six pins, usually. Once the key slid in, and the pins were pushed down, the mechanism released, and with a twist the door would open.

But the pins also reacted to pressure.

Arriving by the Mercedes, Leon took a look either side of him then looked down at the tennis ball in his hand. He'd driven a small hole in the ball with a knife, about the size of a pea, and he twisted the ball so it was showing, then put the hole against the lock of the Mercedes.

Checking either side, he held it to the lock then hit it hard with his right hand, pushing all the air out of the ball and into the lock.

There was a click and he saw all four plastic locks rise beside each window of the car.

The car was now open.

He smiled, then pulled open the door and ducked inside, tucking the ball back into his pocket. All the high-tech shit and gadgets were out there, but nothing worked better than a cheap old tennis ball.

The next part was a bit harder. He pulled a knife from his pocket quickly and removed a small panel under the ignition. He could see three wires, two red, one black. This part worked just like in all the movies. Separate the battery and starter wires, strip off the plastic sheaths, touch them together to spark the current, and job done. The engine is on and you're good to go.

Looking up to make sure no-one was around, he took one of the two red wires and pulled it from the cylinder.

He then started to cut into the end of the wire, removing the sheath.

Back inside the hospice, the six men had just left Fletcher's room, Cobb leading the way as they walked down the corridor. All of them were slightly distracted, thinking about what Fletcher had told them and the revelation about Carver's connections.

They turned the corner, Cobb pushing the release mechanism for the security door, and the group walked back into the reception area. The woman who'd shown them in was back behind the desk, and she pulled the key from her pocket as soon as she saw them, turning back to the locked room behind her and sliding the key into the lock. She looked keen to return the four weapons. Archer figured she thought the quicker she gave them back, the quicker they would all leave.

As she opened the door and the four officers walked around her desk to retrieve their weapons, Cobb turned to speak Jackson, who was looking outside.

But he saw the American's attention was directed at something outside in the car park.

He was frowning.

'What the hell?' Jackson muttered.

Cobb followed where he was looking.

And saw a teenager sitting inside his car.

Leon had just cut off the second red sheath, the two copper inner wires themselves now exposed, and held them close, one in each hand.

'Hey!'

He heard a shout and looking right, saw a dark-haired man in a suit shouting, looking straight at him and pushing open the door. Behind the guy, Leon saw a group of cops, two of them with a sub-machine gun in their hands, turn and look over, just as they slapped a magazine into each weapon.

Oh shit.

He was stealing a cop car.

Without another moment's hesitation, he pushed the two wires together.

And just as Cobb started to run towards his car, the Mercedes exploded.

He was thrown back, the glass on the front entrance smashing from the shockwave. As the car exploded, Jackson's BMW reacted to the blast and went up too in a second explosion, both cars thrown up vertically into the air, erupting into one huge fireball.

The flaming wrecks of both cars landed on the ground with two *thuds* and burned away, smoke billowing out of each, the alarms of other cars in the lot set off by the rippling shockwave of the explosions.

SIXTEEN

At the same moment as the two cars exploded, the seatbelt signs on a Boeing 747 aeroplane which had just finished taxiing on a Heathrow runway clicked off with a *ding*. In the next moment, passengers undid their seatbelts and rose, stepping out into the aisles, stretching, opening the overhead lockers to retrieve their hand luggage and getting ready to disembark.

It was the earliest flight to arrive from Washington, the 4:50 am direct from Dulles to London Heathrow. They'd made good time, the flight five hours and forty minutes in total, the trans-Atlantic wind behind them shaving another forty minutes off the flight. Most of the people on board were businessmen and women or families returning from holidays, lots of suits and briefcases, sunburnt skin and noisy tired kids. Up ahead, the aisles started to clear as the passengers began to disembark, the airline staff standing to one side formally, smiling and thanking everyone for flying with them as they filed past.

A small man dressed in a black sweater and blue jeans with scarring across his face and neck ignored the flight staff as he passed them, moving off the plane and heading swiftly down to the immigration hall. They'd landed at Terminal Five, the newest Terminal at Heathrow. The man was carrying a small holdall as luggage, no suitcase to collect. He didn't even really need the bag, but he figured travelling with nothing could attract unwanted attention, and as he'd murdered someone in the last seven hours he didn't fancy any unnecessary scrutiny from airport security.

After a few moments of walking along the clean corridors, he moved down several escalators and arrived at the passport check hall. All EU members were being directed one way, everyone else to the left, and he headed in the direction of the EU queue. The man had the best fake passport money could buy, and his dark features backed up the Spanish passport's credentials.

When it was his turn he moved forward and passed over his documents to the man at the desk. The guy looked at his photograph, then back at him, and the small man noticed his surprise as he saw his scars.

'Purpose of visit?'

'Visiting friends.'

He could see his scars were attracting the man's attention.

'Boiling water. When I was a child,' the small man said, in as good a Spanish accent as he could muster. He said it with a smile and a look that said *I've had to explain this many times before, but I'll do it again for you.* It'd actually been from a phosphorous grenade that had gone off right by his ear, but he figured it probably wouldn't be a great idea to tell the official that.

After a few moments pause and another quick glance at the scars, the guy stamped the man's passport, handing it back with a nod.

'Enjoy your visit. *Next*,' he called, looking at the next person in the queue.

The small man took his passport and moved on towards the Arrivals Hall.

He walked through Customs under the *Nothing to Declare* banner, seeing the one-way mirrored glass and feeling eyes upon him from people behind. Then he walked through a set of double doors and arrived in the Arrivals Hall.

It was pretty busy, lots of people milling about, sunlight streaming in through the long windows. He scanned the building, looking left and right, searching for a familiar face.

Soon, he found it, a big man leaning against the far wall by the long glass windows, his superior officer, Spider. He was wearing a sweater, but had the sleeves pushed up, and Bug saw the spider-web tattoos covering each of his forearms.

He walked over to the second-in-command of the Black Panthers. Spider saw him coming, and kicked off the wall. The two men shook hands as other passengers and travellers moved past them towards the exits.

'Any trouble?' Spider, asked in Albanian, his voice low, looking down at the smaller man.

'None, sir.'

'The target?'

'Gone. He suffered.'

Spider nodded. 'Good.'

His smiled faded.

'Crow and Grub failed. They're both dead.'

The smaller man turned and looked out the window. 'Shit.'

'Yes. But it's OK. We'll handle it.'

Bug looked around. 'Where's Bird?'

'He won't be here for another few hours. He's flying in from Connecticut.'

There was a pause. Then they both turned and walked across the hall to the exit and the taxi rank. They saw a queue was forming down the pavement to their left, an airport worker ushering people into line, but Spider ignored them and raised his arm to hail a passing taxi. He got lucky with the second one that passed, and the black vehicle pulled up.

Both men stepped inside, pulling the doors shut behind them. Spider gave the driver directions, the man nodding as the Albanian told him where to go, and the vehicle moved off, headed into the centre of London.

Back at the hospice, two fire engines had arrived. A team of firemen were holding the big hose and dousing the two cars, the water spraying over the blackened shells of the vehicles, the flames pretty much extinguished. The cars had been totalled by the explosions, both now just charred skeletons, hundreds of thousands of pounds gone in a second along with the kid who'd tried to steal the Mercedes.

Back inside the hospice, nurses were quickly checking on each patient. Fortunately, the bulk of the rooms were past the security door the other side of the building so none of them had been affected by the explosion.

By the front entrance, Archer took a good look at the smoking wreckage, then walked down the path towards Jackson, who was standing watching the fire-team work, Archer's boots crunching on the smashed glass of the entrance windows as he walked.

'Thank God for thieves,' Archer said to him. 'Never thought I'd hear myself say that.'

'They followed us here,' Jackson replied quietly. 'They must have put the devices under the cars when we were inside.'

Archer nodded, and looked around the car park, sensing Jackson's tension beside him. A small crowd had gathered outside the gates, much as it had back at the ARU's headquarters after the gunfight, but he looked at the tall office buildings around them, every window a possible threat point.

Behind the two men, Cobb reappeared, Chalky, Porter and Fox alongside him, the four men walking outside to join the other two by the entrance. None of them noticed the receptionist glare at them as they passed her desk. They hadn't exactly added to the calming atmosphere of the hospice since they'd arrived.

'Mason and Spitz are on their way with two cars,' Cobb told Archer and Jackson, putting his mobile phone into his pocket. 'We go straight back to headquarters.'

He turned to Jackson.

'From there, you can either stay with us or head back to the Embassy.'

'I'm staying,' he said, nodding his head at the four task force officers. 'Truth be told, I'm liking this armed escort more and more.'

Cobb nodded. 'OK.'

'What about Fletcher?' Archer asked.

'What about him?' Chalky said.

'They'll know he's here by now, Chalk,' Archer said, turning to him. 'He'll be one of the top names on their list.'

'So? The man said he's ready to die.'

'So why don't you go in there and do him yourself?' Archer said, his irritation rising.

'Relax, you two,' Cobb said. 'It's OK. There are two armed officers from an ARV on their way down already. Fletcher is staying. He's too sick to move. But they'll be guarding the desk and his door 'til this is over.'

The group of men nodded, and they all looked back across the parking lot at the smoking ruins of the two cars.

Cobb saw the destroyed shell of his Mercedes.

'Thank God for thieves,' he muttered under his breath.

At the command post across town, the leader of the Panthers was in a foul mood. He rose and kicked his chair across the room, letting out a long stream of expletives in Albanian. It had all started so well. Worm had tailed the group to the hospice, then moved around the building and saw which room they entered. He got a glimpse of the man in the bed before they closed the curtains, and there was no mistaking who it was. Corporal Simon Fletcher, the missing man from the list, the last piece of the puzzle.

Once the curtains were drawn and his view obstructed, Worm had moved back into the quiet parking lot and taking advantage of no-one being around, had quickly placed the two devices under each car. Both charges were hooked up to the ignition, and would detonate once they received a current. Worm had taken up surveillance in a coffee shop across the street, waiting for the men to leave and to watch Cobb and Jackson die.

But then some lowlife kid had car-jacked the Mercedes and blown himself and the two vehicles up, saving Cobb, Jackson and their four-man escort. Worm had slipped away down the street immediately, calling his commanding officer and letting him know what had happened.

The big soldier was furious. Three times these two men had cheated death today. But rather than make him desperate, their run of luck made the man even more determined to kill them. He realised that without these setbacks, this would all be too easy. Their revenge was systematic but not sweet.

He would have to earn the deaths of Cobb and Jackson.

He'd have to get it done himself.

Taking deep breaths and getting a grip on his fiery temper, he walked across the room and scooped up the chair, bringing it back to the table and sitting down. Anger wouldn't achieve anything here. He needed to think clearly with a level head. Feeling his white-hot rage start to evaporate like early morning mist, he leaned back in his chair and looked at the selection of weapons lying on the floor across the dark safe-house. Two of the Kalashnikovs were gone, but they still had five left, as well as all the silenced MP5s, Dragunov, bazooka and thousands of rounds of ammunition.

Looking at the guns, he started to form a plan of attack. They'd gone to visit Fletcher, so clearly they'd put two and two together and realised what this was about. Cobb and the American would most likely head back to the ARU police station. They'd been taken by surprise before, but now would be on their guard and would figure they could foil another attempt. After reconnaissance, Worm had told him that there were armed officers stationed at the entrance of the building, just inside in the reception area. If either Cobb or Jackson left, they would go to a safe-house or into hiding somewhere.

The Panthers had a number of options. It depended on which choice the two men took.

He started running different scenarios through his mind, different plans of attack. Spider and Bug were on their way here, and together with their commanding officer and Worm, the quartet would get this done once and for all.

No mistakes this time.

Both Cobb and Jackson would be dead before midnight.

SEVENTEEN

After Deakins and Spitz arrived with the two replacement black 4x4 Fords MI6 had supplied, Cobb, Jackson and First Team had piled in and left Fletcher, the hospice and the two smoking wrecks of the cars behind. As they got into the vehicles, Cobb ordered the two drivers to take a different route back to the Unit's headquarters, regardless of the time it would add to the journey.

Thirty five minutes later, the men found Nikki waiting for them inside the Briefing Room at the ARU HQ when they walked in. She'd been working hard since they'd left and had drawn up a chart on a board on the wall with the list of names Cobb had given her.

In total, there were eleven photographs stuck on the board, forming a makeshift pyramid. At the top were two men, Cobb and Jackson, the pair who had run Operation Blackout. Both photos were official ones from the file, and they were stuck side-by-side. Below them, the other nine were separated into three columns of three, neatly spaced out.

The team looked at them closely. To the left were the three soldiers from the British Army, half of the rescue team from that night. *Adams, McCarthy* and *King*. Adams' photo had a big *X* over it, but the other two were untouched. In the middle were *Spears, Fraser* and *Webster*, the three U.S Rangers, the other half of the rescue team. There were two big *X*'s over Spears and Webster.

And to the far right were the three former hostages.

Carver, Floyd and *Fletcher*.

Archer looked at the last cluster of photographs, putting faces to the names of the two men. The photos were from some old military file, both guys dark-featured with short buzz-cuts and pale faces. Carver's lips were almost sneering, his brown eyes glinting with arrogance, whilst Floyd's expression was blank, just staring straight ahead. The two faces were forgettable.

Archer pictured them both going berserk with M16s, mowing down women and children in a dark camp somewhere out on the plains in Kosovo.

Not a pleasant thought.

Shifting his gaze, he looked at the photo of Fletcher below them and was taken aback. It was an old photo and not an official one, but nevertheless Fletcher looked like a completely different person from the frail, damaged man in the hospice bed. In the picture he looked strong, healthy and confident, full of vitality, wearing a beret and his combat fatigues and smiling at the camera. He was about a hundred pounds heavier and a hundred times happier. The person in the hospice was just a withered shell of this man, like the skin that was left behind after being shed by a snake.

'Here you are, sir,' Nikki said. 'I hope these are the right men. I heard about the cars. Are you OK?'

'We're fine,' Cobb said, examining the board. 'And yes, these are the right men. I recognise them all. Outstanding work.'

He paused and stepped forward, tapping Webster's photograph on the board. Archer saw he was a blond-haired guy, dressed in desert combat fatigues, a similar photo to the one of Adams. He had a big black *X* across the photograph, concealing most of his face and features.

'They got to Webster?' Cobb asked her.

Nikki shook her head.

'No, sir. He was killed in Iraq, 2004. Stood on an IED.'

Cobb nodded, then stepped back, examining the board with the other men. He turned to Jackson, and Archer saw his face harden.

'So, CIA Deputy Director Carver was behind this?'

'It was classified,' Jackson said. 'You know the way it works. I couldn't have told you.'

'I don't believe this. I was the one running the damn operation. I needed to be given the facts.'

'Oh don't play all innocent, Cobb,' Jackson replied. 'You're telling me you've never withheld operational information before?'

He paused.

'This was a case of national security. Carver was connected. If the press had got hold of what his son did, the damage would have been immense. You think the public would still have supported the war? All this shit happened just after the Clinton impeachment. The entire country didn't know who to trust anymore. The American public had lost faith in its Government. Just picture it; not only does the son of the Deputy Director of the CIA murder an entire village of women and children on a drunken rampage, but then he gets rescued from capture because his father didn't want him to get hurt? Right there in bold print, next to those about the President. Imagine the headlines.'

'I don't give a shit about the damn headlines.'

'You would if it was your son who did the shooting. You would if you had been one of the heads of the CIA. Support for American involvement in the war would have melted away and Carver's career would have been toast.'

He paused.

'We had to shut the whole thing down. If word got out, the consequences would have been irreversible.'

'They've already been damn near irreversible,' Cobb said, jabbing a finger angrily at the ruined glass of his office next door.

There was a pause. Cobb shook his head in frustration and paced to the window. The four armed officers stood there in silence. This was a two man conversation that had fifteen years of weight on top of it.

'OK, so what happened to Carver senior?' Cobb asked, turning back to Jackson. 'Is he still in the CIA? Or is he on his way to the Presidency and sainthood?'

Across the room, Jackson shook his head. 'He's gone. He retired and had a heart attack when he was walking his dog three years ago. They buried him at Arlington.'

Cobb shook his head and cursed, looking at the board. The atmosphere in the room was tense.

'We should've been prepared,' Cobb said. 'If you had told me, we could have put precautions in place.' He tapped Carver's, Floyd's and Fletcher's photos. 'These three men murder an entire camp of women and children and we expect their husbands and fathers to just forget it ever happened? Jesus Christ, Ryan. What did you think would happen?'

'What would you have done?' Jackson fired back. 'Given each of the men bodyguards and armed protection for the past decade? C'mon, think man. We never could have known it was going to go down like this.'

Cobb turned from the board and stalked back to the window. In the silence, Porter turned to Nikki.

'Did you manage to pull anything on the enemy?' he asked her quietly.

Nikki shook her head.

'Nothing apart from the dead guy on the slab at the morgue. But I forgot to mention, another body turned up just before lunchtime. Same kind of tattoos as the man who attacked us here. Forensics think it was the second gunman, judging by the marks on his hands from the trigger guard of the rifle.'

Cobb turned and all the men looked at her.

'How did he die?' Archer asked.

'Single gunshot wound to the head. Self-inflicted. Suicide. About ten bystanders watched him do it.'

'He killed himself?' Chalky said.

'Probably because he failed,' Cobb said.

Porter turned to Jackson.

'The Black Panthers. How many men in a Unit like that?' he asked.

'Eight,' Jackson said.

'So two down. We're looking at six of them left,' Cobb said. 'Do we even know what these men look like?'

Jackson looked at Nikki, who shrugged.

'All we know is they are exceptionally well-trained, extremely tough and according to all official records, don't even exist. None of them have used their real names for over a decade and no-one knows for sure where any of them are. Officials at US airports on the East Coast are on alert in case they try to flee the country, but they don't even know who they're looking for. These men are like ghosts.'

'And they want both of us dead,' Cobb added, looking back at Jackson.

Silence followed. Cobb walked back over to the board and pointed at three photographs; Fraser, King, and McCarthy.

'OK. We need to warn the others. Where's Fraser? The last remaining Ranger.'

Jackson nodded. 'I already called ahead from the car. Two agents are on their way to him now. He works in an office near the Beltway, in DC. We'll get him guarded with round-the-clock security.'

'OK,' Cobb said, tapping King and McCarthy's photos, the two British army soldiers. 'These two are our responsibility. We need to find them before they do. Nikki?'

'King lives not far from here,' she said, reading from the file in the crook of her arm. 'Small apartment in Angel. He works nights as security at a shopping centre. McCarthy is the floor manager at a home supply depot. I tried both their home phones but neither man is picking up.'

'Where does McCarthy live?'

'He has a lease on a house in his name in Notting Hill.'

Cobb turned to First Team, who were standing there silently, listening, their MP5s in their hands, waiting for instruction. Hard as the clean-up team had tried earlier, the floor under their boots was still stained with dried coffee and blood, reminders from earlier in the day.

'Get over to Angel. Get King, then go to Notting Hill and get McCarthy. Bring them in,' Cobb ordered. He turned to Nikki. 'Keep trying both men. Don't stop until you get an answer.'

'Yes, sir,' she said, following First Team, who were already moving to the door. After they left, Cobb turned to Jackson again, the two men now alone in the room.

'If anyone else dies, it's on you. Know that.'

'Spare me,' Jackson said. 'I don't remember pulling a trigger.'

'You knew what they did. You should have told me.'

'Look man, let me ask you something,' Jackson replied. 'If I'd told you what these men did, would you still have been as determined to get them out?'

Cobb suddenly paused. Silence filled the room.

'That's what I thought,' Jackson said. 'We'd have been in this shit regardless of you knowing every detail. So don't try and pin any of this on me. They came after me today too, you know. It's not just you.'

Cobb shook his head angrily. 'Say what you want, Jackson. Whatever will help you sleep at night. But you know as well as I do that a lot of innocent people died today, joining everyone who was murdered in the town that night. If you'd warned me, we probably could have saved most of our guys, or at least given them a fighting chance. If we survive this, I hope you can live with that.'

Jackson turned before he said something he'd regret, and walked to the window, taking a deep breath and watching the four armed officers leave in one of the new black Fords.

I hope you can live with that, Cobb had said.

You don't know the half of it, Jackson thought.

As the four officers of First Team headed out quickly, they passed Deakins on the stairs who was leading an attractive woman in her thirties and two young boys up to the second floor. When they arrived, they moved down the corridor and Cobb saw them coming as he walked out of the Briefing Room. He turned and moving forward, kissed his wife, his two sons staring at the damaged glass of their father's office.

Behind him, Jackson walked out of the room and saw the family.

'I'll check on Fraser's situation,' Jackson said to no-one in particular, excusing himself and nodding to Cobb’s wife. He pulled his mobile phone from his pocket and walked down the corridor, disappearing out of sight.

Standing beside the doorway to the Briefing Room, the tech team working away in the Ops room beside them, Cobb's wife turned to her husband.

'Are you OK? We saw what happened on the news.'

'I'm fine,' he said.

His two boys were looking up at him and he hugged them both quickly, one by one.

'Guys, I want you to go and sit in my office for the time being, OK? I need to talk to your mother,' he said.

The two boys nodded and shuffled round the corner, stopping to look at the damaged glass up close.

Alone, his wife lowered her voice, allowing the concern on her face and in her voice to show.

'Jesus, Tim. Who did this?'

'Come with me,' he said, motioning to the Briefing Room.

She followed and he led her towards the notice-board.

It took him ten minutes or so to explain what had happened. He ran through everything, from Adams' suicide to the anthrax hoax at the Embassy and the unexpected attack on the station. He told her about Blackout and Fletcher's revelations about what he, Carver and Floyd did in that village. And finally, he told her about the men involved in that operation all being killed systematically, picked off one by one, and how the teenage thief trying to steal his car had saved his, Jackson's and four of his men's lives.

His wife listened closely to the whole explanation, then shook her head in disbelief once he finished.

'So they know you're still here? That's so dangerous, sweetheart. They could be back at any minute.'

'I have men guarding downstairs, both entrances. No-one gets in without ID.'

'But these are Special Forces soldiers, Tim, not street-thugs. You need to get out of here. They'll come back for you and try again and again until they succeed.'

'I can't leave. This is our base. Everything we need is here. And besides, what would I tell my men? That I'm going to leave them to fend for themselves?'

'But they aren't trying to kill your men, Tim,' she said slowly. 'They want to kill you.'

There was a pause.

Cobb shook his head, taking a breath and pacing the room. He didn't like his options.

'Your men can handle it. These killers don't want Nikki, or Porter, or Archer. They want you.'

'I won't leave them.'

She moved across and took hold of him, looking into his eyes, putting more emphasis behind her words.

'These men are coming to *kill you*, Tim. They won't stop until they do. They know exactly where you are, and they've almost succeeded twice today. How many times will they have to try before they get lucky?'

Cobb didn't respond.

'You can still command the Unit from elsewhere. Please Tim, I'm begging you to leave. Please.'

Pause.

'And don't forget you're putting everyone else here in danger by staying.'

He looked at her.

He knew she was right.

'Where would we go?' he asked her.

'My family's house. It's off the radar, and none of these men will know about it. They won't have a clue where you'll be. From there, you can organise your team. You can still run the operation and track these men down, Tim. At least you won't still be here, with a big target painted on your chest.'

Cobb thought about what she'd said. His wife came from a wealthy family, and their home was a beautiful Hall an hour or so outside the city. Called Hawkings, after her family surname, it had been passed down from generation to generation over hundreds of years. It was a big place, over two hundred acres of parkland and forestry surrounding a beautiful large manor.

She had a point. None of the soldiers would have any idea about the estate.

'Damn it,' he said, quietly. 'I hate it when you're right.'

'Which is often,' she said, standing on her tiptoes and kissing his cheek.

'I'll explain to Nikki what's happening,' he said, giving in. 'Before we go, I need to call Porter and tell him to take over until I'm established at the house.'

As he turned and headed into the Ops room, his wife watched him go and finally let her abject relief show. Her husband could be stubborn and was so caught up in the current situation she was worried he'd lost perspective.

The enemy he was dealing with here were professionals. All that had saved him so far was a cocky thief and an inch of reinforced glass.

As she watched the man she loved talk with Nikki, she looked over at the damaged panes of his office and felt her anxiety rise.

The dents and pockmarks on the glass told a chilling story.

The same as the bloodstains on the floor beneath her feet.

Hurry, she thought, watching her husband explain the situation. She wanted to get the hell out of here.

Before the men who did that to the glass came back to finish the job.

EIGHTEEN

Across town, former British Army Corporal Nick King was panicking.

The bonus of working nights at the shopping mall meant he had his days to himself. He had the luxury of sleeping in, typically waking up around noon, and had settled into a routine of heading out to the gym for a workout before he came back and enjoyed a late lunch around 2:30 pm.

This Thursday morning had begun like any other. He'd woken, climbed out from under the covers, used the bathroom and brushed his teeth, then pulled on some tracksuit bottoms and a hoodie and headed out the front door to the gym fifteen minutes away. He liked to hit the weights before he put in an hour on the treadmill, some resistance training then a chance to blow his lungs out on a steep incline. He'd seen a lot of his peers, guys who used to serve in the army, slack off once they left the service, but he refused to let that happen to him. Just turned thirty six years old, he still had the body he'd had when he was twenty two, and he refused to let age dictate how his physique looked in the mirror.

He'd been about half-way through his cardiovascular workout on the treadmill, working hard, when the two o'clock news began on the screen mounted on the wall in front of his machine. Seeing as it was a pretty upmarket gym, the television screens all had cable with the one directly in front of him tuned to CNN.

Judging from the opening montage of news-clips, it seemed that it had been a pretty chaotic morning both sides of the Atlantic. The headlines were dominated by reports of two suicides by the Thames and a car-bombing in the US, as well as the discovery of two other men found dead, one in his car and the other in his apartment, in DC and New York City respectively. The last clip and headline from the opening montage showed that there had also been some kind of full-on gunfight at a counter-terrorist police station across town.

Working hard and upping the incline by pushing one of the buttons on the panel in front of him, King had watched the television closely, curious, wiping sweat from his forehead as the newsreaders began with the main headlines.

When he realised that one of the suicide victims was Charlie Adams, his old friend from the service, King had stepped off the treadmill immediately, staring up at the screen. He couldn't hear what the reporter was saying. All of the televisions were muted, dance music from the gym pumping out of the speakers instead, but he read the teletext and got the gist. *A single gunshot wound to the head*, the text said. *Unexpected and tragic*. It damn well was. King had served with Charlie for almost eight years, and he was the best officer he'd ever served under in the army.

But then the reports had moved on to cover the dead men found across the East Coast in America. Their names came up in white letters one-by-one on the black teletext.

Derek Spears.

Jason Carver.

David Floyd.

Under the cool blast of the gym's air-conditioning, King suddenly felt ice cold.

All three names and Captain Adams' suicide were setting major alarm bells off in his head. They instantly took him from the cold cardio room in the posh London gym to a dark barren plain in Kosovo fifteen years ago. His worst fears were confirmed when he saw a dark-haired man giving a report at the police station where the gunfight had taken place. His name and position came up under the shot.

Tim Cobb, Director of the ARU.

Adams. Spears. Carver. Floyd. Cobb.

Five names, random and meaningless to probably everyone else watching the report, but with a chilling significance to King.

Everyone involved in that operation was being taken out.

He'd stepped back, the treadmill beside him still whirring as the running strip continued to rotate round and round. He'd glanced around the gym, suddenly full of fear to see if anyone was watching him. He'd left the building instantly and driven home as fast as he could, trying to stay calm and work out a plan of escape.

Arriving back at his home, he'd raced through the lobby of his apartment building, frantically pushing the button for the lift. Eventually it arrived and he made his way up to his apartment as quickly as he could, making sure no-one had followed him, checking that no-one was waiting for him either side of the corridor when he got up on the 8th floor. Seeing no-one, he'd eased his key into the lock of his apartment, quietly turning it and edging open the door. He stood still for a moment, watching and listening, trying to see if he could sense a presence, anyone hiding in there waiting for him.

The place felt empty.

Shutting the door behind him, he'd quickly checked the entire apartment and to his relief there was nothing unusual, nothing disturbed, no-one there. He'd found a bag and packed as quickly as he could, grabbing the most essential things and leaving everything else. He needed to get out of London immediately, lay low and hide out until someone explained what the hell was going on and got him some protection.

But just as he'd started packing, the phone on his bed-side table started ringing, making him jump, short-circuiting his already wired-up nervous system.

Standing still, his heart racing, he looked over at the phone as it rang.

Its shrill sound echoed around the silent apartment.

Like a warning siren. Or an alarm.

He stared at it.

Maybe it was the police.

Or maybe it's someone else.

Maybe they were waiting for him to answer. Maybe there were explosives hidden somewhere in the apartment, hooked up to the phone line.

He ignored it and continued to throw everything he needed into the bag, while the phone continued to ring. He finished packing, then looked quickly around the room, grabbing his wallet and passport from the top drawer of a desk in the living area. He had enough money to leave the country for a few weeks, and with every passing second that was looking like an increasingly attractive option. He moved through the apartment quickly, checking he had everything he needed to disappear, then headed to the door, still dressed in his tracksuit bottoms and hooded sweatshirt, his t-shirt underneath damp with sweat from a combination of his workout and fear.

He pulled open the door and stepped outside slowly, checking the corridor left and right.

It was empty.

He moved out, locking the apartment quickly, then turned and realised he had a choice to make. The lift or the stairs. He went with the lift. He was on the eighth floor, and it would be faster. Then he could get the hell out of here, go somewhere he couldn't be found, far away from any danger. An old friend of his from the service lived in Spain on the coast, leasing out boats. He could stay with him for a while.

He walked quickly down the corridor, his bag over his shoulder, his mind racing through his options as he arrived at the lift. He went to press the button, but as he did it dinged in front of him, already arriving at the floor.

The light above the door lit up.

He stood there, checking either side of the corridor again, and waited for the doors to open.

Back at the ARU's headquarters, Jackson had left Cobb and his family to some privacy and had just connected to one of the two agents headed to pick up Fraser in Washington DC. It was still mid-morning over there and Fraser would surely be in his office.

The phone held to his ear, Jackson stood behind the tech team in the Ops room, fidgeting and on edge, pacing back and forth. Saving this man's life meant a lot more to him than Cobb and his team realised.

'Hello?' a voice said.

'Agent Wallace?' he asked. 'This is Operations Officer Ryan Jackson. Where are you?'

'We just entered the building, sir. Staff Sergeant Fraser works on the fourth floor. We'll be up there as soon as the lift arrives.'

'You don't have time. Take the stairs. And stay on the line.'

'Yes, sir.'

'Are you armed?'

'Yes, sir. We both have our side-arms.'

'Good. Be ready to use them.'

Across the city, First Team made it to Angel fast, Porter getting them there with typically impressive speed in one of the back-up Fords from MI6. They pulled up outside the apartment building on Holloway Road as Nikki gave them details of the man over the hands-free phone hooked up to the car.

'He lives in Apartment 8B,' she said. *'Blond, six-three, distinctive. He's probably seen the news, so be prepared. If he's there, he'll be twitched or just won't answer the door. He's not picking up the phone, so we might have missed him.'*

The four men nodded and stepped out of the car. They slammed the doors shut, Porter pressing the button on the key and locking it, and all four moved quickly towards the apartment building.

As they pushed open the main doors, Archer saw a tall man coming the other way towards them. Archer checked him out, but saw the guy had dark hair, not blond, so it wasn't King. This man had a harsh face, a beak of a nose and slicked, jet black hair over angry eyes.

Archer stepped to the side to let him pass, but they still bumped shoulders, the man turning and glaring at Archer.

They held each other's gaze for a brief moment, then the man looked back to the street and walked off, disappearing out of sight.

Inside the building lobby it was quiet. No-one was about. Porter turned to Chalky and Archer, who had just joined them.

'Take the stairs.'

The two men nodded and Archer moved across the marble floor, pulling open the door to the stairwell as Chalky moved through it, his weapon in the aim.

The two men disappeared, sprinting up the stairs as Fox pushed the button for the lift. It was already there on the ground floor and once the doors parted the two officers stepped inside, Fox pushing the button for 8 and then hit the button for the doors to close.

Inside the Washington DC office building, former Staff Sergeant Matthew Fraser was indeed at his desk. He worked as a software analyst, a reliable if tedious job, a world away from his past life, but it provided a regular and stable pay-cheque and meant his family had a good standard of living. He'd left the United States Army Rangers in 2010 and in all honesty was struggling to make the adjustment from military to civilian life. Back then, he'd taken it for granted, but the places he'd been and the times he'd had, even in combat, had been some of the greatest of his life. He'd mistakenly figured it would all last forever.

But it hadn't. His wife had become pregnant the year before and although they'd been expecting just one child, they'd had twins. After a decade of being absent and away on operations with the Rangers overseas, she'd begged him to leave the military. She told him she needed him around to help her with the two babies, but he also knew that she wanted her boys to grow up with their father, not just look at images of him in photograph frames or ultimately at a wooden coffin lifted off a plane from some foreign country, an American flag laid across the top as a brass trumpet played on the runway.

He'd relented and mustered out in December, saying goodbye to his fellow Rangers and a career he'd spent sixteen years building. He'd applied and been accepted for the job in this office, offered a reasonable salary and no healthcare. Considering the responsibilities he'd used to carry, like taking on rebel forces in Iraq or performing covert hostage rescues in Kosovo, reviewing software specifications paled in comparison.

He'd arrived just over an hour ago, Thursday, two days before the weekend, and was at his desk examining some emails on his computer, most of them from disgruntled customers asking a question about the company products or claiming something didn't work and demanding action. He reached over and picked up a cup of coffee by the screen, taking a sip and hoping that the more he read the complaint on the screen the more he would end up giving a damn about it.

As he leant back, bored already, he caught a glimpse of some movement in the long window running down the upper half of the door to his office. Leaning right, he saw two men in suits talking with one of the workers out there. The two men both looked his way and then started heading straight for his office, spotting him through the glass. They looked official, definitely government men, and in a hurry, one of them holding a cell phone to his ear and talking into it, keeping his eyes on Fraser. The former US Ranger could have picked them out in a crowd. CIA, or maybe NSA. Square jaws, clean shaven, pistols in pancake holsters hidden under their suit jackets.

He took a long pull from his cup of coffee as they approached wondering what they wanted, secretly thankful for the break in his monotonous routine. He felt his pulse quicken, for the first time in a long time, that old rush, like a junkie scoring a fix.

Finally, some excitement.

Suddenly, there was a smash of glass as something hit the window of his office. The bullet hit Fraser in the side of the head, shredding through his skull and brain and exiting the other side in a bloody spray, killing him in an instant. He was dead before his cup of coffee hit the desk. The mug hit the table side-on, the hot liquid spilling out over the keyboard and the dead man's thighs.

Fraser dropped from his seat, the spattering of his blood and brains a harsh red on the clean white of the far office wall. The two CIA agents in suits saw all this through the window and rushed forward, barging open the door.

Looking down at the dead man, they both pulled their pistols, shouting back at everyone else on the level to get down as they tried to see where the shot had come from.

NINETEEN

Back in London, Archer and Chalky moved fast up the stairs of the apartment building, their MP5s tight to their shoulders and in the aim, scaling the steps quickly and silently. They arrived on 8, and Chalky took hold of the door handle. He looked at Archer, who nodded, and he pulled the door open.

Archer was the first into the corridor, looking straight down through the aimed MP5's hair-trigger.

And he saw King.

The man was slumped against the wall in front of the lift doors, a smeared red stain behind him from where he'd been shot in the head and his body had slid down the wall. He had a carry-on bag next to him on the ground, the bag half-unzipped, clothes spilling to the floor. Archer and Chalky ran down the corridor, coming to a halt by the dead man.

Just then, the elevator arrived and the doors parted, Porter and Fox seeing for themselves what had happened.

'Oh Jesus Christ,' Fox said, moving forward.

King's eyes were still open, staring at the ground, his head lolled to the side, a trickle of blood coming from the entry wound in his forehead.

'We were too late. Shit.'

Chalky pointed at the passport, jutting halfway out of the holdall on top of some clothes.

'Looks like he knew they were coming.'

'Call Nikki, Chalk,' Porter said. 'Let her know. We need a clean-up crew and a body-bag team from the morgue.'

As Chalky nodded and pulled the mobile phone from his tac vest, Porter noticed that Archer had a concentrated look on his face, not listening to the other men.

'What?' Porter asked, noticing his demeanour.

Archer looked over at him.

'You seen anyone else in the building since we walked in?'

'Only the guy we passed at the front door.'

They held each other's gaze.

They sprinted to the stairwell, pulling open the door, taking the stairs three at a time. Archer was the first back down to the lobby and he rushed past a surprised couple towards the entrance. He burst through the front doors, looking left and right down Holloway Road either side of him, but he was too late. All he saw were pedestrians, passing cars, the constantly moving maze of midday London.

The tall dark-haired man with the harsh face was long gone.

Behind him, the other three had arrived. Chalky was already calling in the murder on his phone as he and Fox jumped back into the car. Porter climbed into the front seat, firing the engine and called out of the window to Archer.

'Arch, let's go! We need to get McCarthy!'

Archer took one last despairing look at the street. He cursed himself. He'd looked the killer right in the eyes. He'd even made physical contact with him when they knocked shoulders.

Swearing, he turned and ran over to the car, jumping inside, the vehicle already speeding off as he pulled his door shut.

A hundred yards across the street from Fraser's office in the centre of Washington DC, the dark-haired man who had taken the shot that killed the former US Ranger was already moving down the stairwell of the building across the block.

He'd left the rifle in position on the roof, like a calling card. It had been bought illegally and was untraceable, along with the ammunition, and he'd only ever handled the ammunition and rifle with gloved hands to protect against DNA and fingerprinting. His cheek had touched the stock, so there would probably be something for the Americans to work with, but even if they managed to find anything he'd be out of the country long before anything could be done with the information. No-one knew his real name, or who he was. He was truly anonymous, which was the best thing in the world for a sniper to be.

Arriving on the ground floor, he turned left and moved down the corridor to the fire exit, pushing it open and stepping outside onto the street. Closing the door behind him, he peeled off the two layers of latex gloves on his hands, stuffed them into his pocket and raised his hand as traffic moved past. Moments later a yellow cab pulled up. He stepped inside, shutting the door behind him, and within ten seconds he was speeding away from the scene, camouflaged among all the other vehicles and headed straight to Dulles International Airport and his soon-to-depart flight to London.

Across the Atlantic in London, the leader of the Panthers was preparing to take out McCarthy. This was a job that he'd previously delegated to Crow and Grub, but with both men dead he would have to do it himself. It was an inconvenience, but this change of plan often happened in the field, an operational setback, but one that he would rectify soon enough. Besides, the old mantra definitely held water here.

If you wanted to get something done, get it done yourself.

Rising from his seat at the centre of the command post, the man shot the cuff on his fatigues and checked his watch. He'd just miss Bug and Spider, who were on their way here. They might even pass each other on the road. Bird was already on his way back and Flea would be here by nightfall, once he killed Fraser and got to Dulles for his flight.

Keeping both televisions on but muted, the big soldier walked over to the wall and the line of weapons laid neatly across the carpet. He scooped up a Kalashnikov rifle, pulling back the cocking handle and checking the mechanism inside the chamber. He'd cleaned and oiled all the weapons the day before, and for street-bought guns they were in surprisingly good condition.

He picked up a double-taped magazine and slapped it into the weapon, pulling back the handle and loading it, then picked up a black weapon case. Inside, there was a bazooka and a single rocket-propelled grenade that would insert inside the launcher with a *click*. That was it. Once that was done, it was ready to fire.

Turning, he looked around, making sure everything was in order. As he did so, he caught another *Breaking News* report on the CNN screen.

Man killed by suspected sniper inside office in central DC, the screen said.

The big man allowed a faint smile to creep across his mouth.

Fraser was down.

Then he pulled open the door to the corridor of the empty building and walked out, closing it behind him and making his way downstairs to the car.

The building had a parking lot in the basement, protecting the men and whatever they were carrying from any prying eyes on the street, and as the lift dinged open the commander saw one of his men, Worm, sitting in the front seat of a silver Fiat, the engine running.

He moved forward and tossed the weapons on the back seat, covering them with a blanket. He slammed the door, then climbed into the front passenger seat, pulling the door shut.

'King is dead, sir,' Worm said, in Albanian. 'Shot him in the face. I made it just before the police showed up.'

'Good,' his commanding officer said, adjusting the seat in the car to accommodate his large frame. 'Let's go. We need to get to McCarthy before they do.'

Without another word, Worm nodded. He put his foot down, and the tyres squealed as the car took off towards the exit and the street outside. As they moved up the ramp and into the afternoon sunlight, the commander ticked off both *Fraser* and *King* from the checklist in his head.

Eight down.

Just three to go.

TWENTY

Unlike King, the reason that McCarthy wasn't picking up his phone wasn't out of fear or apprehension. He simply hadn't been at home.

He'd just got back from his girlfriend's place from across town, the time on the clock ticking to 2:30 pm. He'd been asleep all morning after a heavy drinking session last night and hadn't seen or heard anything on the news. He had a half-day today, working the afternoon shift from 3:00 'til closing, and wanted to freshen up and drink some water before he made his way over to the warehouse, his head pounding from the hangover.

Pulling the front door of the house shut behind him, he dropped his keys on a table by the door then walked upstairs, taking off his shirt as he went. Moving into the bathroom, he twisted on the tap for the shower, pulling off the rest of his clothes. He showered fast, peering out from behind the curtain to check the time on the clock across the room on the bedside dresser.

He didn't mind the job at the depot. He was a manager and the pay was surprisingly good, enough to put food on the table and put his nine year old son through a local school. He'd left the army in 2009 as a sergeant, and had bagged the job at the warehouse immediately after he left. Staying in the army hadn't been an option for him. His views and the way he saw things had changed. He didn't agree with the war in Afghanistan and he sure as hell wasn't willing to put his life on the line for it. A lot of his friends were out there at the moment, and he knew it was likely at least some of them would never be coming back.

Turning off the water, he stepped out of the shower and dried off quickly, then brushed his teeth and towelled his hair, taking a few moments to drink as much water as he could from the tap to give his body a hand as it processed all the alcohol from the night before. Once he'd changed into his uniform, he moved downstairs, grabbing a blueberry muffin from a cupboard in his kitchen and heading to the front door. He took a coat from a hook and pulled it on, then stepped outside and locked the door behind him, taking a deep breath of fresh air, feeling his headache start to ease off.

The street was relatively quiet, only a few people about, just another midweek morning in a London suburb. He saw a postman doing his rounds, going from door to door, and a couple of guys carrying out maintenance on the road to his right. He'd lived in Notting Hill since 2004, managing to buy a small property with money he'd inherited from his parents. He'd timed it just right. Given the recession and the increase in house prices, he wouldn't even be able to rent a place here now. He remembered just after he moved here how hectic the street was on a daily basis. Back then, tourists were still visiting the area to see where they'd filmed the Hugh Grant movie several years earlier. Most of that interest had died down now, but at the weekends and on Fridays the place was as busy as it ever was.

He walked along the pavement to his car parked on the street and climbed inside. He put the key in the ignition, firing it, and pulled on his seatbelt as he took a bite of the muffin. Putting the car in gear, he checked over his shoulder for any traffic, then released the handbrake and pulled away from the kerb.

Suddenly, a black 4x4 Ford pulled into view from a side street up to his left, moving fast. It stopped midway across the road abruptly, blocking it from both directions, just as McCarthy was pulling out into the street. He slammed on the brakes, jerking him forward. The Ford was directly in his path.

Angry, he jammed on the handbrake, pulled off his seatbelt and opened his door, climbing half-way out of the vehicle and glaring angrily at the black car.

'What the hell?' he shouted at the driver up the street. 'Get out of the road!'

He watched as the doors opened and four men quickly stepped out of the vehicle, all dressed in police gear, MP5 sub-machine guns in their hands. The lead officer started approaching him quickly.

'Are you Lee McCarthy? Formerly British Army?' he shouted as he moved towards him.

'Yeah. That's me,' McCarthy called back, frowning. 'What's going on?'

'Sir, I need you to come-'

He never had a chance to finish the sentence.

During the exchange, McCarthy had sensed some kind of movement down the street to the left, about thirty yards away. Someone had stepped out of a silver car, a big figure dressed in black.

Distracted, he turned his attention from the cop, and saw the man was wearing a balaclava.

And he had a long weapon on his shoulder.

Aimed straight at him.

The bazooka suddenly whooshed and gave a flash.

McCarthy didn't even have time to blink.

The rocket-propelled grenade hit the fender of the car. The explosion reacted with the fuel in McCarthy's car instantaneously and the entire vehicle exploded in a huge fireball, killing McCarthy instantly. Porter was only just out of the blast radius, which saved his life, but the force of it threw him back hard into the ARU's car.

Behind him, Archer, Fox and Chalky were all knocked off their feet from the explosion too, the fireball billowing out ahead of them. Car alarms on other vehicles on the street were set off as dogs in houses and gardens nearby started barking, adding to the cacophony of sound.

Staggering to his feet, his ears ringing, Archer was the first to react. As the blackened shell of McCarthy's car was engulfed in flames, Archer moved around Cobb's car and saw a man drop a bazooka to the ground. The guy was huge, dressed in black fatigues and had a balaclava shielding his face. *One of the Panthers.* He was next to a silver car, another man in black and a balaclava behind the wheel, and the guy on the street started to run around the car towards the passenger seat.

'Hey!' Archer shouted, raising his MP5.

Hearing him, the huge man paused, reached inside the back of his car and pulled out an AK-47 Kalashnikov rifle. Without a moment's hesitation, he snapped the weapon into his shoulder and started firing as Archer dove for cover, falling to the hard concrete and scraping the skin on his palms as a volley of bullets smashed into the car where he'd been standing. He heard people further down the street who'd been drawn by the explosion, screaming as they ducked down, the brutal echoes of the gunfire echoing off the buildings, the front lights on the car smashing and the glass tinkling to the ground.

The man kept up the rate of fire, Archer pinned down behind the vehicle, Fox and Chalky joining him having dragged Porter out of the line of fire and behind the car. When there was a break in the assault, Archer peered round the back of the vehicle and saw the man jumping back into the silver getaway car.

Archer aimed the hair-trigger of the MP5 and fired back, controlled single shots. The bullets smashed into the side window and front-shield of the car, both the men in balaclavas ducking as the bullets skimmed past them. The driver pulled a U-turn in the road, and the wheels squealed as the vehicle took off down the street, heading the opposite way from Archer.

Behind him, Chalky was already hauling a dazed Porter into the back of their own car. Fox threw himself into the driver's seat as Archer ran round and jumped into the front passenger seat beside him, just as Fox fired the engine.

'Go, Fox, go!' Archer shouted as Fox floored it, and they took off after the two soldiers, speeding down the street.

TWENTY ONE

The two Panthers had a head-start and were already some distance ahead, the speedometer on both cars pushing seventy, parked cars, houses and stunned pedestrians flashing past either side. The silver Fiat pulled a hard sliding right and Fox did the same, not giving an inch. Archer pulled the mobile phone from the pocket on his vest, calling Nikki. It connected almost straight away.

‘Nikki, we need back-up!' he shouted. 'We’re tailing two of the Panthers. They just took out McCarthy. We’re on Ladbroke Road, heading west.'

'Copy that.'

Fox turned a hard left as Archer ended the call, the wheels of the car squealing as the Ford slid south onto Ladbroke Grove. They could still see the Fiat racing ahead of them. Fox put his foot down harder as pedestrians at a passing crossing jumped back, and the car flashed past, keeping the Fiat in sight, weaving in and out of traffic.

Archer turned and looked back at Porter. *'How you doing, Port?'*

He was sitting with his head back, bleeding from cuts to his face and head. He was just beginning to recover some of his hearing, his ears bleeding too. He tipped his head slightly, sensing Archer was looking at him, and nodded, still dazed and out of it.

Behind the wheel, Fox was using every second of his pursuit training and experience in the field. He used to ride in an undercover response vehicle before he joined the ARU, and although it had been a while, Archer saw why he had a reputation as one of the fastest drivers in the Met.

There was a roundabout up ahead, but the silver Fiat carrying the two Panthers barely slowed, racing around it and causing other drivers to brake and swerve. They ignored a red light at the next junction and careered across the intersection, smashing a small VW out of the way. The ARU vehicle followed as the Fiat roared straight on, the street behind them filled with the sounds of blaring horns of cars left in their wake.

Then the two Panthers made a mistake. The Fiat turned a corner too fast. The driver lost control and the car smashed head on into a lamp-post. The impact dislodged the light above which fell onto the roof of the car and shattered into a thousand pieces. The driver tried to throw the car into reverse, but the engine died, so without hesitation, the two soldiers scrambled out, abandoning the car, taking off in opposite directions.

One of them ran onto MacFarlane Road, headed west. The other, the huge guy who'd fired the bazooka, was running towards the Westfield Shopping Centre, one of the largest malls in the city. He still had his AK-47 in his hands. Speeding towards him, Archer watched the guy turn towards them in the middle of the street, aiming the rifle at the front of the Ford.

'Get down!' Archer shouted, grabbing Fox, who ducked and braked at the same time.

The guy opened fire, the bullets smashing into the car and through the windshield, the four officers huddled low and just avoiding the fire, some of the rounds thudding into the seats, white fluff protruding through the black cushions from the bullet holes. He was firing on full auto which suddenly stopped as his magazine clicked dry.

The guy cursed and dropped the empty Kalashnikov on the ground, then turned and ran towards the shopping centre, people on the pavement screaming and running in panic.

Archer threw his own door open, seeing the big guy sprinting towards the galleria.

'Cut him off!' Archer shouted as he jumped out, slamming the door and taking off across the road after the Panther.

Fox roared off up Wood Lane, past the West Side of the shopping mall, the front of the vehicle riddled with bullet holes, Fox doing his best to see through the smashed-up windshield. Dodging through the traffic, Archer sprinted across the street and ran as fast as he could after the fleeing soldier.

Outside the shopping centre, terrified people had rushed for cover when the man in black who'd fired the AK-47 sprinted past them, ploughing through anyone in his path as he headed for the galleria, followed forty feet behind by an armed policeman.

The big man sprinted past a long Debenhams store, then took a sharp left and raced into the shopping centre itself, smashing unsuspecting shoppers out of his way. Archer dodged round a young couple, leaping over a pushchair, and chased after the guy as fast as he could, his MP5 gripped in his hands as he tried to keep pace with the fleeing man.

Inside, the arcade was busy for a weekday, lots of shoppers meandering around. Some people who had been near the entrance to the mall had stopped in their tracks, wondering what the unusual noise was outside. They'd all been taken by surprise as the huge figure dressed in black rushed past them, followed soon after by the young police officer carrying the MP5.

Archer weaved his way through shoppers and kids, racing through the area crowded with people.

'Move! Move!' he shouted.

He saw the Panther racing up an escalator ahead. He moved fast for a big man and Archer was running as fast as he could to keep up, hampered by the MP5. He ran towards the escalator and took the steps two at a time, determined not to let the guy get away. All that morning time in the gym was paying off; he was in excellent cardiovascular condition and he was making up some ground on the Panther.

Archer arrived on the First Floor, looking left and right. He couldn't see the soldier, but there were more shoppers up here, who'd stopped in their tracks when they saw him with the sub-machine gun in his hands.

'*Which way?*' he shouted.

They pointed right. There were lifts and toilets there, but the door to a service corridor was open and Archer sprinted forward, bursting through it and racing down the side corridor.

He could hear the slap of running footsteps up ahead and he chased after them, arriving at a flight of stairs. He leapt down two at a time, down past the ground floor and onto the lower car park levels.

He caught a glimpse of black as the man turned a corner up ahead, and Archer jumped off the remaining steps, sprinting after him.

He rounded the corner, and then instinctively ducked. A steel pipe swung in the air, smashing into the wall where his head had been. From a distance the Albanian Special Forces soldier had cut a large figure, but up close he was huge. He kicked Archer's MP5 out of his hands with his boot, breaking the strap, the gun clattering to the ground, and he swung the pipe at Archer's head again as if he was going for a home run.

The smaller man ducked and hit the man in the face with an overhand right. Although the blow landed, it didn't seem to hurt the soldier at all, but Archer's hand felt like he'd just punched granite. The two men locked up, then the soldier head-butted Archer above the left eye, his head like a rock, smashing into Archer's forehead. Archer staggered back and pulled his Glock from the holster on his thigh, but the man was already out of the door.

Dizzy and disorientated from the head-butt, his eyes watering, Archer staggered and scooping up his MP5, he stuffed the Glock back in its holster and moved into a corridor, just as the soldier disappeared out of the other end, heading into the car park. He took off after him as fast as he could, with blurred vision, and burst out of the door into the parking lot.

Just as he arrived, he heard a loud *thump* and saw the huge soldier run into a car door that had suddenly swung open in front of him to Archer's left. Through blurred vision and watery eyes, he saw it was the ARU car. Fox had pulled round into the underground car park.

Archer saw Chalky jump out onto the dazed soldier instantly, restraining him, Fox racing around from the driver's seat and helping him subdue the large man. Porter was climbing out of the car from the other side, the stains of blood trickling from each earlobe joining the cuts on his head and face. He saw Archer was shaking his head, trying to clear his vision, and moved over to him.

'You OK?' he asked.

Archer nodded, his chest heaving up and down from the exertion as he sucked air deep into his lungs. His vision clearing, he looked down at the Black Panther soldier. It'd taken both Fox and Chalky to restrain the struggling man, and he was pinned to the ground while Chalky bound and zipped up his wrists with a set of plasti-cuffs from his tac vest.

Belly to the ground, the man turned and looked back at Archer. His face was shielded with the balaclava but there was nothing but sheer murder in his eyes.

'What about the other one?' Chalky asked Porter loudly so he could hear him, this knee on the big soldier's back.

'We'll find him,' Porter said. 'Let's just get this one back to HQ.'

*

Fifteen minutes later, Worm watched from a crowd gathered on the corner of MacFarlane Road as tape was drawn up around his ruined getaway car, the damaged lamppost leaning drunkenly over it. He'd fled down the residential streets once they crashed, but doubled back when he realised the cops hadn't pursued him and ditched his balaclava and overalls revealing jeans and a sweater. He blended right into the crowd, but made sure to keep himself well out of sight at the back.

Looking left, he saw the black Ford that had been tailing them appear out of the car park and head towards them, bullet holes on the front windshield and both the front headlights smashed. It pulled to a halt, and a blond man stepped out from the back seat, rubbing a cut above his eye as he walked over to the officers by the ruined car, holding a brief conversation in lowered voices. Worm recognised him as the pretty-boy cop from King’s apartment building, the one he’d bumped shoulders with.

He shifted his gaze to the car and saw his commanding officer in the middle seat. They’d taken off his balaclava and Worm saw his commander's head down, his dark hair ruffled, the huge muscles of his arms and shoulders pulled behind him by a set of handcuffs. Worm swore under his breath in Albanian, then turned and walked away quickly.

He pulled a mobile phone from his pocket and checked the time on his wrist-watch. All the others would be landing, in the next couple of hours, but Spider and Bug would already be here.

He dialled a number and waited, glancing back. Through the crowd, he saw the blond cop step back inside the car and watched it speed off back into the city, no doubt to their police station.

'Sir?'

'Yes, ' Spider’s voice said.

'It's Worm. Where are you?'

'At the command post.'

'Bad news. The English police captured Wulf after we killed McCarthy. We tried to get away, but the car crashed and we had to run.'

Pause.

'Do you know which station?'

'I think it's the team under Cobb. I recognised their uniform. They all have *ARU* printed on the back.'

There was a pause.

'OK. Come back to the safe-house. Bird and Flea will be here soon. We'll get him back.'

'Yes, sir.'

The call ended. Worm turned and moved off down a side-street, away from the crowd and the ruined car, headed back to the command post and his comrades, his mood darkening with every step.

TWENTY TWO

Back at the ARU's headquarters, Jackson was standing alone in the Briefing Room, a cup of lukewarm coffee in his hands, made more out of a desire to give himself something to do than anything else. He was leaning against the drinks stand, staring at the noticeboard across the room with his name on it, deep in thought.

He'd been on the line with Agent Wallace in DC when Fraser had taken the round to the head, mere seconds before they got to him. Coupled with reports from Director Cobb's task force, who'd found King dead in his apartment building, and the most recent confirmation that McCarthy had just been killed, it had quite simply been a disastrous hour. They'd had the jump on the Panthers, but nevertheless they hadn't reacted in time, their officers and agents beaten to the trio by seconds.

And because of that delay, three more men had now been murdered.

Agent Wallace had called Jackson back and told him that Fraser's office building had been completely evacuated. The murder weapon had been located on a rooftop across the street and taken to the lab, along with the spent copper jacket from the bullet lying on the ground to the right of the rifle. They were checking security and street cameras to try and tag the shooter, and were searching for any witnesses.

They had to follow procedure of course, and the lab could come back with something if the rifleman had made a mistake, but deep down Jackson knew he wouldn't have. These men knew what they were doing. And this operation was a one off, not a serial attack like the two snipers back in 2002. The guy had left the rifle behind deliberately.

And Jackson felt as if all that effort in the lab would just be a waste of time. Fraser was still dead, his wife now a widow, his kids left without a father. It didn't matter if they found a hundred fingerprints on the rifle and cartridge.

None of them would bring the man back.

News of both King's and Fraser's deaths had been confirmed moments apart from each other, just as Cobb had been preparing to leave with his family. Two of the armed officers would deliver them to the house in one of the replacement MI6 Ford 4x4s, ensuring they weren't tailed, then return to the station.

Before he left, Cobb had walked into the Briefing Room to speak to Jackson alone. Before he spoke, the atmosphere between the two men had been tense.

'I'm sorry for giving you such a hard time earlier,' Cobb said. 'I was too tough on you. None of this is your fault.'

Jackson smiled. 'No problem. We're all strung out.'

A silence had followed. Cobb had walked over to the board, tapping the photographs of the three murderers, the men who started all this. Carver, Floyd and Fletcher.

'This kind of thing has happened before, hasn't it?' Cobb continued. 'Massacres. My Lai, in Vietnam. Haditha, in Iraq.'

'And those are ones we know about,' Jackson said.

He paused.

'I met one of the soldiers from My Lai back in Virginia just before I went to The Farm. Just before he died. When he spoke about it, he had the same expression that I saw on Fletcher's face earlier.'

Pause.

'I asked him how many women and children died that day in the jungle. He said he lost count. There was never an official number released to the public, but we know the minimum was 347 civilians dead. Women and children. Babies.' He looked at the board. 'The same exact shit that happened here.'

Silence.

'Come with us, Ryan,' Cobb had said. 'Until this is over. We can run the operation from the Hall. You'll be secure. None of the Panthers will have any idea where we are.'

Jackson smiled, and shook his head, looking back at him. 'I need to stay, Tim. To be honest, I don't fancy isolating myself. I need to be near the airports. Once someone realises the connection in these attacks, I'll probably get called straight back to Virginia. But until then, I need to be in the thick of it.'

He saw the look on Cobb's face.

'Don't feel guilty. You have a family to protect.'

He pointed at Cobb's office and at the damaged glass.

'Besides, no-one's taken a shot at me today.'

There was a pause.

Both men looked at the board, the eleven photographs and names, seeing their own faces at the top of the pyramid.

Seven of the photographs now had a big X over them.

'Four of us left,' Cobb said.

At the doorway, an officer from Second Team appeared. 'Ready to go, sir?'

Cobb nodded. He'd turned to Jackson and offered his hand.

'You're sure you want to stay?'

Jackson shook it. 'Positive.'

'OK. I'll see you again soon.'

'Take care of your family, Tim. And keep your head down.'

'You too.'

And with that, Cobb had turned, walking out of the room, and disappeared down the corridor, out of sight.

Truth be told, standing alone in the Briefing Room and with a fresh *X* over the face of McCarthy, Jackson was beginning to regret not taking up Cobb's invitation. Shaking his head, he took a calming breath. There were armed men guarding every entrance here. They'd been unprepared before. The Panthers wouldn't get the drop on them again. And besides, Jackson couldn't leave. He had a personal responsibility to stay here in the middle of this, one that nobody knew about. He owed it to those who had already been killed by the soldiers. If they came for him, they came for him, and the chips would fall where they may.

The thought of the group of men who wanted to end his life made him feel slightly sick. He looked down at the cup of coffee, two sugars, loaded with caffeine. That definitely wasn't helping keep his nerves steady. As he tossed the still-full cup of liquid into the trash beside him, he saw the dark-haired, attractive girl who ran the tech team enter. *Nikki,* he remembered. For a nasty moment he thought she was moving to the board to draw another *X* over Fletcher, but instead she walked towards him standing by the drinks stand.

'Good news,' she said.

'What's that?'

'Our team just captured one of the Panthers, the man who killed McCarthy. He was trying to escape from them through a shopping centre. They cut him off and got him in handcuffs.'

'That's great.'

'They're on their way back with him. Maybe we'll get some answers.'

Jackson nodded as Nikki took a foam cup and helped herself to a small cup of coffee from the stand, more of a shot than anything, some caffeine to spike her blood sugar and keep her alert. They stood there in silence for a moment, then she nodded to him and turned, moving back to her desk next door with the cup in her hand. He watched her leave, then turned and walked over to the window, looking out over late-afternoon London, bathed in sunshine.

In the commotion and panic of the day's events, neither Cobb nor any of his officers had taken a moment to think about Jackson's initial involvement in the case all those years ago. He'd been just as young as Cobb, only twenty six, a junior agent fresh from his training. It should have been obvious. His role to ensure Blackout ran smoothly should have been delegated to someone with far more authority and experience, especially considering the importance and secrecy surrounding the operation.

But none of them had stopped to question why it had been him.

He thought back all those years, back to when he was called into a Senior Agent's office only weeks after he'd moved to London in March 1999.

Hearing what had happened in that small town in Kosovo.

What his cousin, Jason Carver, had done.

How he'd butchered all those women and children. How the Brits would be organising the rescue, but that Deputy Director Carver had insisted his nephew Ryan oversee the operation as both an American and family presence, making sure it ran to plan, making sure they got the stupid boy out of there alive. It was shameful. His uncle was panicking, partly about his son, but mostly about the potential damage to his own career.

Still stunned after hearing the news and sickened by the massacre, Jackson had been passed a phone inside the senior agent's office. His uncle was on the other line from his desk in Virginia.

Get him out of there alive and I'll see to it that your career takes off.

That was all he'd said.

To this day, Jackson's subsequent actions caused him shame. He'd hidden his revulsion at his cousin's deeds, even though he was well aware that if the operation was a success Jason would probably never be punished for what he'd done. Out of some stupid misguided thought of family and national loyalty that he'd regretted every day since, Jackson had agreed to do what he was ordered. Blackout had gone ahead under his and Cobb's supervision and it had been a perfect success. A month later they had a damn ceremony for Ryan in DC, where Deputy Director Carver pinned the medal on him in front of a national audience and the cameras, shaking his hand like he'd done something heroic and patriotic. In hindsight, given the guilt he now carried with him, Jackson knew he should have just said no and walked away. Every promotion he'd ever landed in his career since took him back to that first compromise. No advancement or pay rise had ever been worth it.

They should have left the three murderers to die. The men who did that to innocent people deserved everything they had coming.

It didn't matter if one or all of them were family.

Looking out as the sun started to set across the city, Jackson thought back to when they were kids. He and Jason were the same age and had grown up together in Staunton, playing football, riding bicycles and staying out late, sneaking into the local cinema to watch R-rated movies. In his wildest dreams, he never could have imagined that the boy he'd known back then would turn into an evil, mass murderer of a man. He remembered sitting next to Jason in the cinema and seeing his cousin's feet barely touched the floor from his seat, his eyes wide with excitement at the movie playing on the screen, innocent and a good kid.

Jackson sighed and looked at the buildings in the distance. In the years since the rescue, Jason hadn't been in contact once. He would have been well aware by then that his cousin had helped co-ordinate the rescue operation, that he'd played a significant part in the fact that he was still alive and not cut up into a hundred pieces by the men whose families he'd slaughtered. But he'd never once bothered to pick up the phone to thank him for helping to save his sorry ass, not once in the past fifteen years.

Jackson remembered how the kind, fun and intelligent Jason he'd known as a kid had morphed into a spoilt, arrogant and aggressive teenager. He'd lost all his charm and friendliness, and in short, had become a real asshole. He was cruel and started bullying other kids, picking on anyone at high school smaller than him. He'd left high school with a shitty diploma and hardly any friends, and the next thing Ryan heard was that Jason had signed up to join the Marine Corps. At the time, Ryan had both figured and hoped the training and discipline might straighten him out and fix his problems. But deep down he'd worried about the thought of Jason with a gun and responsibility. Ryan knew that when Jason had arrived back on US soil after Blackout and signed the same secrecy pledge, he'd been honourably discharged. Honourably. Like a damn war hero, his arm in a sling. A second chance, an opportunity to live a full life, a right he'd stolen from all those people in that camp that night. And now, fifteen years later, seven more innocent men had died because of his crimes.

Jackson shook his head, looking out at the city. His own blood had butchered those people, the same gene-pool, his own damn cousin. He liked to believe in the goodness of people and that life usually found a balance, but he knew the reality was often far harsher and a lot less romantic. So far today, two men had been shot at close range. Another had been car-bombed. Another sniped. One had committed suicide. And the latest had been hit in a rocket attack.

More bodies. More death. More innocent people dead just because his idiotic cousin wanted to play the hero, go home and brag about how many people he'd killed during the war, forgetting to mention that they were pretty much all women and children. And now, men who had saved his life, men he'd never bothered to even look up and thank, all dying because of his drunken stupidity and lust for blood.

But then again, life had sort of found a balance. The supposed glory that had awaited him had never materialised. His marriage had fallen apart almost the moment he got back and his father had turned his back on him, disgusted by what he'd done and the threat he'd posed to his own career. Jackson knew his cousin had been living alone in DC for the past eight years. He had no friends and no money. He worked a dead-end job in a sleazy strip-club far from the wealth and importance of the city, getting fatter and older and watching his life pass him by. He was so broke he couldn't even afford to be an alcoholic.

Jackson had caught the CNN report at his office earlier in the day. It said that Jason Carver had been strangled with a wire in his car in the early hours of the morning, no witnesses, no-one around to see him die. His funeral would take place sometime in the next two weeks, and Jackson was as sure as anything that there would be few, if any, mourners

Strangled with a wire.

Jackson nodded. Jason was dead. So too was Floyd, his partner in crime. Although he'd claimed he hadn't pulled a trigger that night, Fletcher's time was also coming to an end due to Nature. It was a fitting end for all of them. Fifteen years on, justice had been served. Even though one of them was family, they deserved exactly what they got.

But the other men who'd died today didn't. The hardest part was, Jackson could understand the rage of the Panthers, the thirst for revenge. If it'd been his family who had been massacred, God only knew how he would feel and what he would do to bring those accountable to justice.

Jackson looked out at the orange-tinted sky on the horizon.

They were out there right now, and Jackson was next on their list. He knew they would die to get to him, to Cobb, and Fletcher in the hospice bed. They wouldn't show mercy, even for a sick man. One way or another, this thing would end with more people dying. More kids left without fathers. More wives left widows. All of them paying for the crimes of three stupid men committed over a decade ago.

And the shame Jackson had carried since that night suddenly felt ten times heavier.

Something outside the window caught his attention, and the CIA agent looked down as a dark Ford pulled into the parking lot. The front of the car looked like it had been damaged from gunfire. It moved swiftly along the tarmac and swung into an empty space near the doors below. He saw two men from the Unit's First Team step out, Fox and Archer, and then watched as another officer opened one of the rear doors and led out a huge man dressed in black fatigues, his hands cuffed behind his back.

Jackson watched the four men lead the captive inside. He was a giant, dwarfing the two officers either side of him. The American studied him as he was led into the building.

Jason had ruined this man's life.

Looking down at the captive, all those feelings of guilt and regret at what his cousin did that night filled him like a balloon full of water, close to bursting. Alone at the window, he watched as the man was led across the tarmac.

'I'm sorry,' he said, quietly.

Then he turned on his heel and headed downstairs to watch the interrogation that would surely follow.

But he'd make sure that the man was securely in the cell first before he moved down the corridor.

Outside, Chalky and Fox escorted the huge man towards the entrance of the building, Porter and Archer checking behind them that they hadn't been followed. Once they all moved inside, Chalky and Fox took the captive through to holdings as the other two officers exchanged greetings with several members of Second Team. Archer touched the cut above his left eye. It was sore and he had a thumping headache. Beside him, he saw Porter still had dried rivulets of blood down his neck that had trickled out of each ear, his face peppered with cuts and blackened from the explosion.

He turned to Archer. 'You alright?'

'I'm fine,' he said. 'Better than you, anyway. Go and get cleaned up, boss.'

Porter nodded and patted him on the shoulder, then walked into the station and headed upstairs. As the two officers from Second Team turned to talk to each other, Archer had time to stop and think for a moment, the first time in a while. Taking his left hand off the stock of his MP5, he pulled his phone from his tac vest and scrolled through his recent *Call History*, finding Katic's number. He pushed the green button and waited for it to connect, turning and walking to the entrance to look out of the windows.

It rang three times, then was answered.

'Two calls in one day,' she said, munching on something. *'Did you miss me already?'*

'Bad time?'

'Lunch break,' she said, through a mouthful of food. *'It's been a quiet day. No-one's robbing any banks.'*

'Don't jinx it.'

'You OK?'

'Yeah, I'm fine.'

'Any news on your situation?'

'We found out that the two guys who attacked our station are from a larger group of eight.'

'Oh shit.'

'We captured one of them. He just got taken inside to the cells.'

'Do you know who they are?'

'Funny you ask. Your family is Serbian, right?'

'Yeah. My grandparents left after the Second World War, but I still have relatives there.'

'You ever heard of the Black Panthers?'

There was a long pause.

Down the line, he heard her stop munching on her lunch.

In the receiver, there was nothing but a period of silence.

'Why do you ask?' she said eventually.

'Apparently they were a Special Forces Unit during the Kosovo war. Part of the KLA.'

'I know who they are.'

He paused. Silence.

'Can you tell me anything about them?'

Another pause.

'My family who are still there, they live in a town called Priboj,' she said. *'It's a small place, less than 30,000 people, towards the border with Bosnia. A few years ago, I went to visit my first cousin, Marija. I stayed at her home, with her husband and two small girls. The first night I was there, we all had dinner together, and then she took the girls off for a bath and put them to bed. I headed upstairs too to have a shower and get an early night's sleep, but from my room I heard Marija telling the two girls a story. I'd never heard it before. It was one of those bedtime stories with a moral that warns children about something. Like the Boy who cried Wolf.'*

'A fable,' Archer said.

'Yes, that's right. Anyway, I heard her talking to them in Serbian. She told them about a family. They used to live down the street, before the two girls were born, and were not nice people. They lied, they cheated, they treated everyone around them badly. They had two boys who would bully all the other children in the playground, punching and kicking them and so forth.'

She paused.

'Anyway, long story short, there was a school bus in the town that came every morning to pick up the children who lived on the street. And one morning, the driver pulled up outside the house of the two bully boys. But no-one came out. The driver shrugged, then drove on and continued on his way. But then the kids didn't show up the next day. Or the day after. So eventually, the police went round to their house. And they found that the family was gone. Vanished into thin air, the father, the mother, the two boys. But the sheets on their beds were rumpled, blankets half on the floor, chairs knocked over. As if they'd been snatched in the night.'

'OK,' Archer said, confused, not sure where this was going.

'Marija told the two girls that something came for the family. She told them that because the family were so cruel a monster came in the middle of the night and took them away, and no-one ever saw them again. She said the beast had a name, called the Crno Kuguar. *The* Black Panther*, in English.'*

Archer frowned, touching the cut again over his eye.

'I don't understand.'

'After Marija shut the kid's bedroom door, we went downstairs to get a drink and I told her I'd overheard her story. I didn't grow up in Serbia so had never heard it before. I asked her if it was a famous old tale or something she made up.'

She paused.

'Then she told me it was actually true.'

'What?'

'Well, not the monsters thing. But I swear to you, as Marija swore to me, that during the war people just went missing from all over the area, in the town and in the surrounding countryside. She assured me that the family she spoke of had existed, and all four of them had vanished. Rumours had spread about who was responsible for these disappearances. She told me it was a KLA Special Forces Unit called the Black Panthers.'

'They stole people?'

'That's what everyone there still thinks, even the adults. No-one ever found out what had happened to those who disappeared. But not a single one was ever seen again. Rumour had it the Panthers were arrested and put on trial in Belgrade after the war. And after that happened, no more people went missing.'

'That's right. That's what we were told.'

'So the story was actually based on reality. It scared kids into behaving because of that. And Marija told me that no-one ever knew what had happened to the Black Panthers. Like their victims, they just disappeared too.'

'Not anymore,' Archer said.

She paused.

'Whoa, wait a minute,' she said. *'Are you telling me these are the men who attacked your station?'*

'Yes. They're trying to kill my boss.'

'Why?'

'I can't say.'

'Jesus Christ, Sam. These men are the stuff of nightmares in Serbia.'

Archer went to reply, but he heard a whistle from behind him. He turned and saw Chalky in the doorway of the lower corridor, gesturing at him to join him.

'I need to go.'

'Archer, listen to me,' she said. *'There's a lot of bullshit back home surrounding these men, but somewhere the myths mix with the truth. To this day, grown men in Priboj are scared shitless at the mention of the Panthers. Be careful.'*

Archer nodded. 'Is there anything else you can tell me about them?'

'Yes.'

'What?'

'They must have been desperate to kill your boss.'

'What makes you say that?'

'They attacked during the day. That's very unlike them. That's the opposite of the fable, in fact.'

'Why was it unlike them?'

She paused. He looked out of the windows of the police station at the setting sun.

'Because they come for you at night.'

TWENTY THREE

'They'll have taken him back to their police station,' Worm said, in Albanian, as the group of soldiers gathered at the command post. 'I recognised their uniforms. Each man had lettering on the back of his vest. ARU. The same Unit that Grub and Crow attacked.'

In the dark room, illuminated only by the glare of the two televisions, Bug, Bird and Spider listened closely.

'You know where this place is?' Spider asked, also speaking in their native tongue. When they'd set-up the operation, Spider had been in charge of the US-based foursome and was unfamiliar with locations this side of the Atlantic. Worm nodded.

'Yes sir. But I also have good news. I followed Cobb and Jackson and the officers earlier. They arrived at some kind of hospital. I couldn't follow them inside, but moved around the building into the garden and saw them before they shut the curtains. I saw who was in the bed.'

He paused.

'Corporal Simon Fletcher.'

The men looked at each other. Bug hawked and spat on the floor.

'Son of a bitch,' Bird muttered.

'That is good news,' Spider said to Worm, nodding.

Silence followed. His piece said, Worm looked over at Spider. With their commander gone, Spider was the new man in command, but the soldiers had just as much faith in him as they did in their commanding officer. Spider was the kind of lieutenant that would never challenge for the top position, loyal, willing to die to save his leader. The perfect right hand man, and a good soldier in his own right.

'OK,' he said, in Albanian. 'We arm up, then go to this police station. We take back our leader, and kill anyone who gets in the way. Then we go to the airport, pick up Flea, then head to the hospital and kill Fletcher. You said there is a long garden outside this man's room?'

'Yes, sir,' Worm said.

'Good. Flea can take him with the rifle. We won't need to move inside.'

'What about Cobb and Jackson, sir?' Bird asked.

'They won't still be at the station surely,' Bug said. 'Only a pair of fools would still be there.'

'So what do we do?' Bird asked.

Spider smiled in the darkness.

'Never underestimate human stupidity. We take a good look and see if they are there. And if they aren't, we'll get one of the other policemen to tell us where they are.'

*

At the ARU's headquarters, the atmosphere on the lower level of the building was one of both apprehension and excitement. The capture of the soldier felt like a big victory, even though they all knew there were five more of these men still out there. After Fletcher's warnings about the squad and their aura of being Special Forces, the wattage of their perceived invincibility had been dimmed slightly. With one of them in handcuffs, it was physical proof to the team that these men were mortal, the same as the rest of them, and that they could be subdued and arrested like anyone else.

The captive had been placed inside one of the interrogation cells, alone. The room was simple, two chairs either side of a desk. The lights in the room were bare and bright, throwing harsh light into every corner and over the soldier in the centre of the room.

The ARU was a squad that dealt with terrorists and hardened criminals on a regular basis, so they were used to dealing with some of the toughest and most violent men out there. But they'd never encountered a Special Forces commander like this before.

Staring straight ahead, arms bound behind him by Chalky's plasti-cuffs, the man cast a hulking, intimidating figure. He hadn't said a word since he got captured, but just by sitting there his sheer physical presence emanated danger.

No officer or detective had gone in to interrogate him yet. Time was on their side. Cobb was at the safe house, Jackson was here and Fletcher was being guarded at the hospice, all protected and prepared. Porter had ordered that they wait, so they'd left the

Panther in the cell for over an hour. The man in the interrogation room and his team had enjoyed the element of surprise when killing their seven victims so far.

That wouldn't happen again.

With Cobb gone for the time being, Porter had assumed leadership of the squad. He was standing outside the cell in a dark viewing room, alongside the rest of First Team and Agent Jackson, who'd come downstairs after they'd first brought the captive in. Down the corridor, Deakins and Second Team were still guarding the building, both front and rear entrances, but each officer was still wearing his throat mic so they could all communicate at a moment's notice.

In the room adjacent to the holding cell, shielded behind a one-way mirror, Porter pulled his mobile phone from its home on his left collarbone and pushed Cobb's number as the other men examined the Panther through the glass. The phone rang once, and was answered.

'*Port?*' Cobb said.

'Evening sir,' Porter said, turning to one side. 'I have some news.'

'Talk to me.'

'I'm afraid it's both good and bad. We captured one of the Panthers. He's in one of the interrogation cells right now. We think he might be the leader.'

Pause.

'The bad?'

'We didn't get to McCarthy in time. They killed him.'

'Shit. How?'

'Bazooka attack. Hit his car in the street.'

Pause.

'Is everything over there secure?' Porter asked.

Silence. Cobb didn't respond, and the connection went fuzzy.

'Sir?' he repeated.

'Sorry,' Cobb's voice said, the line cutting in and out. *'The connection's bad. We're almost at the house. My in-laws are away, so we have the place to ourselves. Blessing in disguise.'*

Pause.

'We need to get this man talking. Find out where the rest of his team are. Who's going to lead the interrogation?'

'I was thinking Fox or Archer, sir. Since Frost retired, those two have taken the brunt of it. They're both pretty solid.'

'OK. If one of them can't get through, use the other. But tell them to stay on their guard. We know how dangerous this man is. And keep me posted. How's Jackson?'

Porter glanced at the American, who had his back turned, watching the captive closely through the glass.

'He's fine, sir.'

'OK. Keep me in the loop.'

The call ended. Porter turned to Jackson and the rest of First Team, who were standing there in a line watching the soldier, like a jury.

'Cobb's almost there,' Porter told them.

Jackson nodded. 'Good.'

Porter looked over at Archer. 'Ready for some face-time?'

Archer nodded, feeling the cut over his eye from the head-butt the soldier gave him. He'd had a headache ever since.

'Let's do it.'

TWENTY FOUR

The Special Forces soldier didn't react when Archer entered the room.

It was totally silent in there, the lights glaring down from the roof-light, bright and quiet. Archer closed the door with a click that echoed around the room. He had no folder in his hands. There was no tape recorder on the table between him and the soldier. The recording equipment was rigged up in the room already and every word was recorded from outside. Normally, in interrogations such as these, the handcuffs on the prisoner would be off already, but this time they were definitely staying on.

Archer moved forward, taking the empty chair across from the man.

A long silence followed. The lights in the room were stark and unforgiving, and they gave Archer an opportunity to fully examine the soldier in front of him up close. His physical presence was intimidating. He was wearing black combat overalls and black boots, and the seams of the clothing were tight around his shoulders and arms as his hands were pulled back behind him from the cuffs. He was built like a doorframe. His hair was dark and ruffled from the balaclava, and he had rough stubble on his chin and cheeks.

'What's your name?' Archer asked him.

The man looked at him.

His face was strong and hard, chiselled from stone, dark eyebrows.

He had dark, blue, unemotional eyes, as cold as Arctic frost, and they settled on Archer's face.

'In English, my name would be Wulf,' the man said, his Eastern European accent strong, his voice deep.

'Is that your real name?'

The soldier paused. 'You mean the name my parents gave me?'

'Yes.'

'No.'

Pause.

'You and your team have killed seven men today. I saw you kill McCarthy. That's a life sentence in prison.'

He paused.

'But you guys also murdered people in the US. Former soldiers. Unlike us, the Americans still have the death penalty. They'll push for extradition. Then the lethal injection. For you and all your friends.'

'Where is the man called Cobb?' Wulf asked, ignoring him.

'He's here. He's outside, watching.'

'You're lying. Only a fool would stay here.'

Pause. Wulf's eyes examined Archer's face, and his expression.

'You think you've won, don't you, young man?'

'Sure feels that way, doesn't it?'

'Does it?'

‘Take a good look around you.'

Wulf smiled.

It was unnerving.

'You haven't won. Everyone in this building is going to die.'

'That seems pretty unlikely right now.’ Pause. ‘Besides, what did we ever do to you?'

‘You got in the way.’

Pause.

'Where are the rest of your friends?' Archer asked him.

'Where is Cobb?' Wulf asked back.

'You're in no position to ask questions.'

'Yes, I am. You should respect me, boy. You are just a police officer. Someone like you wouldn't last an hour in our life.'

'Is that so?'

Wulf looked at him, his blue eyes almost freezing over with frosty contempt. 'Look at you. You are soft and weak. You live in comfort. My parents died when I was a child. I killed my first man when I was eleven. I spent fifteen years in a prison where you wouldn’t survive one night. And you think you can beat me?'

He laughed, filling the silence. It was harsh and deep, and echoed around the room.

'I'm going to kill you. All of you. Then I will execute Cobb. Wherever he is, wherever he is hiding, I will find him.'

Pause.

The room was silent.

'Cobb had nothing to do with what happened.'

'He freed the men who did it. That makes him guilty.'

'It wasn't his fault. He didn't know what those men did.'

'He should have left them to die. But he gave them freedom. And they put me and my men in jail. They murder our families and we are the ones who are punished for it.'

'Move on. You can’t change the past.'

'They shot both my children in the head. They were twins. Three years old. A boy and a girl. My wife was killed as she tried to protect them.'

'I'm sorry. But move on. Cobb didn’t pull the trigger.'

‘Tell me where he is.'

Pause.

‘Why did the KLA expel you?’

The man looked at him. Said nothing.

‘They abandoned you. And I think your men have abandoned you too. You’re all alone.’

Wulf went to reply, but suddenly, the room went dark.

The lights had cut out.

As Archer looked around in the sudden blackness, confused, he heard that laugh again, deep and threatening, rumbling around the pitch black like distant thunder.

'They're coming,' Wulf said. 'You're going to die, young man.'

'What the hell was that?' Deakins said, out by the reception desk.

He was with two other members of Second Team, all three standing in the darkness, their visibility slightly better than down the corridor due to the lights from the streets outside. A few moments later, Agent Jackson and Porter appeared through the door from the corridor, both of them looking anxious.

'Power cut?' Porter asked.

'No, it-'

But before Deakins could respond, there was a smash of glass.

Beside Porter, Jackson was thumped backwards, blood sprayed all over the wall and onto Deakins and Porter, as the CIA agent took a bullet in the neck.

He fell back, collapsing on the ground.

'Shit!' Deakins shouted.

The whole team crouched low and took cover, hustling fast through the doors back into the dark corridor of the holding cells. Porter grabbed Jackson's collar, pulling him into the corridor, blood smearing on the ground under the wounded man as Porter dragged him behind the cover of the door. Jackson was clutching at the wound, his eyes wide with shock and fear, and blood pulsed out of him through his fingers, already soaking the top of his shirt and suit jacket and leaving a stained crimson trail on the white floor.

'C'mon Port!' Deakins shouted, helping him with Jackson.

There was a *thump* and a kick of plaster as another bullet hit the wall by Porter's head and he fell back into the corridor with Jackson, Deakins locking the door.

Heaving Jackson over his shoulder, Porter and Deakins hustled down the corridor, towards their team-mates, most of whom were standing in the corridor, confused.

'Get back!' they shouted.

Behind them, the door suddenly exploded, as it took a rocket from a bazooka head on. The force of the blast smashed it off its hinges and the twisted frame flew down the corridor, coming to rest in a smoking dented heap on the floor. The officers had their MP5s to hand but were forced to scatter for cover, ducking into holding and interrogation cells as automatic gunfire suddenly erupted down the corridor from the far end, the silhouettes of three men lit up in the smoke and streetlights, muzzle flashes of automatic weapons lighting up the smoky darkness.

Moving out into the corridor from the viewing room of the interrogation cell, his MP5 in his hands, Chalky crouched low and tried to take a closer look at who was coming.

Three men, dressed in black fatigues, and each had a Kalashnikov rifle in their hands.

Chalky and Fox started to fire back, but the three men had the corridor and they unloaded with the AK-47s, pinning the team further and further back, the air filled with the brutal flash and echo of automatic gunfire, bullets tearing into the corridors and smashing windows. Chalky and Fox were forced to retreat, bullets smashing into the walls and glass panels on doors.

Back inside the interrogation room, Archer turned in the darkness to try and locate Wulf.

But he heard the sudden scrape of a chair as the man moved and then something smashed into the back of his head.

As Bird and Bug kept the rate of fire up in the corridor, Spider pushed open the door and moved inside. Wulf was in there, standing over an unconscious blond policeman. Spider raised his weapon at the officer's head, but Wulf shouted *No* in Albanian. *Cobb,* he mouthed afterwards, tapping his temple. He turned, laying his hands on the table behind him, and his lieutenant pulled a knife and cut through the plasti-cuffs.

'This way,' he shouted, over the gunfire in the corridor.

Wulf nodded, but on his way grabbed the young cop, dragging the unconscious man with him by the collar. They moved back out into the corridor, moving fast towards the exit.

A young woman with dark hair and glasses was cowering by the stairs. Spider hit her in the face hard with the butt of his rifle, knocking her out instantly. He caught and then dragged her with them too as she started to fall to the ground.

Down the far end of the corridor, the ARU were returning fire but hadn't put any of the Panthers down. Chalky risked a glance and saw the man called Wulf rushing towards the exit with another soldier, as the two other Panthers kept up their fire to pin the ARU officers back.

He saw Wulf was dragging someone behind him, a limp figure.

Archer.

'They've got Arch!' he shouted.

Turning, he ran across the corridor and up a flight of stairs into the Ops room, bullets shredding into the wall and just missing him.

Upstairs, the tech team were all huddled in Cobb's office behind the safety glass again, but Chalky ignored them, sprinting over to the smashed windows from the gunfight earlier in the day. He ripped the brown paper covering the holes out of the way and started firing down on the soldiers who were at their vehicle, a white van. The men dove for cover as Chalky's bullets hit the car, smashing the windows and the brake lights. The other two soldiers started returning fire as they ran to the vehicle and Chalky was forced to take cover.

Looking back down, he saw them pile into the van, pulling the doors shut, and he ran for the stairs, sprinting down them and running through the front door into the parking lot as the Panthers sped off towards the exit. He paused, lifting his MP5 and firing on full auto at the van, blowing out one of the tyres and smashing the rear brake lights. Once the sub-machine gun clicked dry, he dropped the weapon and pulled the Glock and sprinted after them, racing across the parking lot as fast as he could.

The van screeched out into the street, turning a sliding right, and Chalky ran through the exit and turned, sprinting after them down the road. One of the soldiers fired back, hitting a car beside Chalky, but the car gained speed and started to pull away. No matter how fast Chalky sprinted, he was losing ground.

In desperation, he continued to chase after it but the driver put his foot down and the van sped off into the night.

Chalky staggered to a halt, completely out of breath, desperate and scared, knowing Nikki and Archer were in the van with the four soldiers.

He looked down the road but all he saw were streetlights.

They were gone.

He turned and kicked a parked car in frustration.

'Shit!'

Back inside the building, Fox raced back into the interrogation room that had held Wulf, smoke and the smell of cordite from the gunfight in the air. He had a red boxed first-aid kit in his hand, one he'd snatched from the viewing room next door. One of the officers had got to the reserve generator the other side of the building, hitting the switch, and it suddenly kicked in, dim lighting coming back on with a buzz and a flicker, showing the destruction and damage to the lower corridor of the station.

Inside the interrogation room, Jackson was lying on the ground, his head on Porter's knee, the ARU Sergeant desperately clamping his hands at the wound at the American's neck to try and stop the bleeding, blood pooling under them both. Fox ran forward and dropping to his knees, pulled out some bandages from the open box. He and Porter desperately started packing the wound on both sides, compressing it, trying to stop the constant blood flow. They were both kneeling in blood, the red liquid all over their hands, knees and boots, as Jackson's body started to tremble.

'Someone call an ambulance!' Fox shouted, as he and Porter compressed the bullet wound either side.

But the blood kept coming, soaking the pads, staining their hands, spreading out over the white floor.

He looked down at Jackson, who was shivering.

'Hang on, buddy,' he said. 'Stay with us.'

After a few more moments of desperate effort to stem the flow, the American looked up at Fox, who was holding one of the bandages to his neck, clamping it in position, the pad dark and soaked with Jackson’s blood. As Fox pushed it firmly, he looked down into Jackson's eyes.

The CIA agent gently shook his head. Almost imperceptibly.

He knew.

The blood was pumping out of him.

They couldn't stop it.

Fox looked over at Porter, both of them doing all they could, kneeling in the warm life-blood of the wounded man.

But before either of them could say a word, Jackson spoke.

'It's OK,' he said, quietly.

His face was calm, some of his blood smeared on his cheek, the back of his hair damp from it, his body no longer shaking. Although he spoke at almost a whisper, the silence of the room made every word clear. After a pause, Fox looked at Porter, who nodded. He leaned back, releasing his grip on the blood-soaked bandage. Jackson lay there, his face calm, the red puddle around them slowly increasing. If it wasn't for the blood silently pooling out of his neck to the floor and his complexion that was growing paler every minute, he would have looked quite serene, not a man in the last moments of his life.

Porter looked up and saw Deakins watching from the door silently. He turned and pulled the door shut respectfully, leaving the two officers and the dying man alone.

The three of them stayed there in silence, just the sounds of Porter and Fox's breathing audible. Fox reached over and gripped Jackson's hand, his own stained with blood, comforting the dying man.

The CIA agent flicked his eyes at him and gave a faint smile.

In the silence, blood continued to pool under Fox and Porter's knees, maroon in the dim light from above as it pulsed out of Jackson's body.

Then the American suddenly spoke, quietly.

'I have to tell you…something.'

Fox looked down at him.

'What's that?'

'Jason…Carver was my cousin. Did you know?'

Pause.

'No. We didn't,' Porter said.

'Spent my…whole life…trying to make up for what he did….to those poor people.'

The two officers nodded. Jackson blinked, trying to see.

He was finding it harder to focus.

Then he smiled, faintly, and spoke. His voice a whisper.

'It doesn't hurt anymore.'

Fox gripped his hand tight, as they stayed there in silence.

He felt Jackson give the faintest of squeezes back.

Then his grip relaxed.

And he died.

TWENTY FIVE

Sometime later, Archer blinked his eyes open and instantly winced.

His head hurt.

He was in a dark room somewhere. Alone. It was almost pitch black, but a chink of light creeping under the door allowed him some visibility.

He blinked, looking round, trying to clear his head and figure out what had happened. And where he was.

Am I still in the interrogation room?

Looking down, he saw in the dim light that he was still in his dark blue overalls and white t-shirt. He tried to move, but realised his feet had been duct taped to the chair.

And his hands were similarly bound behind his back.

Moments later, he heard footsteps outside the door and then a key jangle as it slid into the lock.

Then he remembered what had happened back at the station.

The door was pushed open and a man stepped into the room, Archer squinting from the sudden light. When his eyes adjusted, he looked past the man into the room beyond, but couldn't see anyone else out there. The man shut the door, and the room was dark again.

They were alone.

'You're awake,' the man said, same kind of accent as the man called Wulf. 'Good.'

Archer had re-gathered his senses and started thinking fast, assessing his situation. The binds around his hands and feet were tight. He was all alone.

He was in seriously deep shit.

'Do you know who we are?' the man asked, just a voice in the darkness, his accent rolling the r of *are*.

Pause.

'Yes.'

'Good. That will save me some time.'

The man flicked a switch on the wall and a light bulb above Archer flickered on. He blinked from the sudden light, then looked across the room.

He saw the dark, hard-faced man from King's apartment building, the one he'd bumped shoulders with. The man read the look of recognition across Archer's face and smiled.

'Remember me?'

Archer didn't respond, but glanced down at the man's hands instead.

He was grasping something in his right fist.

A long, wickedly-sharp knife, the edge of the blade serrated.

'Here's how this will work,' the man said. 'I'm going to ask you a question. I'll only ask you this one time. But if you don't answer it, I will hurt you. I will inflict pain like you have never experienced. Before long you will be begging me to kill you. And I promise you, you'll tell me everything I want to know. Do you understand?'

Archer didn't respond.

In the harsh light, he saw the man's mouth crease into a smile.

'I also suggest you start giving me some answers before the rest of my team returns,' he continued. 'Luckily for you, they've gone to pick up our last man from the airport and then kill Corporal Fletcher. But they will be back soon. And for your sake, you don't want to still be holding information from me when they return.'

Archer stared up at the man.

'Here is my question, ' the man said. 'Tim Cobb and his family were not at your police station, or at his home. Where is he?'

Archer looked up at him.

He said nothing.

'Do you remember what I just told you?' the man said.

Archer didn't react.

The man stepped forward.

'Typical. This normally happens. Men like you start out tough. They end up like children, soon enough.' The man walked forward, then stopped, putting his hands on his knees, his harsh face inches from Archer's. 'Look at you. You are quite something. You're a handsome man. But too pretty to be a soldier.'

The man leaned forward closer, looking into Archer's eyes, his dark hair slicked back, his nose like a beak over his stubbled sneer.

'As you can tell, I was never attractive. Women never lusted after me. But I guess they all like you. You must be - what's the saying- *beating them off with a stick*. That makes me jealous. So I'm going to make you as ugly as me. I'm going to take that face of yours and cut it off.'

The man reached forward and grabbed Archer's chin, who bucked and twisted away.

'Hold still,' the man said.

Gripping the knife, he pulled back Archer's hair and started to cut from the centre of his brow across the top of his hairline, a long jagged cut to the right. Archer roared in pain as he felt the blade slice into his skin, cutting across the top of his hairline. The soldier had a strong grip and Archer tried moving, but he felt the knife cutting open his head, unable to move, tied to the chair.

Eventually he managed to twist himself out of the man's grip, his head burning. Blood poured down his face, into his eye, and started leaking to the floor, his head and face feeling like it was on fire, the red staining his white t-shirt and navy blue overalls.

The man with the knife stepped back, looking at his helpless captive.

'That's a start,' he said. 'I feel better already. But I'm not going to do it all at once. I'm going to take it a piece at a time until you tell me where Cobb is.

And if you don't tell me, I'm going to cut your entire face off.'

Archer looked up at him, blood pouring down his face, blind from the blood in one eye. Some of it had gathered in his mouth and he spat at the beak-nosed man with the knife.

The guy didn't react.

'Oh, I forgot to tell you,' he said. 'You're not the only person from your station here. There is a woman next door waiting for me. She is beautiful. Dark hair, dark eyes. I'm going to go talk to her. Or I might just skip the talking and do something else with her. These walls are thin. You'll be able to hear. But I'll be back soon.'

He paused. Archer blinked, feeling the hot sting of blood running down the side of his face and his neck. He could feel the cut on the top of his forehead, and it burned and throbbed intensely as blood flowed from the jagged wound.

'You know, I lost my girlfriend and my son that night,' the man with the knife said. 'Both of them were in the first hut the two sons of bitches attacked. They were the first ones to be killed.'

He paused.

'Do you have a wife, or a girlfriend? A woman you care for?'

Archer looked at the ground, blood pouring into his eyes and dripping onto his lap. Hard as he tried to ignore the man, an image of Katic flickered into his mind, like a television screen with bad reception catching a signal.

He saw her dark hair and brown eyes, smiling at him.

She looked beautiful.

'I want you to think of her,' the man said. 'And know that you're never going to see her again. That's a promise from me. Because I just changed my mind. When I come back, I'm going to take your eyes out. And after the woman next door tells me where Cobb is, I'm going to cut your throat, from ear to ear. Then we'll see if you are still so pretty, you piece of shit.'

The man spat at Archer, then turned and walked towards the door, switching off the light. Archer was left in the dark, blood dripping down his face and soaking his t-shirt, half-blinded.

Tied up and all alone.

'Where the hell are they?' Chalky shouted to the re-gathered team in the Ops room back on the second floor of the ARU's headquarters. 'They'll kill them!'

Most of the squad had gathered up there, but without Archer, Cobb and Nikki. They were three of the core members and the room felt empty. Unused to combat situations, the remaining members of the tech team were still shell-shocked and traumatised. They were used to the safe and secure confines of the building, but the headquarters had already been attacked twice in one day. With the captive gone, as well as Archer and Nikki taken hostage, the mood in the room was dark. They were running on emergency power and the lights were still dimmed. In the low light and in Cobb's absence, Chalky was desperately trying to get the team going and thinking straight.

'C'mon! Someone think of something!' Chalky shouted.

He turned to the members of the tech team, all of them sitting in their chairs.

'Do you have access to traffic cameras?'

'Of course,' one of them said.

'Then find the white van that left here and tail it. We need to know where they took them. *Do it now!* If we wait, Archer and Nikki will die!'

The tech team turned and started tapping away on their computers, glad for something to do to help. Fox and Porter stood there in silence, both of them still covered in Jackson's blood, as Chalky paced back and forth. His normally jovial demeanour was gone, his face hard and his brow furrowed with anxiety. He'd seen the kind of men they were dealing with here. He'd heard Wulf's threats to Archer, watching them through the glass of the viewing room downstairs.

And he knew if they didn't find them soon that Nikki and his best friend would die.

Across the city, in a dark car speeding through south-west London towards Heathrow, the commander of the Panthers thought about the young officer who'd tried to interrogate him. He'd been telling the boy the truth. Since he could remember, everyone had called him Wulf.

He'd been named Ibrahim as a baby, but his nickname had stuck as a child. Nicknames in his squad and in the KLA were common, especially using names of animals due to the time they spent living out on the plains and in the valleys. Sometimes the naming was apt, other times it was because of mannerisms or physical appearance. Bug was named because of the scarring on his face and torso. A Serb phosphorous grenade had gone off right by his ear and had scorched that side of his face to leave scaly burns and webs of scarring. Flea, the best sniper in the KLA, was named because of his disproportionally small head. Worm because of his tall and lanky build and the way he crawled across the ground when out in the field. And Spider because of the tattoos on his body. He had two large black-widows inked on his elbows, the webs spreading all the way up his arms.

Wulf had been born in Albania, but had moved to Kosovo as a four year old boy. It was a humble place to grow up, farming country, tough land and cold weather. He'd matured early, forced to fend for himself. He remembered the first time he killed a man. The thief was trying to steal some cattle from his grandparent's farm, in the middle of the night. With no time to alert his grandfather, Wulf had taken his .22 rifle, loaded it and shot the man through the forehead from his bedroom window. By the time he was nineteen, he was an integral part of the Black Panthers, the Special Forces team that carried out the toughest of assignments for the KLA. Before he was twenty two, he was leading them, Spider his second in command.

When the war broke out, he and his team had been ordered by the KLA command to bring the fight to the Serbs, to take back what was theirs. They operated in the Drenica valley, mostly at night, roaming in the darkness and shadows as they hunted the Serbs, often not returning to the main KLA camp for weeks at a time. During the war they'd inflicted hundreds of fatalities on the enemy, but Wulf had never lost a single man, something he took immense pride in. The only real casualty had been to Bug when that grenade went off. But he'd survived. These were his men, his sons, his brothers. He would die in an instant for them, and he knew they would do the exact same for him.

Before long, the war had started to swing in the KLA's favour. They had support from NATO and they'd hammered the Serbs, pushing them back towards Belgrade. Wulf and his team were a big reason why the KLA offensive was so successful, and word had quickly spread, their legend and reputation growing not only on their side but with the enemy.

However, Wulf wasn't a stupid man. He knew the war wouldn't last forever, that he and his men couldn't spend the rest of their lives out there on the plains, hunting down Serbs and being paid close to nothing by the army command. Kosovo was not an area of wealth. There was nothing to steal, and no-one to bribe, and as their offensive had started pushing the Serbs back, Wulf had wracked his brains trying to think of a way he could ensure his men were sufficiently compensated for all their efforts in the war.

And one day, in December 1998, he'd found it.

Or more correctly, it found him.

He and his team had just returned from four days out in the field, performing hit and run raids on Serb outposts and camps, and Wulf had seen the headlights of a car approaching them on the dust track that led to their makeshift camp. He'd raised a bazooka to his shoulder, ready to fire if the vehicle came any closer, but the driver had stopped eighty yards away so as not to draw fire. A man in a white doctor's coat had stepped out then began walking over to the camp, his hands in the air, making a point that he wasn't a threat. Seven sub-machine guns and a bazooka pointed at him, the small man had moved into their camp and approached Wulf, asking him to take a walk with him.

He had a proposition for him.

Once the man was frisked and checked for weapons, Wulf had lowered the bazooka and grabbing his Kalashnikov, turned and walked with the small man, dwarfing him as they strolled side-by-side away from the camp and out of earshot.

The doctor began the conversation by explaining who he was, a University graduate who'd been fired from his job when the war had started due to being Albanian. He'd retreated into Kosovo and been left broke and out of work. With the war breaking out around him his prospects were bleak. However, he said that being fired from his job was the best thing that could have happened to him. In any country, war changes everyday rules and common practices, he'd said. Nations fall apart and are restructured when conflicts were resolved, like Nazi Germany after the Second World War.

But in that period of confusion and lack of structure, there is the potential for significant money to be made. Amongst so much violence and atrocity, the police and the government were distracted. Illegal activity could flourish, like dry earth under a monsoon, soaking up profit and collateral like dry soil sucked up water.

The doctor had explained that the war would be over soon, looking at Wulf through his spectacles. Order would be restored, and the opportunity for illegal earnings would become far more difficult. The doctor was looking to the future, much like Wulf, and told him of a new trade he'd just entered into, one that was already earning him fabulous amounts of money.

Organ harvesting.

Smuggling drugs, weapons and women were common practices all over Eastern Europe, the doctor had told him. They had been for years. One could make a handsome living selling any of the three, but the cash return would never be substantial given the increasing competition out there.

But apparently, the rarest of things to be traded were healthy human organs. Hearts, kidneys, livers and lungs, to be exact. Pure, living, pulsing, fleshy gold. Bags of rare blood types were going at thousands of US dollars each, and a full set of healthy human organs were going at close to fifty. The small doctor explained that he was running a trade with smugglers back in Albania. He would supply the organs, iced and packaged, and the smugglers would then traffick the coolers out of the country through the airport in the capital city, Tirana. The boxes would travel as hidden cargo through to the Ataturk International Airport, in Istanbul, Turkey. All the appropriate workers at each airport had been bribed so seizure of the coolers wasn't an issue, and from Istanbul the organs would then be transported out and shipped across Eastern Europe to the highest bidder.

The amount of money available was crazy, the doctor told him. $45,000 per body, at least, usually more. All that money just for one plastic cooler.

The doctor said that he and the smugglers had been doing this for almost three months, but had recently run into some problems. Namely, supply and demand. The operation couldn't flow without healthy bodies to harvest. Basically, what he needed from

Wulf was to not kill every enemy combatant he and his men engaged out on the plains. The doctor needed hostages, prisoners of war, people who figured they would be held for ransom and returned at a later date after negotiation. In return for the capture and delivery, the doctor said he was willing to give Wulf a ten per cent cut. Four and a half thousand US dollars per captive. Wulf had considered the offer, but like any shrewd businessman, he knew it couldn't run without his help. They'd settled on his cut being twenty five per cent. Over $11,000 per body.

Once they returned to camp, Wulf had gathered up his men, informing them of the proposed deal and asking what they thought. He emphasised how the war wouldn't last forever, that they needed to think of the future. Given their faith in him as a leader, the whole team had agreed on the plan straight away. He'd turned to the doctor and said they had a deal. Once delivery arrangements and locations had been agreed, the two men shook hands and the doctor had got in his car and driven off. After he was gone, the eight man team sitting around a fire, a discussion began concerning the acquisition of the bodies to be harvested. Spider had then come up with a great idea.

Why try to capture the enemy during a gunfight when you could just kidnap them instead?

The deal with the doctor and the traffickers had started working perfectly. Given that the Panthers were away from the main KLA camp for weeks at a time, no-one back at command usually had any idea what they were up to or even where they were. They'd gone deep into Serb territory, targeting the rural areas towards Bosnia and a town near the border called Priboj. The late-night covert entry-and-kidnap raids were always followed by a meeting on a dirt road with two smugglers sent by the doctor, both dressed as KLA soldiers. They told the hostages they were being taken to a detainee camp in northern Albania, and from there an exchange and ransom would be arranged with the Serbian government in Belgrade.

However, the captives were taken to a long, secluded house near the border instead. Once they arrived, their hands bound, they were shepherded out of the vehicle and then executed with a single bullet to the head, no-one around to hear the gunshot or see the bodies fall. Meanwhile, the doctor was inside the house, preparing for surgery, and hours later a fresh set of organs would be bagged, tagged and iced, already on their way to the airport in Tirana, the body of the host buried on the journey in an unmarked grave that no-one would ever find. Sometimes there was also a request for blood, so some of the bodies were drained by the doctor and the blood bagged and sealed. Before long the profits had started to come back to Wulf and his men, and they were handsome to say the least.

The trafficking had continued successfully for months, Wulf becoming wealthier and wealthier as each body was delivered to the doctor and harvested, the money deposited into an offshore bank account. Wulf wasn't a greedy man and kept his men fully informed about the exact amount of money they were making, promising to divide it up when the war was over, giving each man a foundation from which to buy a home or set up a new life.

Through January and most of February, they'd snatched and traded a hundred and fifteen of the enemy, mostly men but sometimes women and children, the entire family set. Once his men got a taste for it, they'd wanted to keep up the supply of bodies and the cash return and so the rules were loosened slightly. They'd been forced a few times to kidnap people from their own side, not something Wulf was proud of, but he had to look at the bigger picture and their futures.

But then everything had changed. It happened the night the two US Marines and the British Army soldier had arrived at the camp holding their families in March 1999.

Wulf and his team had just been returning from a late night trade on the road with the two smugglers disguised as KLA. The radio on Spider's uniform had suddenly started squawking, a guard at the camp where the women and children were based saying that they were under attack by three men, all of them NATO soldiers. Once Spider had raced back to camp and told Wulf, the entire team had piled into their cars and roared across the valley. They'd seen a

NATO Humvee up ahead, coming from the camp and on its way along the dirt track. Bug had stepped out and hit it first time with a bazooka, the rocket whooshing through the night and hitting the reinforced metal plate on the side of the truck, smashing it over with a large explosion.

They'd moved in and captured the three men inside, binding their hands and feet. Wulf had sent Crow and Grub to the township and the two men had returned devastated, confirming that everyone there had been killed. The squad had then proceeded to stamp, punch and beat the trio of murderers, kicking them in the face and pistol-whipping them. Every member of the squad had wanted to kill all three of them there and then, disembowel and crucify them, leave them nailed to trees with their intestines hanging out. But Wulf had ordered no. He'd said that was too quick a death. He wanted their deaths and pain to last weeks, months.

So he and his men had taken the murderers to their camp and thrown them into one the huts. Then the next night they started on one of them, taking away a piece of him at a time, the man screaming like a girl, the men laughing as they removed his toes one by one, a different one each night. They left them gathered in a pile there on the earth, letting the guy get a good look at them every night before they took another one.

But then disaster had struck. The three men had been rescued. Wulf still couldn't believe it had happened, how it had been done, right under their noses in the night.

Soon after, he and his team were arrested by Serbian police. The chief of security at the Ataturk airport had been tipped off about the smuggling, and had contacted the Serbian police who'd ambushed the doctor at the house and Wulf and his men at one of their roadside trades. They'd walked right into the trap, and an entire division of armed police sprung on them, taking them completely unawares. The game was up.

They were taken back to Belgrade, imprisoned and put on trial and charged for war-crimes. Ethnic cleansing, kidnap, murder, and organ harvesting. Once the KLA heard about it, they officially expelled them, turning their backs and forgetting all the hard work the Panthers had done for the Army in the war. The Serbian government were similarly outraged by the conspiracy, and were desperate to keep the harvesting a secret from the rest of the world, so the entire squad were sent away for life to *Ferri*, the darkest, most remote prison in the country, a place that wasn't on any map and that virtually no-one knew about.

A man didn't go to *Ferri* to serve time for his crimes. He went there to die.

Back in the car speeding through London, the thought of the far away prison made him shudder and Wulf brought his attention back to the present, looking out of the window at the road and the area around them. He and three of his men were on their way in two stolen 4x4s to the airport to pick up Flea, who would have just landed from Dulles, Washington D.C. Once they had him, they would make a stop at the hospice on the way back, kill Fletcher, then head to the safe-house and see what Worm had got out of the prisoners before executing them both.

Spider was behind the wheel beside Wulf in the lead car, driving fast, just as he had out on the plains all those years ago. They pulled around a roundabout and moved up the ramp towards the Arrivals lane of Heathrow Terminal Five, golden streetlights breaking up the shadows either side of the road. As they drew around the corner at the top of the ramp, Wulf saw Flea standing there outside the Arrivals hall, waiting, a token bag over his shoulder.

Spider drove forward and the vehicle pulled to a momentary halt. Flea walked over and pulled open the door, climbing into the back.

The moment he shut the door, Spider put his foot down and the vehicle sped off back into the night.

TWENTY SIX

Back at the ARU's base, the tech team were working away frantically, running through the security cameras. They'd found the stolen white van on the monitors and were now tracing its path sequentially across the city. Behind them Chalky, Fox and Porter were standing, all three of them anxious, watching the minutes tick away and desperate to get some clues. Downstairs Second Team were still recovering and doing their best to re-establish some form of protection on the doors, but the entire team was still shaken, bullet-holes and bloodstains covering the lower level of the headquarters, a recently-arrived medical team taking Jackson's body and zipping him up in a body bag.

'C'mon,' Chalky said, looking at the screens. 'We don't have time. Give us something!'

They continued, tapping away frantically, speeding up the tapes.

Suddenly, the guy on the far right made a breakthrough, a blond man called Rhys.

'There!' he said, tapping his screen. 'See.'

Chalky and his team-mates rushed over, looking closer at the screen. Rhys was right. The van had stopped outside a ten-storey office building.

'Zoom in,' he said, and Rhys turned, pulling up a white rectangle and pulling it over the van, then tapping a few buttons. The shot enhanced.

Up close, they saw the soldiers pull open the back of the van and pull out two limp bodies.

Archer and Nikki.

And they watched as they dragged them into the building and out of sight.

‘Bingo,’ Fox said.

'Are they dead?' one of the tech team asked.

'No. Not yet,' Chalky said. He ran his finger along the screen, at the GPS co-ordinates. 'Where is that?'

'It's down as a new office building, finished recently. It’s fifteen minutes north from here.'

'Send us the directions,' Chalky said, turning and running for the stairs, Fox and Porter close behind. Moments later they were already outside, climbing into Jackson's old car, and firing the engine, they pulled out of the lot with a screech and zoomed off down the street into the night.

At the command post in the building ten miles away, Worm stepped out of the bathroom and closed the door, smiling to himself, tossing his knife onto the desk. He took a mobile phone from his pocket and pressed *Redial*, walking out into the dark centre of the safe-house.

The call connected.

'Sir, it's me. I'm at the command post,' he said, in Albanian.

'Did they talk?'

'Yes, sir. The woman did. Cobb and his family are at a big mansion south of the city, in Surrey. It's called *The Hawkings*. She said it's a big place - you can locate it on the map. Can't miss it.'

'Good. Very good. Did she play tough?'

'At first. Then she opened up like an opera singer. Did you find Fletcher, sir?'

'We're on our way there now. Once he's gone, we'll go straight to this house and kill Cobb.' Pause. *'Are they all still alive?'*

'Yes, sir.'

'Wire up the safe-house, then come meet us at this house. The explosives will take care of them.'

'Yes, sir.'

The call ended. Worm walked across the room, flicking a switch on a wad of plastic explosives that had been set up on one of the desks. He thought for a moment, then set the timer to *2:00*. That would give him enough time to kill the pretty boy then get out of here before the safe-house went up. It would vaporise the bodies and any evidence that the Panthers were ever here.

He pushed the button, and the timer started counting down.

1:59.

1:58.

Walking quickly across the room, he put his knife back in its sheath, then picked up a 9mm Beretta from the desk by two flickering televisions, pulling back the top-slide and checking the chamber. The cop had spat at him. Worm would shoot him in both testicles, then the chest, then the head.

He smiled and twisted the door handle, pushing the door open, stepping into the room, raising the pistol.

But he frowned and froze.

The blond man wasn't in the chair.

He was gone.

At that same moment, Archer slammed the door from the other side into the man, smashing him into the door frame. The pain and anger from the wound to his head and the man's threats had unleashed a terrible rage and Archer yelled with anger as he slammed his shoulder into the back of the doorframe again and again, smashing the soldier in the gap, his chest and head pounded and thumping against the frame.

Archer had never been so angry. He roared with rage and hit the torturer with the door again and again, slam after slam, as hard as he could, in a violent frenzy, the pain from his head fuelling the fire. He must have hit the man about twenty times. He only stopped when he finally ran out of breath.

He stepped back, wheezing from the exertion, and heard a slide and a thump as the soldier collapsed to the ground behind the door to his left.

Archer's hands and feet were no longer bound. The chair he'd been tied to had been damaged at some point and a screw was jutting out of the back where the seat met the chair. Archer had sawn frantically through the tape binding his wrists. Once he'd freed his hands, he'd unwrapped his ankles and wiped his face off with his shirt, holding it there to try to stem the flow. It was useless. Blood was pouring from the wound. He felt light-headed and dizzy. There was no other way out of the room than the door, so he'd waited the other side for it to open then attacked like his life depended on it.

Which it did.

He moved around the doorway, looking down at the torturer. The guy's pistol had spilled from his hands. Scooping it up in his hands, he checked it was loaded then dropped down to his knees and checked the man's pulse.

He was dead. Archer had killed him.

He saw that the man's head and body were severely damaged from the metal doorway, his face bruised and smashed and bloody, his ribs and neck surely broken. Archer's rage had given him unprecedented strength. He'd beaten the man to death with the door.

But he didn't give the body a second glance. Stepping over the dead man, he ran through next door. He barged it open and heard a stifled scream.

Flicking on the light, he saw Nikki there alone in a white bathroom, her face a picture of terror, duct-taped to the metal chair. She then realised it was him, but her eyes remained just as wide. His face and white t-shirt were covered with blood, and with the gun in his hand he must have looked like something out of a nightmare. He saw that she was unharmed though.

He rushed forward, dropping the gun, then pulled the tape off Nikki's mouth, blood running down into his eyes and down the side of his face.

'Are you OK?' he asked quietly.

She nodded frantically, looking at his face.

'What happened to you?'

'I'm fine,' he said. 'It's just a cut. Looks worse than it is.'

'Where is he?' she asked, scared.

'He's dead. We need to get out of here. They'll be back any minute.'

As he undid her ankles, she shook her head. 'No. They won't.'

He paused and looked up at her.

'Why?'

'Because I told him where Director Cobb and his family are.'

Archer looked at her as her chin quivered. Tears brimmed in her eyes and fell down her cheeks.

'I'm sorry, Arch. He told me he'd kill you if I didn't tell him where they were. Then he put the knife to my stomach. Said he was going to cut out my ovaries and show them to me.'

'It's OK. He's gone. C'mon.'

He helped her up, wiping blood from his eyes.

'Wait,' she said, grabbing a towel from a hook beside her with her free hand. She pushed it to Archer's cut, and he held it there, trying to staunch the flow of blood. Gun in hand, he took the lead and moved out into the safe-house, keeping her behind him protectively.

The place had been abandoned. The team were gone. He could see two televisions set up on a desk, silently playing the news, the one to the right showing a fresh report of the second gunfight at the ARU's headquarters.

But he saw something else in the distance in the dark.

A series of red numbers.

Counting down.

And they were at *1:01.*

1:00.

00:59.

'Oh shit,' Archer said. He turned to Nikki. 'Stairs! Go!'

She ran forward towards the door to the stairwell. Archer went to follow her, but suddenly stopped. Nikki burst open the door to the stairwell, and turned back.

'Arch, we have to go!' she shouted.

'Wait!' he shouted.

In the silence, the room was still, the only activity the two muted televisions and the red numbers ticked down. But Archer heard something else, faint but unmistakeable.

Whimpering.

There was another door beside the bathroom, a store cupboard of some sort. He ran forward, wiping blood from his eyes and pulled it open.

A woman and a boy were in there, both bound and gagged with duct tape.

They stared at him in terror.

TWENTY SEVEN

The garden of the north London hospice covered about three acres, centred around the duck pond that provided some quiet space for the patients and their visitors. The outer fence was there both to provide privacy and a sense of security to the residents at the hospice, but also as a soft deterrent to anyone who was tempted to access the park from the outside.

The whereabouts of the English soldier had been a puzzle for the Panthers squad. They'd kept his dog tags from the night they kidnapped him, so they knew his name, but the fat CIA analyst who'd pulled the information on the others hadn't been able to come up with anything on the guy. In the car on the way here, Wulf told Flea that once they'd arrived in England, the group had scoured everything they could think of. Phonebooks, internet, everything they could access. But nothing. No-one had any idea where he was. They'd reluctantly come to the conclusion that, like the American soldier Webster, Fletcher had died in the years since. There was no way he'd still be a soldier, not without seven of his toes.

However, when Worm had tailed the two cars leaving the police station earlier, they'd led him here. And after he moved around into this garden, just before the police shut the curtains in one of the rooms, he'd seen a familiar face lying in the bed.

Corporal Fletcher.

Flea scaled the outer fence of the hospice garden with ease and had crept forward, the dark shrubbery and trees providing perfect cover. He was lying prone on his front, the Dragunov Tigr hunting rifle set up towards the building, his shoulder in the stock. The Dragunov was a Russian weapon, semi-automatic and gas-operated, and despite being bought illegally on the street was in pretty good condition. The end of the barrel was fitted with a flash suppressor, which made it a good choice for covert shooting. The rifle was effective at over 1000 metres, but Flea was less than 100 from his target. He'd made shots like these thousands of times, and could almost do it with his eyes closed. Being a perfectionist like most snipers, he would have liked to have had some practice with the rifle, zeroing the sights and getting used to the feel of the weapon, but right then he didn't have a choice. On the way here in the car, he'd loaded four spare NATO 7.62 bullets into the magazine of the weapon as extra insurance should he do the unthinkable and miss.

He had his cheek resting against the stock, his right eye looking down the scope. It was a PSO-1 Optical Sight, a modern scope which had features such as bullet-drop compensation, a rangefinder grid and also a reticule that allowed target acquisition in conditions without sufficient light. His position gave him direct sight into the room, and the crosshairs on the scope were at that moment resting on Fletcher's face. The curtains had been half shut but there was slight gap and it gave Flea ample view of his target. Through the scope, he looked at the man up close and recognised him instantly, despite how sick he looked.

He remembered helping take seven of his toes.

His eye behind the scope, the crosshairs on Fletcher's chin who was totally unaware that he was about to die, Flea smiled.

He lived for this.

As a boy, his father had been a sniper in the Albanian army, and had educated his son about the craft of sharpshooting. He told him how two men called Hiram Berdan and Robert E Lee were the first in history to set up units of designated sharpshooters in a military force, during the American Civil War. How the Germans had been the first to use specially-trained marksmen during World War One. How the Russians had taken it further and started using two man teams. How in the Vietnam War, the average amount of ammunition used for each kill with the M-16 assault rifle was over 50,000, but for their snipers it was just 1.3. How in World War Two, a Nazi sniper with sixty confirmed kills would be rewarded with a personal hunting trip with Hermann Goring. Snipers were valued and treasured like walking gold in conflicts and wars. They'd been responsible for some of the most defining moments in military and world history.

Speaking of history, Flea's own hero was a Finnish sniper named Simo Hayha. During the Second World War, this small Finnish farmer had joined his nation's army and had gone into the forests with his rifle to take on the invading Russian forces. In below freezing conditions, dressed in simple white camouflage, Hayha killed over five hundred Russian soldiers in less than a hundred days.

505, to be exact.

The Russians had sent entire task forces and counter-snipers into the regions to find and take out Hayha, but he'd killed them all. Entire squads and units of some of the best men the Red Army had to offer went out there and never came back. And the amazing thing was, Hayha did it all without using a scope on his rifle, using a simple bolt-action iron-sighted shooter instead. In Flea's eyes, he was without a doubt the greatest sniper who'd ever lived. The Russians had dubbed him *White Death*. What an honour, to have such a name bestowed on you by the enemy. Most nights Flea dreamt of the same thing happening to him.

During the war, Flea had tried his best to go after Hayha's record. He'd spent weeks out in the Kosovo plains and valleys, hunting the enemy, desperate for kills and the chance to build his own legend. He'd done pretty well, his confirmed kill-count up to 321, but that was a lifetime of work so far, not achieved in under four months like his hero. Three months before they were captured and thrown into prison, Wulf had also ordered that they start taking the enemy alive instead of shooting them. That had damaged Flea's kill-count somewhat.

Most of his targets during the conflict had been moving or shielded by cover, but this next shot was just like target practice. He kept his breathing even and saw the target lying there in the bed, fast asleep. One of the men who was responsible for murdering the only people Flea had ever loved. In the camp that night, his father had been staying with Flea's wife and two children.

All four of them had been killed.

In one smooth, gentle motion, he took the slack out of the trigger and gently squeezed all the way. The weapon kicked back and gave a muffled cough and there was a smash of glass in the window ahead. He watched through the scope and saw the target's head jerk, a white puff of feathers from the pillow behind his head joining the red blood as the round passed through his forehead and the back of his head exploded.

322.

Flea didn't hang around. He rolled to his right and found the empty shell casing, then picked up the rifle and moved back to the fence, scaling it quickly and dropping down the other side.

On the street, two cars were waiting, the five surviving members of the squad aside from Worm in each. Bird was waiting in the front car, the engine running. Flea climbed in beside him, laying the rifle on the foot-well and covering it with a blanket. He looked over at the other man and nodded.

'He's gone,' he said, in Albanian.

'Time to go get Cobb,' Bug said, from the back.

Bird took off the handbrake and swung a U-turn in the road. The car moved off into the night, Wulf and Spider following them close behind.

Across town, Porter was speeding at above sixty down the street towards the safe-house, Chalky and Fox in the car with him. Jackson's dried blood was still all over his hands, maroon in the grooves of the edges of his fingernails, the harshest of reminders of the kind of enemy they were dealing with and what awaited Archer and Nikki if they didn't get there in time. Second Team had stayed with the tech team back at the HQ, guarding their base. The building had been attacked twice in a day already and they had no idea if there would be a third attempt.

'Hurry, Port, hurry,' Chalky said, jiggling his leg anxiously.

The streets were already flashing past, and barely slowing an inch, Porter turned left, speeding down a side road. He then cut across the next road, weaving through traffic, and headed into a car park, the building ahead of them. As they arrived, the three men saw there was no sign of the white van that had brought the two hostages here.

That wasn't good.

As Porter slammed on the brake pedal and the car skidded to a halt, they saw the lobby door to the building suddenly burst open. Archer and Nikki were rushing from the building together, but with two other people, a woman and a boy. Archer was carrying the kid on his hip, sprinting as fast as he could. His face was a mask of blood, his white t-shirt covered in it. He had a gun in his hand as he, Nikki and the other woman sprinted away from the building.

'What the-', Fox started.

Behind them, there was suddenly a huge explosion. The eighth floor of the building detonated above them, fire billowing out of the windows. The group were flung to the ground, landing heavily, Archer rolling to his side as he fell to protect the boy from hitting the concrete. Up ahead, the three officers rushed out of the car and ran over towards the group, the eighth floor ablaze, smoke pouring out of every window and sliding up the building.

'Arch!' Chalky shouted, running over. His friend's face was covered with blood. 'Jesus, what happened?'

'I'm fine,' he said, kneeling and wiping his eyes with his t-shirt. He turned to the boy. 'Are you OK?'

The boy started crying. Behind him, Nikki removed a set of binds from the other woman's hands and the moment they were free the woman rushed forward and hugged her boy, crying herself.

Chalky helped Archer to his feet, whilst Fox checked Nikki.

'Are you OK?' Fox asked, concerned, checking her.

'I'm OK,' she said, coughing, and he gently helped her stand.

‘Who are you?’ Porter asked the woman they didn’t recognise.

‘Kate Adams,’ she said through her tears.

‘Are you OK?’

The woman didn’t respond. She just hugged her boy close. Porter turned to Archer.

'Where are the soldiers?' he asked, as the shrill fire alarms on the building behind them started to sound, echoing in the London night.

'They're gone. They know where Cobb is,' Archer said loudly.

Fox and Nikki had joined them as Chalky went over to try and comfort the woman and boy. After hearing what Archer had said, Fox swore.

'So let's call ahead and warn him,' he said.

Porter was already doing so, but turned to him, his mobile phone in his hands.

‘I can't get through. There’s no signal his end,' he shouted.

'So let's go!' Fox said. 'We need to take a shortcut or beat them there.'

'We don't have time! They’re already way ahead of us,' Porter said.

‘What about these two?’ Nikki said, pointing at the distraught woman and boy.

Porter thought for a second.

‘Right, everyone in the car. It’s going to be a squeeze.’

Chalky and Fox guided the woman and boy to the car while Porter tried calling Cobb again.

'I still can't get through,’ he said, climbing into the driver’s seat and firing the engine.

'So what can we do?' Nikki asked, sitting on Chalky’s lap in the back seat and pulling the door shut. 'We have to do something. They'll kill him and his whole family!'

'Wait,' Archer said, from the front passenger seat.

The group looked at him.

'Go back to the station.’

'What?' Porter said, firing the engine. 'Why? We need to get over there, Arch.’

‘I know how we can get there ahead of them.’

*

Twenty minutes later, the streets of London morphing into countryside and fields shrouded by nightfall, the Black Panthers were making good time as they headed for Cobb's safe-house. They couldn’t miss it. Bug had found it on the map, isolated, a significant estate, no neighbours nearby or anyone to hear Cobb scream.

The men were in two cars, all of them now dressed in black combat fatigues, silenced black sub-machine guns in their hands, magazines in the chambers, their faces grim. In the front passenger seat of the front car, Wulf shot his cuff, then lifted his mobile phone from his pocket and redialled Worm's number, keeping his sub-machine gun in his hand.

It rang through.

No response.

'Damn,' he said, in Albanian.

'What is it, sir?' Spider asked, behind the wheel.

'Worm isn't picking up the phone.'

'Maybe it's the signal. Pity. He's going to miss out.'

Wulf nodded.

'Drive faster.'

Spider put his foot down and the car roared on through the winding country lanes, heading closer and closer to Cobb and his family twelve miles away.

Who had no idea they were coming.

TWENTY EIGHT

An hour's drive south of London, Hawkings Hall had been in Eleanor Cobb's family for almost seven hundred years. The property was stunning, surrounded by 200 acres of woodland and forestry, the main Hall itself built just at the end of the 14th Century. The building had been developed and added to over the years, and it had been passed down through the family from generation to generation.

The Hall had twelve bedrooms, six bathrooms and three separate floors, but the pride of the house was a magnificent drawing room. With its large fireplace, antique furniture and beautiful mahogany walls hung with both family portraits and expensive paintings, the room was the centrepiece of the home, the jewel in the crown. The Hall had been featured in many magazines and newspapers over the years as one of the most famous of its type in the country, and given that Eleanor Cobb was an only child with no living male relatives, the entire property would one day be inherited by her and then on her death, passed on to her eldest son.

Upstairs, her husband had just finished putting his two boys to bed in two of the bedrooms. The boys were twelve and nine, and loved the times they were able to stay with their grandparents at this house. On the way here their father had told them nothing of the seriousness of the situation, merely saying he'd been granted an extra few days holiday and that he'd decided they should all go to stay at Granny and Grandpa's house whilst they were abroad.

But downstairs, out of sight of the two boys, Cobb's smile had faded.

He'd methodically checked every possible entrance to the house to make sure they were all secure, ensuring every door and window was locked, a Glock 17 pistol from the ARU gun-cage gripped in his right hand. His wife had wanted to draw the curtains on all the windows but Cobb had refused. Not yet. If anyone was coming, he wanted to see who they were well in advance, friend or foe. It was a full moon tonight and it was low in the sky, which, despite some occasional cloud cover, was already lighting up the gardens and outer park of the estate like a giant silver floodlight. Given the Hall's position as the nucleus of the estate, Cobb wanted a heads up if anyone approached the house.

Having just checked in the long kitchen and one of the back doors, he walked down the main corridor and moved into the drawing room. He found his wife standing there quietly, looking out of one of the windows, her arms folded. He also saw that rain had just started to fall gently outside, drops of water tapping against the glass, sounding like someone drumming their fingers on a table-top, each droplet clinging to the window then sliding down the pane. Cobb nodded wryly. It looked like their run of good weather was over. This was April in the UK, after all.

Making sure the safety catch on the Glock was on, he tucked it into the back of his waistband, and came up behind her, sliding his arms around her waist protectively, looking out into the darkening garden, still well lit by the moonlight despite the shower of rain.

He glanced at a clock across the room. It had just gone *9:31 pm.*

'All done,' he said.

She nodded gently. The two of them stood still, in silence, watching the drops starting to rap against the pane.

'Everything OK?' he asked her.

She sighed, and he knew before she answered that everything wasn't.

'They're out there, somewhere, right now, looking for you,' she said, quietly.

'My men will find them,' he said. 'They don't know about this place.'

There was a pause. Behind her, he looked out across the lawns and into the trees beyond.

'When will it be over?' she asked.

'When we arrest them. We already have one of them at the station.'

'These men won't just roll over and let you put the cuffs on, Tim. You said one of them killed himself before you could take him. And another committed suicide after he failed.'

'Then they'll all die. That's how it will end.'

'But who's going to stop them?'

A long silence followed. She was right. They'd never dealt with men like this before, highly-trained killers. His men were taught to arrest and question, to preserve life whenever possible, not shoot to kill and ask questions later. Whatever happened, this was going to end with more people dying.

Possibly him.

His wife went to speak again, but she stopped.

'What?' Cobb asked her, feeling her tense up in his arms. 'What is it?'

She turned to him and frowned.

'Listen.'

Cobb listened. All he heard was the pattering of the rain against the window.

But then, he heard a faint sound. It was a thumping, or a whining, a mix of both, faint amongst the rainfall but definitely audible.

He listened closer, as the noise grew stronger.

Then Cobb looked at his wife, her eyes wide with fear.

'Get the boys,' he said.

A hundred yards above them, Fox flew the ARU helicopter over the main Hall then started to bring it down on the south-side of the house, the opposite side from where the Panthers would surely arrive on the only road in and out of the estate. Beside him, Porter, Chalky and Archer had all finished adjusting their throat mics and tac gear on the journey, reloading their weapons, and the three officers waited anxiously for the helicopter to land, eager to get on the ground.

The house was still, and there was no sign of any vehicles. It looked as if they'd beaten the Panthers here. During the flight, Chalky had gone to work on the wound on Archer's head with a first-aid kit that the helicopter carried. Given the unpredictable movement of the vessel and Chalky not being known for his medical skills, Archer now sported a bandage wrapped three times around his head in a haphazard fashion, the bleeding stopped by gauze but the wound still throbbing and painful.

The helicopter touched down on the wet grass and before Fox could switch off the engine his three team-mates were already out of the doors, ducking low and running across the green lawn towards the house through the rain. Fox switched off the equipment and grabbing his MP5 from the foot-well, he secured the door behind him and sprinted across the soaked grass after the others, the rotors of the helicopter slowly coming to a halt behind him.

At a window, Cobb had the Glock in his hands but relaxed as he saw the black Unit helicopter touch down; he moved down the corridor to let his men in. He unlocked the door, pulling it open, and the men ran inside, fully armed, Fox catching up and joining them. The rain was starting to fall harder now and the men's wet boots slapped on the stone floor as they ran into the old house.

'What the hell’s going on?' Cobb asked, as Fox shut and locked the door behind him quickly. 'You're meant to be back at the station.'

‘They’re coming for you, sir,’ Porter said quickly. ‘They know you’re here.’

‘What?’ Cobb said.

‘We need to secure the house.’

Cobb looked at them for a moment as realisation dawned, then nodded.

‘This way.’

He led the trio into the Drawing Room to their left. Cobb’s wife was standing waiting there with the two sleepy boys, looking worried.

‘What’s happening, Dad?’ the eldest boy asked, seeing the tension on his father’s face.

‘Is there a cellar?’ Fox asked. 'We need to get you all out of sight.'

‘Yes,' Cobb's wife said. 'But the-'

Before she could finish the sentence, all the lights went off.

The house was plunged into darkness, the only light from the moon shining in through the open windows.

Both Chalky and Fox swore simultaneously, their MP5s in their hands.

‘It’s OK,’ Cobb’s wife said. ‘The power has been cutting in and out recently. Old houses. Nothing to be worried about.’

'No,' Chalky said quietly. 'They're here.'

He was right.

The Black Panthers were already in the house.

Rather than use the main drive and alert whoever was inside that they were coming, Spider and Bird had turned left once inside the gate and parked a hundred yards from the house in the woods, hiding the vehicles amongst the trees. The team had collected their kit and moved on to their target in the gathering darkness, the same routine they'd carried out so many times in the past. None of them spoke, but all of them felt that same thrill that they had all those years ago, the squad out in the field again, hunting an enemy.

They'd stalked their way around the left side of the estate in the shadows, using the shrubbery as cover. Second in the line behind Bird, who was on point, Wulf saw that the curtains to the Hall had been left open and some lights were on. In the moonlight, he could make out fresh tyre tracks on the driveway outside, slowly being washed away by the rain.

Cobb was here.

Under normal circumstances, the team would have liked to have infiltrated from above, through a roof light, but given how wet and slippery the walls were, scaling was impossible. They would have to go in from the ground. Start one side and sweep their way along.

The lock on the west door was old and big and easily picked by Bug, but as he worked on it, they'd heard a helicopter approaching. Taking cover in the shadows, they'd seen the chopper arrive and fly over the house, *ARU* printed on the side. Looking up at the vessel in the rain, Wulf silently cursed the fact he didn't have an RPG. He could have taken the chopper out there and then. But it seemed some of these policemen couldn't keep away.

They hadn't learnt their lesson from the police station.

Once Bug got the door open and the men moved inside the house, after a brief search Bird had located the big fuse-box in the cellar. He pulled the main switch and the entire Hall plunged into darkness. On cue, the men pulled down the visors of their night-vision goggles, their view of the house now tinged with green but clear as crystal through the lenses. They'd also discarded the big and brash AK-47s for quieter weapons.

Each man had a silenced MP5 SD3, the same weapon as the police officers, only with an integrated suppressor on the end of each to hide muzzle flash effectively and make the weapon ideal for night-time operations. Although relatively heavy, weighing in at seven pounds alone without ammunition, the silenced sub-machine guns each held a 30-round magazine full of polished 9mm Parabellum bullets, two more clips on each man's fatigues. The weapons guy down at the Docklands had outdone himself.

Considering the weapons were illegal in the UK after a Firearms act banning all sub-machine guns, six of the MP5 SD3s with sufficient ammunition for four thousand pounds had been a very good deal. Given each man's training and experience, in the darkness the Panthers were damn good.

But with the night-vision goggles and such high-quality weapons, they were close to invincible.

Bird climbed the stairs from the cellar to join the others, pulling the door shut gently behind him. Wulf turned to his men, motioning a sequence of silent orders with his hands. They acknowledged and separated, the three of them moving off in separate directions into the dark and silent Hall, their faces smeared with dark camo paint, dressed in black, brutal silenced sub-machine guns in their shoulders.

Alone, Wulf stood still for a moment, his eyes closed, tuning his senses, listening.

Then he began to creep along the lower corridor, his dark boots printing mud on the floor.

He felt his heart-rate rise with anticipation. Cobb was here somewhere, the last one of the group who had haunted his dreams every night for fifteen years in that prison. The men who'd murdered his family, who had taken everything he'd ever loved from him. Ten of them were now gone. And with this last execution, revenge and justice would be complete.

He could die fulfilled and at peace.

Wulf moved through an open door silently and entered a long and quiet kitchen, the MP5 SD3 locked into his shoulder, a huge dark figure, an apparition, something out of a nightmare. Pots and pans hung from hooks along a long steel sink and table, gleaming silver in the fading moonlight from the windows and reflecting a distortion of the large black figure. He figured Cobb would be armed and his family may be here with him, but that would only sweeten the deal. Wulf would take his family just as he took his. An eye for an eye. A family for a family. Blood for blood.

He felt his anticipation and excitement rise, but took a deep breath, gently loosening his grip on his silenced MP5.

The Hall was silent.

But it wasn't empty.

Cobb was here somewhere.

Wulf had been waiting fifteen years for this night.

With the MP5 SD3 as steady as a rock in his shoulder and his vision as clear as day through the goggles, the Albanian Special Forces commander moved off into the dark house.

TWENTY NINE

In the drawing room, Fox had remained with Cobb and his family, his MP5 clutched in his hands. The power-cut meant they didn't have time to get to the cellar, the access to which was the other side of the house. Cobb had whispered that the fuse box was down there, so once the power went out they knew the Panthers would be coming in from that side. Porter and Chalky had left them in the Drawing Room, moving off into the large dark Hall, playing the deadliest possible game of hide and seek.

Huddled behind a chaise-longue, Cobb's wife had her hands over her two boys' mouths, who were crouched shivering in their pyjamas, terrified. Fox knelt in front of the chaise-longue protectively, his MP5 locked and loaded, Jackson's blood still on his overalls and hands.

Cobb stood beside him with the Glock, both men staring at the two separate doors that led into the room.

The Hall beyond was eerily silent. The only sound they could hear was the rain tapping against the glass.

They waited, knowing there were other men in the house, hunting them, coming to kill them.

Outside the main door, there was a sudden noise. Very faint, but audible. There was a muffled whimper from one of the boys behind them in response.

Fox looked at Cobb, who nodded. The ARU officer rose and crept towards the door slowly, his MP5 in his shoulder.

To his left, the curtains were open.

The moonlight illuminated the room with its cold light, breaking through the grey clouds as the falling rain continued to drum against the windows.

Suddenly, there was a smash, thud and a tinkle of glass.

Fox fell to the floor, as the two boys gave muffled yelps under their mother's palms.

Cobb dropped down too, his eyes raking the windows. Fox had dropped his MP5 and was clutching his leg, blood already pooling on the floor around him, a bullet deep in his left thigh.

Cobb belly-crawled along the floor to the wounded officer, his pistol in his hand. Fox's eyes were wide with shock and pain. Cobb could feel the warm blood on his stomach as he lay by the man. He pulled off his tie and wrapped a tight tourniquet around Fox's leg as best he could.

Then he grabbed his officer's hand and dragged him back across the ground, making sure to stay low and out of view of the rifleman outside who had taken the shot.

Upstairs, Spider was creeping along the corridor, his footfalls silent on the carpeted floor. He'd just cleared two bedrooms, one by one, moving inside each, ready to shoot anyone inside, man, woman or child. He knew Cobb's family were here, but he would have no hesitation killing them too.

However, the two beds had been empty. The sheets were disturbed however, recently used, the covers thrown back, the pillow warm and imprinted with someone's head.

They were here.

Somewhere.

He stalked on. Glancing out of a window to his left, he saw the dark shape of the helicopter on the lawn. There were policemen here somewhere too. No matter. They were used to street arrests and broad daylight. The dark and the night were the Panthers' world. They would be irritations, only. With his night-vision goggles and his silenced MP5, his strength back after all those years in the prison, Spider felt invincible. Many men had tried to kill him before. None had succeeded. And tonight would be no different. English police officers were no match for him and the rest of the Panthers.

The door to the next room was ajar and Spider pushed it back gently with his toe, moving inside, checking left and right.

This room was different from the other two bedrooms. It had been rearranged, a cluster of chairs, stands and a desk gathered in the centre of the room away from the walls. The curtains were drawn but as he slowly checked out the room through his goggles he could see there were white sheets and blankets laid around the place, some cans of paint on the floor beside rollers and brushes, a paint-stained radio resting on a brown desk, plugged into a small generator on the ground. He saw that the room was being redecorated.

Beside the paint cans and roller trays, he could make out the metallic sheen of some black floodlights, the reflector behind the dark bulbs silver and covered by long lens caps.

The painters weren't here. The place was quiet and still, the only sound the constant drumming of raindrops on the shielded windows.

He saw a closed door across the room and stepped forward softly towards it.

Then he heard a *click*.

Suddenly, the room was filled with blinding light. It seared into his retinas through the goggles, and he fell back, tearing them off, his eyes burning with pain.

Across the room, Chalky took his hand off the generator button for the lights. He moved fast round from behind the desk and shot the big soldier through the head.

The man dropped like a marionette with the strings sliced, his weapon clattering to the floor, blood and bits of skull sprayed all over the floor, splinters flying from the wall as the bullet buried itself in the old wood behind him as it exited the back of his head.

The gunshot echoed around the house, faded and then was gone.

Chalky clicked the switch on the generator, the lights turned off again, and he waited, aiming at the far doorway, willing another of the Panthers to walk inside into his crosshairs.

But no-one came.

He moved forward silently, keeping his weapon trained on the doorway, then stepped to the side, pushing the door shut with the softest of clicks. He looked down at the dead soldier at his feet.

Kneeling by the body, Chalky pushed the pressel on his uniform, the only other sound the constant rain hitting the window behind him.

'This is Chalk,' he whispered. *'One down.'*

Ripping the night goggles from the man's head, he quickly wiped off the blood and brains that were on the back leather strap.

Then he pulled them over his own eyes, and raising his weapon, his vision now clear as if it was daylight, he moved on into the dark mansion.

A hundred and sixty yards outside the front of the house, Flea lay motionless on the earth, his Dragunov rifle in his shoulder, his breathing long and slow and smooth.

When they'd arrived, pulling off the main road and parking in the forestry, the rest of the team had headed off to the house whilst Flea moved right, taking up a position facing the giant Hall just beyond the main lawn.

The rain was falling harder now, drenching him, droplets of water flicking onto the scope. But he remained still and focused. He was pissed at himself that he'd snatched at the shot of the cop in the main room, but then again he was unfamiliar with this rifle and the guy had moved just as he fired. He'd only hit the man in the thigh.

However, hopefully he may have hit an artery, or even if he hadn't, the guy would need urgent medical attention or he would bleed to death there inside the house.

Then he would be another kill to Flea's name. 323. Another step closer to Hayha's record.

He'd also just heard a faint gunshot from somewhere inside the house. Good. It meant another of the policemen would be dead. It was inconceivable to him that any of them could kill one of the Panthers. They were cops, not soldiers. They were hopelessly out of their league, and had sealed their own fates by coming here to defend Cobb when they should have left him to die.

At that moment, through one of the large ground floor windows, he saw another of the officers from the police unit creeping along a corridor on the lower level. He moved ahead, tracing the man's path, predicting where he would move, leading the target.

He had a feeling for the rifle now, and adjusted his aim accordingly.

This time he wouldn't miss.

He lay as still as if he was dead, his pupil looking down the scope, ignoring the heavy rain obscuring the moonlight and falling on him from above.

He saw the man had stripes on the shoulder of his uniform.

A sergeant.

Flea smiled as the reticule moved just ahead of the man.

And his finger tightened on the trigger.

Moving silently down the main corridor, Porter glanced out of the window to his right, looking out into the dark and wet night. He kept walking slowly, checking behind him, making his way to the drawing room.

The door was slightly open.

Taking a deep breath, he ducked in, then froze.

The big man they'd held captive, Wulf, was in there, looking straight at him. He was wearing a set of night-vision goggles, the visor pushed up, his face smeared black.

And he had a gun to Cobb's head. Beside him, a smaller man with scarring all over the side of his face and neck had a silenced MP5 against the temple of Cobb's wife, the two kids standing beside them, terrified and helpless. He saw Fox lying on the ground, unconscious, bleeding from a wound to his leg, blood all over the floor. Porter knew from the amount of blood on the ground that he'd need medical attention soon if he was going to survive.

'Drop your weapon,' Wulf said, in English, only the whites of his eyes visible to Porter. 'Or they die.'

'If I drop it, they'll die anyway,' Porter said, his MP5 trained on the man.

'You don't have a choice. You're alone. No-one is coming to help you.'

'Yes, they are,' another voice said, from the left.

Porter glanced to his left and saw Chalky had entered the room, his MP5 aimed at the two men. He had a pair of night-vision goggles over his head which he ripped off with his left hand and tossed across the room to the carpet.

'I just killed your friend,' Chalky said. 'So much for the Black Panthers. You guys are like pussies.'

They stood there, in a stand-off. Through the sights of his MP5, Porter saw Wulf's eyes narrow at the insult. Chalky moved and Wulf and the other soldier tensed, but all he did was move to his right, towards Porter, keeping his hair-trigger on the smaller man beside Wulf.

'If you kill them, I'll kill you,' Chalky said, speaking along the stock of his MP5.

'So what. We have nothing left to live for. Our work here is almost complete.'

Pause.

'Let him go. He didn't know what those men did until today.'

‘But he saved them,’ Wulf said, pushing the gun harder into Cobb’s temple.

He pulled back the hammer.

‘Don’t do it,’ Chalky said, his MP5 tight, the trigger aimed at Wulf’s eye. 'Or you die.'

Wulf didn’t respond.

He smiled, victory in his eyes.

And Chalky felt something cold and metallic touch his neck.

‘Drop it,’ a voice said.

Chalky glanced over at Porter, defeat in his eyes.

'Drop the guns,' the voice said again.

Porter looked at Chalky. They were beaten.

And together, the two men dropped their MP5s, the sub-machine guns clattering to the carpet, as a third Panther held a pistol to Chalky’s neck.

THIRTY

Across the room, Wulf smiled. Bird had got the jump on the cocky cop. Reaching to the cop's thigh, keeping the muzzle of his pistol jammed in the kid's neck, Bird pulled out what looked like a Glock pistol from a holster and tossed it to the rug. He then pushed the cop over towards the group huddled by the far wall.

Wulf released Cobb and moved forward, keeping his sub-machine gun on the other officer, the sergeant. He removed the man's Glock from his thigh holster, then suddenly swept forward and hit him in the gut. The guy wasn't expecting it and it winded him, bending him double and dropping him to the ground in the blood beside his unconscious fellow officer.

'Against the wall. All of you,' Wulf ordered, pointing his weapon at the officer on the floor.

The two men had no choice. As Bug released the woman and moved forward to join Wulf and Bird, the entire group ended up in a line against the wall. The officers ended up side-by-side with Cobb and his family, his wife hugging her boys close protectively.

Wulf holstered his pistol and swung his sub-machine gun around from a strap over his shoulder. The three soldiers had taken up staggered positions in front of them, their MP5 SD3s in their hands, and all three had lifted the visors on their night-vision goggles.

The trio of soldiers stood there for a moment just staring at them, their dark faces emphasising the whites of their hate-filled eyes.

Wulf's burned into Cobb and the two men made eye contact.

'This is for my family,' he said, looking into defenceless man's eyes. 'You son of a bitch.'

'Please, don't do this,' Cobb's wife said, crying, holding her two boys tight.

'You should have stayed away from here,' Wulf said to her. He pointed at Cobb. 'We would have let you all live apart from him. But you didn't. You came into our world.'

He raised his weapon to his shoulder, aimed at Cobb's chin.

On cue, the other two men did the same.

'And here, heroes don't exist.'

But before Wulf shot, he noticed something. The two police officers in the line-up didn't look worried.

Quite the opposite.

The smaller one who claimed he'd killed Spider was actually smiling.

Wulf lowered his MP5 SD3 a hair, looking at the man, genuinely baffled.

'Something funny?' he asked.

The man grinned at him. 'Yes.'

'You seem very calm for a man who is about to die,' Wulf said.

The man nodded.
'So do you.'

What came next happened in a flash. It happened so fast it took everyone but Porter and Chalky by surprise.

There was a smash of glass and a thump and the small Panther with scarring on his face fell back, shot in the head. A second later, the same happened to the second Panther, the one in the middle. He fell back, shot in the head, dropping to the ground.

Wulf froze for a millisecond in disbelief. Then he turned and looked out of the long window of the room to his right, human instinct, trying to locate the danger.

And a hundred and sixty yards across the lawn, Archer shot him between the eyes with the PSG1A1 sniper rifle.

Just after he pulled the trigger, Archer watched the bullet smash through the glass window and hit the huge soldier right on target. There was a burst of red behind him as the rear of his head exploded, and he dropped out of sight, an instant kill, one the SAS instructors would have approved of. Archer kept his eye to the scope of the rifle for a moment longer, watching Cobb gather his family into a frantic and strong hug, Porter and Chalky dropping to the ground and tending to Fox, who was lying there, hopefully still alive.

Beside him, out there in the rain, the Black Panther sniper was dead.

When they'd got back to the ARU's headquarters earlier, the team had rushed off in different directions. Nikki had taken Kate Adams and her boy inside, the three of them severely shaken up but safe. Fox had raced up to the roof to fire up the chopper with Porter and Chalky, as Archer ran down the damaged corridor of the lower level, rushing past clean-up crews and stepping on spent cartridges and bloodstains. Officers from Second Team saw him and were asking if he was OK, seeing the blood on his face and t-shirt, but he didn't have time to stop and explain.

He'd snatched a new tac vest from the locker room, replacing the one he'd had taken off him by the Panthers and destroyed in the explosion. He'd gone to the gun cage and taken an empty MP5, then reached for a magazine. But he'd stopped. He'd found himself staring at the two PSG1A1 rifles. He'd placed the MP5 back on the rack, grabbed the PSG1A1 after checking the serial number and making sure it was the weapon he'd fired earlier in the day, then took three clips of ammunition and ran to the roof, blinking blood out of his eyes.

Once the Eurocopter had touched down on the lawn and the other three officers had run to the house, Archer had taken off for the undergrowth on the east side of the Hall. He saw that all the curtains were still open and the lights were on. It didn't seem like the Panthers were here yet.

But a few moments later he'd watched as all the lights went out.

He was wrong.

They were already here.

As he moved around the outside of the manor in the darkness, he'd suddenly seen and heard the Black Panther sniper take the first shot from the shadows. He'd seen Fox go down in the main room from his viewpoint in the shadows. Although he was just under a hundred yards away and the undergrowth was dark, the muzzle flash from the rifle had told Archer exactly where the man was.

Archer had flanked the sniper, the rainfall dulling the sounds of his footsteps and once he'd got around the man's shooting position and moved forward, he'd found the man lying there on the ground, focused and unsuspecting. He was prone and in close to his own rifle, concentrating on his target and not on what was behind him. The soldier hadn't bothered with cover or a ghillie suit and he was just lying there on the grass and earth five feet from Archer, soaked by the rain.

The hunter became the hunted.

His face and bandage around his head camouflaged and smeared with mud, Archer had lowered the PSG-1A1 and crept up behind the man. He'd taken a Glock from the gun-cage and tucked it into his thigh holster earlier, but he didn't want to use it and alert anyone in the house. But Archer felt a coldness settle over him. His head throbbing, the front of his fatigues and t-shirt stained with blood, he was still enraged by the torture from earlier and watching Fox get hit. He wasn't going to read this man his rights.

This sniper was about to die.

The soldier had started as Archer started choking him. He tried everything to break his hold, bucking and thrashing. Archer knelt on the man's back and pushed his face down into the mud, his hand on the back of the man's head like a clamp, depriving him of any oxygen, ramming him down with considerable force, his fingers spread over the damp black hair on the back of the guy's head. The man had fought and gargled as water and mud filled his nose and mouth, but Archer had kept him down, keeping the pressure on like he was trying to close a packed suitcase. Within thirty seconds of thrashing, the sniper had fallen unconscious as oxygen to his brain ran out and Archer continued to hold his face down until he died.

Once he released the man's head and checked that there was no pulse, Archer had pushed the sniper's rifle into the undergrowth and rolled the dead body out of the way. Moving back and retrieving the PSGA1, he'd set up in the exact same position where the sniper had been lying with his own rifle.

He'd looked down the scope and seen the hole in the main room window from where Fox had taken the bullet. Archer had fired this rifle earlier that day and already knew it was zeroed, but he’d had to wait and take long slow deep breaths, willing himself to calm down, the crosshairs of the scope dancing around all over the place as the rifle responded to his adrenaline-spiked heart rate. Killing a man with your bare hands wasn’t the best thing to do before sharp-shooting, but he willed himself to calm down, using the breathing exercises he'd memorised, long and slow, one after the other.

While he was steadying himself, he’d watched the entire situation in the living room unfold. He’d seen Porter and Chalky enter, just after the two Panthers. When the soldiers had entered, Archer had been on the verge of firing, the crosshairs still rhythmically thumping off target by his heart-rate, but Porter’s arrival had seen the two men forced to turn and put their weapons on Cobb and his wife to cover themselves and get Porter and Chalky to drop their weapons.

He’d watched helplessly as the third Panther had entered behind Chalky. For a horrible moment, he thought the guy was going to pull the trigger straight away, but they’d disarmed Chalky and Porter instead and pushed them across the room to join Cobb and his helpless, defenceless family. Watched them get blindsided and disarmed. He saw the last three Panthers take up staggered positions, facing Porter, Chalky, Cobb and his family, three sub-machine guns in their hands. The crosshairs of the scope were no longer jumping around. Archer's breathing was smooth. His view down the scope was still.

Aiming at the smallest of the three Panthers, Archer had gently taken his left hand and pushed the pressel on his tac vest, looking down the scope into the room. The radios had a radius of seven miles transmission, so his voice spoke into the earpieces in Porter and Chalky's earpieces like he was right there in the room with them.

'I'm right here,' he'd whispered. *'The moment I shoot, go for your weapons.'*

The way that everyone was positioned couldn't have been better. The three soldiers were stood there like targets on the range. All that practice and time came down to this.

He'd taken aim on the smallest soldier, the one to the left and put the crosshairs on the side of his head. He'd emptied all the air from his lungs, just as he saw Wulf lower his weapon slightly and say something to Chalky.

And he squeezed the trigger.

The moment after he fired, he'd already moved onto the man in the middle. He fired again, calm, just like range practice and hit him in the head too.

As he swept the rifle to the third man, Wulf, he'd seen the giant soldier turn front on and look straight at him. His face was smeared black with camo paint, but Archer had seen the surprise in his eyes. He'd centred the scope on the bridge of the man's nose.

And he'd fired.

He'd snatched the second shot slightly. But they were three shots, three headshots.

Three kills.

He reckoned Chalk owed him another twenty quid.

Looking down the scope, he saw Chalky rise and reappear and motioned at him through the windows to come over fast. Climbing up in the muddy earth, Archer scooped up both the PSGA1 and the Panther's rifle and ran towards the house through the rain.

Behind him, the dead sniper lay there on the sodden earth on his back, looking sightlessly up at the dark sky, raindrops falling onto his face and body.

He and his team-mates had set out to murder ten men today.

They'd taken out nine.

But all the Black Panthers were now dead.

And Cobb and his family were safe.

THIRTY ONE

Six weeks later, on a bright and sunny May morning, Archer stepped out from a black taxi outside the Armed Response Unit's headquarters. Dressed in a simple white-t-shirt and blue jeans, his blond hair hung down over a white rectangular plaster on the upper left of his forehead, the strap of a black holdall bag looped over his shoulder. He paid the fare and thanked the driver, then turned and looked up at the newly refurbished building in front of him as the taxi moved off towards the exit behind him. From where he was standing, it looked like all the repair work was almost complete.

Since that day of chaos, funerals for all ten men who had died that day had taken place on both sides of the Atlantic. The entire Unit had gone to Clark's service at a church not far away, and Cobb had flown to Virginia the next morning to attend the service for Ryan Jackson. Porter went with him and insisted on paying out of his own pocket for the flight. Jackson had died in the line of duty, so there was an anonymous small star now on the wall for him inside the CIA's headquarters. Porter had told the rest of the team of Jackson's revelation as he died, that he was Jason Carver's cousin and of the immense guilt he'd felt at what his cousin had done. It explained his behaviour and the look on his face Archer had noticed when Fletcher had told them what happened that night. As he lay dying, apparently he'd told Porter and Fox that he'd spent his whole life trying to make up for what his cousin did that night in Kosovo.

The star on the wall inside the CIA's headquarters was forever proof that he had.

The medical team who had arrived at Hawkings Hall that night were surprised and somewhat taken aback to find a critically wounded police officer and five dead bodies of anonymous men all covered in strange and foreign tattoos, dotted around the property. Four had been shot in the head, and one had been suffocated outside in the mud. They removed the bodies from the site under Cobb's orders, without asking too many questions, and the corpses were all disposed of, no record of their existence or any of the events that had happened that night finding its way onto any official report. Fox was rushed to the hospital by helicopter, the medical team already working on him on the way there. Later that night, news came in that he was going to be OK. The bullet had missed his femoral artery by a hair. If it had hit, he would have bled to death right there and then.

Eleanor Cobb's parents had returned to their family home from their holiday in Verona to find the floors freshly cleaned and some new panes of glass in the drawing room windows as well as some new mahogany panels on the walls both down and upstairs. They thanked her for the surprise maintenance, and even though her father sensed something else was afoot he chose not to pry or ask questions. The two boys were also recovering well from the ordeal. Rather than be traumatised, the youngest was already telling Cobb that he wanted to apply for his father's police unit when he was eighteen.

Kate Adams was coming to terms with everything that she and her boy had endured, including the death of her husband which she hadn't been aware of until someone broke it to her gently at the ARU's headquarters. She was a tough woman, made of similar mettle as that of her late husband, but the boy was still young, only six, and it was going to take a long time for him to recover, hopefully without any long-term damage. Nevertheless the two of them were still alive. On a day where countless innocent people had died, that was the most important thing.

Pulling open the front door, Archer walked into the ARU's headquarters and nodded to the new officer on the front desk, a man he didn't know. He signed the form, showed his ID and passed through the barrier as it buzzed. He walked down the repaired corridor all the way to the locker room on the right. Walking inside and swinging a bag from over his shoulder, Archer opened his locker and took out a couple of spare t-shirts, some spare trousers and some other items, tucking them into the bag.

He turned and took a good look at the room. He nodded, then walked out, heading along the corridor and out the door, turning right and heading up to the second floor.

The ARU's headquarters had been the victim of two separate gunfights in that twenty four hour period, and much of the building had been damaged by the rounds. Despite the cost, Cobb had been given the go ahead from the top to revamp the entire building. Maintenance crews had started work the following day, repairing and reinforcing the downstairs of the building, with a separate team coming in and replacing the glass of Cobb's office with fresh, equally bulletproof panes. A paint team had recoated the walls, a floor team re-carpeting the rooms, removing any outward signs that the day of terror had ever happened.

Arriving at the tech team's centre, Archer saw them working away, fingers tapping on keys, Nikki with her back to him taking charge of them all. She'd recovered well from that day, both physically and mentally, and they were all proud of her. It had even seemed to have made her more determined in her work, and they'd all noticed she was attacking each day with a renewed vigour. Looking at her, Archer guessed the saying was true.

Whatever doesn't kill you definitely makes you stronger.

He turned right and headed for the door to Cobb's office. The glass was looking good as new, and through the crystal-clear panes he saw his boss sitting there behind his desk, sipping on a cup of coffee. Archer knocked on the door and Cobb nodded. The young officer entered, closing the door behind him.

'Morning, sir.'

'Morning. How's the face?'

'It'll be OK. I just came from the doctor. He said it'll heal up well. Only a faint scar under my hairline, which my hair should cover anyway.'

'Good.'

Archer grinned. 'He asked me the cause of injury and I told him *torture*. Don't think he knew if I was joking or not.'

Cobb smiled.

There was a pause.

Archer stood there, his holdall in his hand. Cobb took a drink of coffee and looked at him.

'So this is it then,' he said.

Archer nodded.

'Yes, sir. I guess so.'

'You're sure this is what you want?'

'Yes, sir. I'm sure.'

There was a pause. Cobb saw the look on Archer's face.

'Don't feel bad. I understand. Truth be told, I've seen it on your face ever since you got back last summer. You've got itchy feet.'

'It's not this place,' Archer explained. 'I love it here, sir. I love the team, everyone here. Being under your leadership. But I'm half American. I can't deny that. That's my home too. I want to work there whilst I'm still young. I have to. Right now feels like the right time.'

Pause.

Cobb nodded.

'You know that I'll always have a spot for you here, no matter what,' his boss said. 'All you need to do is pick up the phone. I mean it. Any time of day, month or year. You've earned that with everything you've done, everything you did for me and my family and the rest of the men.'

He nodded.

'I knew the moment you walked in for interview during selection that you were special. And you've outdone every expectation I ever had for you. You've done some amazing work here, Sam. I've watched you grow up, literally, in front of my eyes these past two years.'

'Thank you, sir.'

'Are you sure I can't convince you to stay?'

Archer smiled. 'I'll be back someday. If you'll take me, of course.'

'You know I will. I look forward to it.'

Pause. Archer stood there, his bag in his hand, ready to go.

'So where next?' Cobb asked.

Archer smiled. 'Honestly?'

'As always.'

'I was thinking New York City. I was thinking the NYPD.'

'That sounds perfect. I know some people over there. I'll provide my recommendation and see if we can get things moving for you. You'll have to retrain of course, but that should be a breeze for you.'

'Yes, sir. Thank you.'

There was a pause. Then Cobb rose from his chair and walked round his desk and offered his hand. Archer shook it.

'Good luck, Arch.'

Archer nodded. Then he turned and walked out of the freshly repaired office.

He walked into the Briefing Room and saw his team-mates there, all of them save for Fox and Chalky. He said goodbye to them all one by one, embracing and shaking hands, then turned and headed downstairs to the exit. By the stairs, he saw Nikki was waiting for him. He walked forward and stood there in front of her, both of them looking at each other silently. Then Nikki moved forward and hugged him.

'Thank you,' she said, quietly, into his ear.

After a few moments they parted and she wiped tears from her eyes.

'Shit. This is embarrassing,' she said.

'It's OK. I have this effect on most women,' he joked. She laughed, then her smile faded and she looked at him.

'Come back soon, you hear?'

'I will.'

He smiled and reached forward, taking her hand and squeezing it. Then he released it and headed down the stairs towards the lower floor and the exit.

He took a last look down the corridor, then pushed open the main door.

And ran into Chalky, leaning against the wall outside.

He was standing there alone in the morning daylight, dressed in jeans and a navy blue polo shirt.

'There you are,' Archer said. 'Thought I'd missed you,'

Chalky shook his head and kicked off the wall, standing there beside his best friend. There was a long silence, the distant sounds of early morning London filling the air. Chalky broke it.

'So you're really leaving?'

Archer nodded. 'Yeah. Afraid so.'

'When will you be back?'

'I don't know. But guess I'll have to come back sometime soon. You need someone here to keep you out of trouble.'

Chalky grinned.

'Tell you what, I think that guy with the knife did you a favour, Arch,' he joked. 'I always told you your face needed some work done to it.'

There was a pause as Archer smiled.

Then the two best friends stepped forward and embraced. They parted, stepping back, and shook hands.

'And thanks,' Chalky said.

‘For what?’

‘For everything.’

Pause.

'I'd better head up. Don't want to piss off Cobb or Porter or I’ll be joining you,' Chalky said.

He nodded.

‘Take care, Arch.'

'You too.'

Archer nodded as his best friend turned and headed into the building, moving up the stairs and disappearing out of sight. Slinging his holdall back over his shoulder, Archer took one last look at the police station, the Armed Response Unit, his home for over two years. He smiled and took a deep breath of fresh air. He felt good.

Ready.

Excited.

Then he turned on his heel and started walking through the parking lot towards the exit. Suddenly, he heard a voice call after him.

'Your girl never did meet someone else, did she?'

He turned and saw Chalky back at the front door.

Archer looked at him for a moment. He grinned.

Chalky shook his head.

‘You always were a bad liar,’ he called. ‘Ask her if she has any hot friends.’

Archer smiled and waved. Then he turned and walked across the parking lot. He turned right down the street, and headed off into the morning London sunlight.

His bag slung over his shoulder and his eyes looking straight ahead.

THE END

###

About the author:

Born in Sydney, Australia and raised in England and Brunei, Tom Barber has always had a passion for writing and story-telling. It took him to Nottingham University, England, where he graduated in 2009 with a 2:1 BA Hons in English Studies. Post-graduation, Tom moved to New York City and completed the 2 Year Meisner Acting training programme at The William Esper Studio, furthering his love of acting and screen-writing.

Upon his return to the UK in late 2011, Tom set to work on his debut novel, Nine Lives, which has since become a five-star rated Amazon UK Kindle hit. The following books in the series have been equally successful, garnering five-star reviews in the US, UK, France, Australia and Canada. The Sam Archer series has had over a million books downloaded worldwide and each title is currently being adapted into audiobook format.

Tom spends most of his time back and forth between the US and the UK. He can be contacted at http://www.tom-barber.co.uk/

Blackout is the third novel in the Sam Archer series.

Follow @TomBarberBooks.

Read an extract from

Silent Night

By
Tom Barber

The fourth Sam Archer thriller.
Now available on Amazon.

*****

ONE

No-one was in Central Park to see the man die.

It was Friday 17th December, a week before Christmas. New York City was a majestic place during the summer but it was equally captivating in the winter. Festive cheer was everywhere. Shop windows were adorned with imaginative seasonal displays, each store trying to outdo the other. Bars served strong punch containing warming liquor, fruit and spices. Speakers were rigged up on lampposts in several neighbourhoods in the outer boroughs through which familiar carols were played during the day. And saplings planted in small soil patches on the sidewalks all over Manhattan were decorated with lights, contributing to the red and golden hue the city adopted every twelfth month of the year.

With soft snow powdering the grass and golden lights sprinkled in trees all over its 843 acres, Central Park epitomised the feel-good seasonal ambience of the city. During the day and early evening, the ice-skating rinks in the Park were in constant use. People could either rent skates or wear their own, some gliding around the ice gracefully, others wobbling their way round far less confidently, treating each completed lap as a small victory. There was the constant *click-clock* of horse's hooves as they pulled carriages along the roads, tourists or couples sitting in the back, taking photographs or enjoying a romantic tour. Small two or three-piece brass bands took up positions beside the paths and worked their way through a repertoire of Christmas songs. And amongst all this, there was a constant stream of people just exploring the sights and admiring the scenery around them. Thirty five million people made their way into Central Park each year and a significant portion of that number came during the winter months.

Nevertheless, once the sun went down the Park started to quieten. A few remaining horse-drawn carriages trundled past, but the activity from earlier in the day quickly decreased as the air grew colder and the night got darker. The Park was open until 1am, but it had been a chilly December and that particular Friday evening was the coldest of the month so far. People were not inclined to hang around.

Coming up to 10pm, the lamp post-lit paths and sidewalks were now eerily quiet.

Snow had just started drifting down from the sky again, adding an extra layer to the white powder that had already blanketed the grass and naked branches on the trees.

During the summer one of the most popular areas in the Park was Sheep Meadow, located to the West between 66th and 69th Street. Fifteen acres in total, the large field hosted hundreds of people every day from early May to the end of September, but apart from the paths running around the perimeter it was shut off during the autumn and winter months to protect the ground and preserve the grass. That night the Meadow was dark, empty and quiet.

Save for the falling snow and one solitary figure.

At the north perimeter, a groundsman was slowly trudging his way along the fence, heading west. He was working alone. Before starting his shift he'd wrapped up well. He was wearing four layers of clothes accompanied by a scarf, a thick set of gloves and a knitted woollen hat. He'd read somewhere that a human being could lose something like fifty per cent of their body heat through the top of their head, so during the frostier months he always made sure that the beanie was firmly in place before he started work.

Being of Mexican descent, he didn't enjoy the New York winter for a number of reasons. One of them was the emptiness of the Meadow at this time of year. Even though the summer period tripled his workload he still far preferred the warmer, and therefore busier and more sociable time of year. Some places were designed for activity; without it, they seemed neglected and forlorn.

Pausing by the fence, he looked out at the dark field. It had the same deserted feel of a large school on a break for the holidays or an airport Terminal at night.

It was unnatural.

He didn't like it.

Six hours after beginning his shift, the groundsman was almost finished for the evening. He had a number of jobs to attend to in his area of the Park, but emptying the trash cans would be the last tonight. When he was done, he'd punch his timecard, take the A train back up to Spanish Harlem and enjoy a bowl of his wife's homemade soup. He walked along the fence pulling a wheeled cart behind him, a handful of black trash bags tossed inside. Just two more bins to empty. The drop-off point for removal of the bags was at the south-west corner of the Meadow, so once he'd gathered the last two he would dump them all there, return the cart to storage and get his ass home.

He approached the penultimate can, his thick boots crunching in the snow as he walked. He could see the black bag inside was about three quarters full. Coming to a halt, he pulled the bag out of the can, tied off the ends and then tossed it into the cart behind him to join the others. He drew a fresh bag, pulling it off a roll he'd stashed in the cart and replaced the old one.

But just as he was about to move on something on the ground caught his eye.

It was pretty well camouflaged by the snow. He'd almost missed it.

Stepping forward and bending down, he wiped off a layer of snow with his glove.

It was a black shoebox. It looked like someone had tossed it at the trash but missed and walked away, leaving it there on the ground. He was about to scoop it up to throw it inside the newly-replaced bag, but hesitated. He could hear something.

The box was clicking.

The groundsman looked around. All he could see was falling snow and a dark, quiet Park. Whoever had left the box here had long since gone.

Maybe there's an animal inside, he thought.

It was common practice in the city for unwanted pets to be dumped like this. He couldn't just leave the poor creature out here to freeze to death.

He reached forward, pulled a string securing the box and lifted the lid.

The moment he did, the clicking stopped.

There was a *whump.* A small cloud of yellow gas spewed from the box and hit him directly in the face. He instinctively recoiled but inhaled at the same time, the mustard-coloured gas sucked into his mouth and nostrils.

And immediately, he started choking.

He couldn't breathe. Coughing and gagging, he was suddenly overwhelmed by a horrific pain in his chest. It felt as if it was on fire. Every desperate breath he tried to take made the searing, burning sensation worse. He coughed harder, his whole body starting to jerk, blood spraying out of his mouth onto the white snow. He staggered back then collapsed to the ground, doubling over. He curled up in a tight ball in a vain effort to stop the agony, but it was getting worse.

He started to retch, his body spasming violently, blood and pieces of lung tissue spewing from his mouth onto the snow around him. The agonising and uncontrollable spasms increased in intensity, contorting his body and growing more and more violent. Suddenly, there was a loud *crack.*

His spine had snapped.

Immediately going into shock, the groundsman gargled as fluid filled his ruptured lungs.

And thirty seconds after he'd inhaled the gas, the man drowned in his own blood.

His jerking and convulsing ceased.

He was still, blood and bits of lung spattered both on his clothes and on the ground around him.

Crimson against the white.

He was the only person in the Meadow. No-one else was around.

And the snow continued to fall silently from the sky.

Across the city, they'd been working on the guy for almost three hours before he cracked. There were two people torturing him, a man and a woman called Wicks and Drexler. Inside the dark house Wicks walked over to the bed and put his hands on his knees, looking down at the bloodied man who was strapped to the frame. The guy had lasted longer than they'd expected. They'd worked their way through every sharp implement they could find in the kitchen, and by the second hour had gotten creative.

Wicks reached forward and ripped a strip of duct tape off the dying man's mouth. He did it fast, like pulling off a band aid. Then he peered in close. The guy's eyes were hazy from blood loss and shock trauma.

'Something you wanna tell us?' Wicks asked.

The man coughed weakly, blood around his mouth, his arms and legs taped securely to the wooden bed posts. He mumbled something that was just a whisper.

'Louder.'

'Macy's.'

'Go on.'

He coughed.

'B..Bryant Park,' he said, blood bubbling out of his lips. He must have ruptured a lung.

'And?'

'Pier...17.'

'What time?'

'Around...11. 30.'

Wicks looked into the man's eyes for a moment, then rose.

Drexler stepped forward, a suppressed Glock 21 in her hand and gave the man on the bed six slugs, three to the chest, three to the head. She pulled the trigger fast, the man's body jerking as he took each round, splinters coughing up from the bed frame and floor under the bed as the bullets buried themselves in the wood. The spent cartridges jumped out of the ejection port, tinkling to the floor, each one bouncing and eventually rolling to a stop. Looking at the dead man, Wicks pulled his cell phone and dialled a number. Someone answered on the fourth ring.

'It's me. He talked. We're in business.'

He listened, nodding, then ended the call and slid the phone back into his pocket. Then he turned to Drexler.

'What time is it?'

Still holding the pistol, the dark-haired woman shot her cuff. '6:25. The sun'll be up soon.'

Wicks nodded.

'Let's go,' he said. 'We've got work to do.'

****

Printed in Great Britain
by Amazon

10854817R00214